The
Upstairs
House

ALSO BY JULIA FINE

What Should Be Wild

The Upstairs House

a novel

Julia Fine

HARPER

An Imprint of HarperCollins*Publishers*

THE UPSTAIRS HOUSE. Copyright © 2021 by Julia Fine. All rights reserved. Printed in the United States of America. No part of this book may be used or reproduced in any manner whatsoever without written permission except in the case of brief quotations embodied in critical articles and reviews. For information, address HarperCollins Publishers, 195 Broadway, New York, NY 10007.

HarperCollins books may be purchased for educational, business, or sales promotional use. For information, please email the Special Markets Department at SPsales@harpercollins.com.

FIRST EDITION

Library of Congress Cataloging-in-Publication Data has been applied for.

ISBN 978-0-06-297582-9

21 22 23 24 25 LSC 10 9 8 7 6 5 4 3 2 1

For my children, my best and most true things

The Upstairs House

November 1950

Death flaunts itself on every tree, and Margaret looks out the hospital window, calling it beautiful.

Typical, thinks Michael. The others have gone to the washroom, to interrogate the nurses, to the hotel to retrieve a fresh shirt. Margaret has stayed. Margaret is here. Margaret helps Michael align the clasp of the necklace to the protrusion of bone at the back of her neck. Margaret looks at her and says, "Oh yes, Rab," *Rab* for Rabbit, Michael's pet name. Margaret is *Bun*, short for Bunny. "Lovely."

Michael knows the appropriate word is not *lovely*. Once lauded as the most beautiful woman in America, in recent years she's shed a body's worth of bulk, finally completing the transformation from her former self—Blanche Oelrichs of the gilded Newport Oelrichs—into the legend she deserves to become: Michael Strange, poetess, actress. At twenty-four, she'd felt the literary urge, needed a nom de plume to publish. The name came to her in a dream, not just a pen name, but a better self, the leading lady role of any lifetime—Michael Strange, iconoclast and luminary. Michael Strange, the benevolent sun.

Now sixty, Michael Strange is dying.

For years she's been told that leukemia will kill her, but the prognosis is so antithetical to Michael's self-conception, she's refused to take it as fact. All summer into hospitals, then out of them. No one believed she'd return to the lecture circuit. No one thought she'd make it up to Maine. During the thirteen-hour ride north on the Bar Harbor Express, Michael had begrudgingly written out the details of her funeral: "Dress me in my pleated robe—white with gold trim—and lay me in the living room at Under the Hill." The prelude to Wagner's *Parsifal* will play on loop as the guests are received, "and if the musicians grow tired, replace them."

That was July, and here Michael is now, in November. The doctors underestimated her natural resilience, her joie de vivre, her stubbornness. All traits that she'd been known for in her youth. All traits that thrived once she was free of Margaret.

Margaret. Always Margaret. Margaret bent over the bed, face leaner than Michael remembers, lines webbing out from her eyes. If only someone would marry her, take her off Michael's hands.

"Rab, what else can I do for you?" asks Margaret.

The others trickle in: Michael's housekeeper, her one surviving son, a few old friends, Charles Shaw and Ted Peckham.

"Go home and rest," Ted says to Margaret, but Margaret stays. Margaret is loyal. Margaret is executer of Michael's estate, and she has sworn she'll recite Michael's poetry nightly. No doubt Margaret will sit herself down in their shared rooms at East End Avenue, or in her writing studio—that silly Cobble Court—or in that ridiculous cabin in Maine, and summon Michael. Will that be enough to bring her back? After all, that is the spirit: in ink, in the poetry. That is the soul.

Michael is afraid to die. Only the foolish aren't afraid of the unknown. But here are her admirers, hovered above the hospital bed, seated on the windowsills, legions of angels. Michael still conducting her own life. *If the musicians grow tired, replace them.* And here, around her neck, heavy against her sunken breast, is the thick double strand of pearls her friends so envy. Centering her, weighting her to the earth.

AFTER A WHILE, Ethel the housekeeper whispers, "We'd better take them off her before somebody else does."

Part I

I MEANT WHAT I SAID IN MY LETTER THE ONLY GIFT MY SOUL WILL
ACCEPT FROM YOU AT THIS POINT IS ABSOLUTE SILENCE STOP

—telegram sent from Michael Strange to
Margaret Wise Brown, November 1949

1

October 2017

I'm sure that Clara noticed the balloon, though it was dark and all the books claimed that at three hours old she couldn't see more than three feet in front of her. Still, there she was, reaching her pruny fingers toward the shadow at the window.

"The beginning of your life as a woman," I said. "Being told you couldn't have seen what you're sure that you saw."

"Oh, stop it," said my mother. She was sitting on a bench that folded out into a bed. Clara was nursing, or attempting to nurse: burrowing and gumming and ramming her face into my chest.

"You'll have to position her," the nurse had told me. "She can instinctively seek out the breast, but she'll have trouble seeing it." So I'd positioned Clara, and she had promptly rejected that position, preferring, it seemed, to rub her forehead vigorously against my collarbone.

"Remember when you swore there was no man without his pants in our back alley? I was staring right at him. He was peeing on Mr. Novak's car."

"You're delirious," said my mother.

"I was seven. I wasn't blind."

"Feed your child."

But it wasn't as easy as that. Nothing about motherhood was as easy as that. This I knew from the moment they moved Clara from the bloody sheet and up onto my belly. "There is nothing like the bond you will feel upon first meeting," said Mrs. What-to-Expect. "The rush of love will overwhelm you." I looked at Clara, a puffy little larva, mouth pulsing, and I waited for the bond. I waited for the rush of love. There were needles still stuck in my arm. Maybe they were interfering.

"Isn't she beautiful?" said Ben. "Isn't she perfect?"

I thought she had been perfect while inside me. Despite the many imperfections of my pregnancy, Clara herself had been perfect as a small, fertilized egg, and she'd been perfect as a fetus when we watched her through the ultrasound monitor, flailing her little legs. Perfect while we'd built her dresser and her crib, and ironed stickers to the wall for her to coo at when she lay on her deluxe organic mattress. She'd even been perfect while she contracted my uterus, through the searing pain of the car hitting potholes and sudden red lights as we rushed to the hospital downtown. She was perfect when the triage nurse reached in to check my dilation, and perfect when I got the epidural, and so perfect while I pushed until the top of her head appeared in the massive mirror the nurse had brought so I could monitor my progress, fully perfect, perfect hair all covered in perfect white goo.

And then she was here.

I said, "I'm tired."

WE'D TAKEN A tour of the hospital several weeks prior, but half an hour after the birth, when they moved me from the labor to recovery room, nothing looked familiar. A baby factory, Ben had called it, and I'd pictured all the little baby parts on a conveyor belt, eyeballs popped into sockets, fingernails glued onto fingers, a pile of dud arms and legs. My nine months in and out of hospital complexes—stepping on and off of scales, peeing in cups, having my blood drawn—had made me macabre. But I found comfort in the thought of each little part of Clara pieced thoughtfully together, of Clara as one of many, which made me one of many, which kept me safe.

The nurse wheeled me through an empty waiting area toward my recovery room. The lobby's massive windows looked out onto the fog of the city, a gray day casting a gray light onto teal plastic chair cushions and whitewashed walls. Outside, a balloon drifted past—a face with squinted eyes and a Charlie Brown smile. The attached corkscrewed ribbon, having failed its only task, fluttered pitifully against the glass.

Ben was still downstairs with Clara. She was forty minutes old. We couldn't all fit in the elevator together to leave the labor floor, and I was scared to be alone, away from Ben. When the anesthesiologist made everyone else leave so she could give the epidural, I'd panicked to see Ben go, clutching his T-shirt and making him promise to read through all the paperwork after I signed it. It had been a relief to see him peek his head back into the room, and it was a relief now to see the elevator doors open to display him next to Clara in her clear plastic bassinet with the wheeled wooden paneling. Ben was staring down at her, in awe. Frowning in the way I knew meant he was overjoyed, the way he'd been caught frowning in the photos of our wedding. I felt like a voyeur.

"Ben," I said. He looked up, and he was mine again.

"We did good, babe." Ben let the nurse take Clara, and came out to squeeze my shoulder. "*You* did so good." A bit of the joy that I'd wanted sparked quietly in my stomach. I tried to fan the flame.

"We did, didn't we?" I reached up for Ben's hand, but it was gone.

He grabbed the wheelchair handles and swiveled me away from the IV drip, so that the tape on my forearm lifted and the needle tugged flesh. It was a brighter pain than the pain of the birth, which had been raw and deep and muscly. The nurse smiled at him and wheeled Clara toward us. This was how it would be now—the three of us. This was how it had been, I supposed, for the previous nine and a half months, I just hadn't really known it.

My recovery room was just off the elevator. Ben knocked me into the privacy curtain that hung behind the door.

"Whoops!" He was giddy, eyes rimmed red from lack of sleep. There was a bed with papery sheets, and a bench that folded out for Ben to sleep on. A massive computer sat behind a jumble of tubes and wires, which the nurse connected to the IV pole, still firmly connected to me. I folded over onto the mattress, my legs rubbery with anesthesia.

"Maybe you should try to walk around?" Ben suggested.

I shot a panicked look at the nurse pressing buttons, who pretended not to notice. My thighs were massive, doughy and spreading. I stuck a fingernail in one, and felt nothing.

"The mesh panties are in the bathroom," said the nurse, adjusting Clara's swaddle. "And so are cold packs, and a squeeze bottle to rinse. You have to slap the cold packs around a few times before you use them. Don't be afraid to ask for as many refills as you need."

Clara's eyes were shut. She made a little mewling yawn. I wondered what her breath would smell like.

"We'll have to feed her soon," I said.

"Let's get some rest." Ben rolled Clara closer, so that when I tilted the bed back I could still reach the side of the bassinet. I put a hand on the plastic and turned to the window. There it was again, that lost balloon with its leering Mylar smile.

I WOKE UP to a different nurse adjusting my bedding.

"Blood pressure still good." She had thick hands, capable, squeezing my wrists. Her smile felt routine. "How's the pain?"

"Just in general?" I blinked at her. My stomach was still bloated, but instead of a fully pumped ball, it had slightly deflated. Stitches were tightening at the back of my vagina. My biceps burned from holding up my legs while I pushed. "Okay, I guess?" I could almost hear my mother telling me not to uptalk.

"Okay, good. You get your Motrin now. I'll write it on the board, but don't worry, when we switch shifts your night nurse will keep track of it."

"Do I need to—" I paused, still hazy, unsure of what I was asking.

"We'll try feeding her again in a half hour or so. You two will figure it out. I'll stop back in to help you soon."

I didn't understand. Would we figure it out, or would we need her assistance? How much of this was instinct, the two of us minnowing up through the water for air? How much was I supposed to be afraid of? I turned to the window to find that the balloon hadn't moved. Its face was pressed against the glass, flattened features like my sister in a sheet mask, the eyes half-moons, the nose too large. Annie would be here soon—they all would be here soon, and there would never be another of this moment.

"Wait," I said, "I think there's something the matter."   •

The nurse pressed down on my abdomen. "It all feels fine. Totally normal."

"No, I mean—" Ben was coming into the room, rolling the bassinet in front of him. He looked so happy, so perfectly content. "Never mind," I said. "I must just be tired." The nurse smiled again, parted the curtain, and walked out the door.

"Do you want to hold her for a minute before the family gets here?" Ben asked, passing Clara over before I could respond. I wanted to want to hold her, so I nodded even while realizing that I didn't want to hold her. But here she was, in my arms. Little tufted eyebrows, skin so loose she wore it like a coat.

"She seems smaller," I said to Ben.

"It's normal to lose weight right after birth," he said, "remember?" I didn't.

"Is she supposed to be so . . ." I wasn't sure what I was asking. Clara wasn't what I'd expected, but I couldn't say how. I'd held

Ben's brother's kids just hours after they were born, so I knew that the baby would feel soft, that she'd be squinty, that her hair would be crusty with afterbirth. I knew she would be me, but also not me, Ben but not Ben. She sighed, and her nose wrinkled. I was on the cusp of something—some emotion, some metamorphosis, some deep realization. Then my mother walked in.

My mother didn't knock, just swept in as if entering her own living room, hair freshly dyed and nails just painted. She was wearing a magenta wrap dress with a plunging neckline that displayed her freckled cleavage. Grabby fingers, thick perfume.

"My grandbaby!"

"You didn't have to dress up. You shouldn't have dressed up." I frowned.

Ben mouthed something from across the room: *Your father.* Of course. It must have been a good six years since she'd seen him. I thought it highly unlikely that he'd make it to the hospital today—or really any day—but who was I to tell her that she'd wasted her best dress on us and Clara?

"Well, aren't you just divine? Aren't you a treat?"

"Do we have more of those ice chips? I'm thirsty."

"I can run out and—" Ben started, but I shook my head furiously, determined not to let him leave me. The balloon was laughing at us—me and Ben, my mother. I didn't mind, but my mother hated being laughed at.

"It looks so familiar," I whispered.

"What?" My mother had scooped Clara from my arms and was inhaling her.

"The balloon," I said.

"The what?" She glared at me before turning back to coo at Clara.

. "Never mind. I don't understand why everyone says babies smell so good."

"Aren't you just delicious? Aren't you just divine?" My mother's face was so close to Clara's that I worried she would smear her with concealer.

"Let her be happy," said Ben softly. I shrugged.

I knew where I had seen that balloon before. We'd had one like it in the undergrad office waiting for Steve, the adjunct, when he got back from his four-day paternity leave. I wasn't yet pregnant. I'd looked at his rumpled button-down and milky red-rimmed eyes and felt superior: because I could, if I wanted, sleep ten hours straight. Because I didn't smell like spit-up. Because I didn't have another life tethered, yet, to mine.

"Can't someone get rid of that thing?"

"Get rid of what?" said Ben.

"The balloon that keeps banging on the window."

"I haven't seen any balloon," said my mother.

"Can't you just open the window and grab it?"

"Megan, we're thirty stories high. This is a hospital. The windows don't *open*." My mother's mascara was clumpy, and prompted in me an unjustified rage.

"Can we call the nurse back and see if—"

"Megan, it's fine. It'll float away."

"It's been on me since I got upstairs."

"Megan, it's nothing."

2

Before the baby was my body getting ready for the baby, a preparation both physical—swollen ankles, leg cramps, nausea—and mental. I worried about everything. What if the fumes from the carpet cleaner in the condo next door came through the vents in our bathroom and poisoned our daughter? What if she was born with some new genetic disorder that they couldn't catch with prenatal tests? What if the dog hated the baby and we had to get rid of the dog? What if the dog attacked the baby while we weren't looking, and we had to have the dog put down, and then the neighbors got mad because they all loved Solly and they tried to kick us out of the condo association for being bad parents and bad dog parents and who would want to live next door to those?

"They would understand," said Ben when, at eight months pregnant, I played out this scenario. "In the incredibly unlikely event that our dog turns vicious and attacks our newborn, I'm sure that everyone will understand why we have to get rid of her." Solly was splayed on the floor next to the couch, and he reached down to scratch between her ears.

"But I don't want to get rid of Solly."

"Then good thing we don't have to."

"I feel like you're not taking me seriously."

"I feel like you're not being serious." My face fell. Ben softened.

"Everyone has babies," he said, which wasn't true. "People have babies all the time. We're in one of the best cities in the world, and we have the best doctors. There's nothing to worry about."

None of this was true. If we had stayed in New York, or moved to Paris, maybe then at least some of it would be true. But after fifteen years away, we'd moved back to Chicago, forty minutes from Ben's parents, twenty-five from mine.

"What are you so scared of?"

"I don't know."

If I let myself linger—and I tried very hard not to—I did know. What scared me was the being known, the knowing. This baby would forever be bound to me: How would I hide myself from a part of myself? I knew my own mother in ways that I hoped my daughter would never know me. I pitied my own mother, and never wanted to be pitied. I'd seen my mother's C-section scars and her sweat stains, knew the smell that she left in the bathroom. I'd heard her ugly laugh and seen her swear at waitstaff and watched her cry in the dark at our old kitchen table after spilling her fourth glass of wine. Motherhood was not a role I'd envied. It was not a job I wanted.

But I didn't *not* want it either. I didn't actively push it away. We hadn't been trying for a baby; I could've hidden the news from Ben and handled everything discreetly, but I didn't. There was a piece of myself I wanted to cultivate, a version of myself I wanted to be. I could pack sack lunches and bring Gatorade to soccer practice, make trifold science fair projects and polish tiny toenails. I could set aside the dissertation that had started to bore me. Best of all, I barely had to *do* anything. I could choose without actively choosing: here was my body letting us know that we could have this thing, this future, if we wanted it. I could make something of myself, a literal second self, a second living breathing someone who would need me. I supposed it would be nice to be needed.

If I went to the clinic, I would bleed. If it was just the pill, just a needle, just a quick anesthetic, I thought I might have done it. But I didn't want to bleed. Bleeding would have been so messy, too obvious a metaphor. I was an academic, and I lived in a world of eternal incubation—always one more semester, one more grant. To bleed would have commemorated finality, an active commitment for which I was not dispositionally prepared.

So Clara was born.

WE PUT HER in the car seat and the nurses had to correct the straps, which retrospectively seemed like the beginning, although maybe it was the balloon that was really the beginning, or that the back of the nursery bookshelf cracked when Solly stepped on it while I was putting it together, or my writer's block, or the stubbed cigarettes the workmen dropped onto our balcony when patching the roof.

"You have to put her feet through here," the nurses told us as we readied Clara to leave the recovery room, and Ben's eyes got wide and worried.

"They fixed it, see?" I said.

Ben worried that my milk hadn't come in yet. He worried about traffic. He had to go to Houston in a week, and his guilt was manifesting as anxiety. He adjusted the blanket that was draped over the car seat.

"We should have gotten one of those specially made covers."

Clara's eyes were open. They were a dark blue that would probably turn brown. She had wispy hair and a little birthmark just above her left eyebrow. She looked very small in the car seat, and because of this the whole project of parenthood suddenly seemed manageable.

Still, we stood in the lobby of the hospital, unwilling to embark. Ben frowned, then laughed, then wiped his eyes. He'd never done as well as me on little sleep—on our honeymoon he had to spend the first full day of jet lag at the hotel with the blinds shut.

"Okay. Yes. Okay." Ben slapped his fist into his palm. "Okay, we got this."

"Of course we do," I said, "Now get the car."

I sat in back with Clara. It was three thirty on a Thursday, which meant traffic, which meant Ben could drive slowly and no one would complain. I felt each stop and start in my pelvis, but compared to the contractions on my previous car ride, it was nothing. I was close enough to trauma that the small things couldn't hurt me; I could still consciously access each moment of the birth. Clara was thirty-five hours old. I had an ice pack shoved into my massive mesh diaper.

At home we gingerly walked her up the stairs from the garage, leaving our overnight bags in the trunk. She was asleep, and had another half an hour before she needed to wake up and eat—until she was back up to her birth weight, we had to feed her without fail every two hours.

Ben held the car seat while I unlocked the door.

My sister had used our spare key to come by and pick up Solly—she'd brought flowers and hung a banner that read "Welcome, Clara" in pink and purple marker on top of the TV. There were muffins on the counter and casseroles in the fridge. Our couch pillows were fluffed and Solly's corner freshly vacuumed, almost free of hair.

"We should set up the swing," said Ben.

"Tomorrow."

I went to an armchair, lowered myself slowly. It hurt to sit down. The air-conditioning was blasting loud and cold, and the sun coming in from the open blinds hit me right in the eyes. For a moment I felt outside my body, past it, looking down from above. *Where am I?* I wanted to ask Ben. But I knew where I was; I just didn't like it. What had we done? Why had we done this? I had a chapter about Gertrude Stein to incorporate into my dissertation. I had a recipe for sous vide rack of lamb I'd been dying to try. With another forty hours, I might beat Ben's ninja video game.

"I think I need to change my . . . you know," I said. "Those cold packs we took from the hospital bathroom . . . can you get them? They're still in the car."

Ben stood wide-eyed, breathing heavily, holding Clara away from his body, not at all the way the nurses had shown. He kept bending his knees as if he might put her down, then standing straight again, then bending. His panic flickered toward me. What was wrong with us?

"I'll go down to the car," said Ben. "And I'll just leave her . . . ?" Neither of us had yet been alone with Clara. There was always my mother or sister, the button that summoned the nurses on call. But this wasn't sustainable, this togetherness. I looked at Ben. We laughed. He just had to run to the car for our bags.

I heard Ben taking the back stairs, his weight making the same dull echo that annoyed me when he came home late, or when our downstairs neighbor went up to the roof: a hollow, metallic sound that usually lasted a few seconds, until whoever was walking had made it from the unfinished stairwell to the carpeted hall. But now the echoing continued—light and peppery, like someone walking in stilettos. *Tap TAP tap TAP tap.* Maybe Arthur from downstairs had a friend. Maybe it was some kind of maintenance and we had missed the e-mail. Clara started to cry.

I popped a breast out of my T-shirt and squeezed. Leaning forward made my pelvis ache. Colostrum eked out of my nipple, orange and sticky, and from somewhere deep inside me a watery red sopped through my industrial-grade maxi pad, wetting my maternity leggings, staining the chair. Clara's mouth found food. I bit my lip and tried to hold my pelvic floor. The *tap TAP tap* continued.

"What the fuck is Arthur doing up there?" I said when Ben returned.

"What do you mean? Arthur's car's not in its spot. I think we're the only ones home."

"Well, then what's making that noise?"

"If you want me to take her and try . . ." Ben trailed off, because there was nothing for him to try, there was just me and Clara's slippery gums, and the milk that my body would be making. I'd never been this consistently close to another person. I'd never had this much power. If I stood up, Clara would fall off my lap, off my breast. And if I held her neck just so . . . I had so much control; I had no control at all.

The upstairs banging came again, and when I winced, Ben asked if there was something he could bring me.

"It's so loud," I said. "Has Arthur always been this loud?"

Ben studiously examined the casseroles Annie had left in the fridge, pulling up the tinfoil, then re-covering. There was an unfamiliar feeling to the condo, like someone had been here—not Annie, who'd let herself in to make beds and wipe counters, but someone else who had come after. I shivered. I was a disciple of Mrs. What-to-Expect, whose bible I'd dog-eared and underlined and put in a place of honor on my nightstand. She warned of preeclampsia and babies being sunny-side up and hyperemesis gravidarum and complications stemming from an epidural and checking for wet diapers and umbilical infections and SIDS. She said nothing about noises being louder, about the air in your home feeling colder.

"Can we bring Solly back now?" I asked.

"I thought we said we'd leave her with your sister for the first few days." Ben brought me a pillow, tucking it behind my head. I was still leaking, but at least Clara had latched. I had another forty-five minutes until I was supposed to take my Colax. I hated it when people said "I thought" and meant "I know."

"I just think it would be comforting to have her here," I said.

"We'd have to walk her."

"You would have to walk her."

"That's what I meant. Do you want me to look for the nursing pillow? Do we know how long she's going to eat?"

The noise upstairs augmented, more persistent. "Is there something you can do about that?" I asked him.

"About the mess? About the pillow?"

"About the banging. Can't you just go talk to Arthur?"

"Megan, I told you he's not home. There's nothing to do."

"Just because his car is gone doesn't mean he is."

"Megan, stop it."

He'd snapped at me. Ben never snapped at me. Ben was even-keeled, the opposite of Annie's awful ex-boyfriend Calvin, the opposite of my awful ex-boyfriends. I felt a momentary thrill of unease.

And then: "I'm sorry. I'm sorry for yelling." He hadn't yelled, but I didn't see any use in correcting him. He rubbed my shoulders and the pressure wasn't firm enough to feel good, just a flaccid, perfunctory tickle. I had to summon deep reserves of patience not to shake him off.

The crashing came again, this time immediately above me. I jumped at the sound. Clara shifted her position but didn't complain.

"Are you okay?" Ben asked. He was looking toward the kitchen—the opposite direction of the noise—as if trying to meet the eye of someone waiting there. As if there was a button he could press like the one that rang the nurses at the hospital, and when they came, he could throw up his hands. He'd say, "I don't know how to make her stop," and the nurses would say, "Have you tried rocking her?" He wouldn't know how to tell them that the *her* he'd meant was me.

"Megan," Ben said, "are we okay?"

He didn't mean it in jest, but I couldn't help laughing.

And maybe that was the beginning—the noises from upstairs, the first crack in Ben, my laughter. A dawning recognition that the anxiety I'd felt during my pregnancy was only going to increase now that Clara had come out of me. The dry, itchy skin. The sensitivity to light. The word *sensitivity* comes from the Old French *sensitif*, which means "capable of feeling." In a way I supposed it was good, to know that I was and I could.

3

I was the one who'd insisted on the condo. We'd bought it three months earlier from a family of four, marveling at how they fit both of their preschool-age children into such a small, closetless second bedroom. Our thinking was that by the time Clara was two or so, we'd upgrade to a house—by then we would be ready to move out to the suburbs, where we could afford a nice big place on just Ben's salary. Well, that was Ben's thinking. That was Ben's justification for humoring me and buying a home in the city that we knew we'd soon outgrow. He wanted to buy close to his parents, wanted a yard and some trees that would be ours, wanted a garden that we'd have to go and water. Having never had any of these things, I didn't miss them. I told Ben that I'd rather not be alone, to which he replied that in the suburbs I'd have Clara and a lot of other family to help me. He couldn't understand why I found this so funny.

Ben never talked about how our money was actually his money. He traveled a lot for work, and we had tacitly decided that my major household contribution was not begrudging him that travel. In the end, I used his schedule as leverage. I said, "I'm pregnant, and I'll be at home more often, and Deerfield is too close to your mother."

That was that. We bought the small two-bedroom duplex with the mauve kitchen backsplash we both hated. We lived above Arthur Ocampo, who was twenty-six and painfully attractive. Arthur

welcomed us with a mango icebox cake his mom had made but that
he didn't want in the house because of his diet, which we guessed
was just protein shakes and whatever he was always outside grilling.
We were in the back of the building, facing the alley, and we shared
the roof deck with Arthur. We didn't interact much. We weren't
going to be friends. For three months our occasional contact was
limited to pulling our cars into the shared garage at the same time,
or when I went up to the roof and he was already there with a beer
and his laptop. The comfortable stasis we'd established was partly
why Ben was so adamant we shouldn't ask him to be quiet.

"I won't be able to get any work done," I said to Ben on our first
full day at home, "with all that knocking." My T-shirt stained with
spit-up, my ass numb from sitting. I couldn't remember the last time
I'd washed my face.

"You can't feed the baby? You can't do her diapers?" Ben was
trying to be sweetly facetious.

"I can't lie in bed and cry," I said, and his smile faded. "Sorry. I
don't mean to be . . . I mean my dissertation."

"Hey." Ben crouched down to meet my eyes where I sat holding
Clara. "I didn't mean to imply that what you're doing isn't work. Or
that you won't ever get back to your project." Another clang came
from above us. He was waiting for me to respond. I wanted more—
for him to tell me that he'd go and quiet Arthur, or that he was angry, or worried, or that I was imagining things. I needed something
to grab on to—something sharp that could shock me back into a
self that was more than a headache and cracked nipples.

"You don't have to worry about your research now," Ben said.
"Focus on Clara."

I didn't have to be told to focus on Clara. All I did now was focus
on Clara. I fed her. I burped her. I swapped out her diapers. I barely
slept because of her. I sweated under her heat. I smelled like yellow
milk and urine.

My half brother once did a school project on rabbits that ate their own progeny. Newborn rabbits looked like little sausages. The mother rabbit had desperate pink eyes. She had to work hard to chew.

ON CLARA'S THIRD day of life, we took her to the pediatrician to be measured and weighed, and the radiant heat steamed like a sauna and she cried the whole time. A nurse took blood from her heel, and it looked like spilled wine. When we got home, the stairwell sounds were louder.

"Don't you hear that?" I said. Ben shrugged. He went to microwave a frozen burrito. "They're better in the oven," I said. He ignored me, and I said, "God, stop ignoring me. Stop ignoring fucking everything."

"Megan," he said, but that was all. He turned away and the microwave beeped. Clara peed through her onesie. Ben scraped the wet tortilla off his plate. "Arthur really isn't making much noise," he said, finally facing me. "And if you think you hear him, then I'm sure he's also hearing Clara crying."

I FELL ASLEEP. I woke up. I considered taking a shower. I forced myself to eat.

IF YOU THINK *you hear. If you think*. Perhaps I heard the sounds so clearly because I spent all day sitting perfectly still, holding Clara while she slept. Nursing her. I did not enjoy nursing. Nobody—not my mother, not Mrs. What-to-Expect—had warned me how much nursing would hurt.

"It feels nice," my mother insisted, even as I cried through the pain of it in front of her. "It's a nice bonding experience." She'd come over to help cook or clean—it wasn't clear which, and since she'd spent the morning either staring at Clara or googling where to buy the best gluten-free cupcakes, it didn't seem likely either task would be accomplished. Scrolling through my phone, I saw that several members of my graduate school cohort were headed to Berlin—I had never been to Berlin and felt now that I would never go to Berlin, because I'd be sitting here with a baby latched to my tit and my mother droning on about the best type of cream to prevent wrinkles on the backs of my hands. I was still fat. I would now be fat forever. Clara was four days old, and when she was sleeping I was wide awake, and when she was awake I wanted to be sleeping. I made a little squawk of pain as she gnawed around to get a better latch. My mother looked at me quizzically. It would be easier to buy formula. Then Ben could help.

The women on the What-to-Expect message boards insisted that I shouldn't buy formula: that the proteins in my breast milk were entirely irreplaceable, that formula-fed babies would be thinner at first, and then develop into ugly, obese toddlers. Though only a lurker on these message boards, I took their collective wisdom as gospel. After all, most were second-time mothers; they knew. So I suffered. I chewed my lip. I pumped to up my milk supply, saving each ounce, watching the fat rise to the top of all the little lined-up bottles. I rubbed lanolin on my nipples, which did nothing, but gave the illusion of action. I listened to my mother list off natural ingredients in a daze that was only broken by the sound of our downstairs neighbor, traveling constantly, angrily, up the stairs to the roof.

"Fucking Arthur and his motherfucking banging."

"What are you talking about? Don't swear at your baby."

"Don't tell me you don't hear it either."

"You should be happy that she doesn't have colic," said my mother.

AS A BABY, I had colic. I'm told I wouldn't sleep, wouldn't be held, wouldn't nurse. My parents ran the fan in the bathroom to mimic the sound of the womb and drove me in circles around the block, hoping for peace. I don't think that my mother intended to use this against me, but each time she mentioned my difficult infancy, I felt she was referring to a debt that was accruing. She'd follow with "Now Ann was such an *easy* baby," an epithet with its own expectations, its own weight. Already, to be sisters close in age is to invite comparison, to be cast as the pretty or the plain one, the brains or the brawn. You'd think each gene, once expressed, could never be replicated, the way we talk about sisters, the way we set sisters against each other. Because I was good at school, Annie was necessarily average. Because I practiced piano more often, I was the musician, no matter that both of us played. Do brothers feel this way, as if a basket of traits must be doled out between them, each attribute in limited supply? My father was a swimmer in college—not so fast that he broke records, but talented enough to make the team. My uncle Brian swam too, and in one fifty-meter freestyle they finished at exactly the same moment. Could such synchronicity even be possible of sisters? All my life I had felt Annie struggling to push past me, and each boost I offered her meant I myself slipped further back.

My mother knew them both in high school—my father and his younger brother, Brian. She found something in my father that she didn't see in Brian, some quality that attracted her. The way he could look at you as if he truly saw you, the way he was willing to reposition himself to best help you shine. When you were in his sights, you were incandescent. The trouble was that when he looked away, you turned off.

"Has Dad come by to see the baby?" my mother asked, subconsciously tapping her long fingernails to the beat of the upstairs sounds. He'd had his other family for more than twenty years, and yet my mother still thought of herself in relation to my father, was still caught in his orbit. I didn't want to be fifty-five and still in thrall to the man who'd destroyed the future self I had imagined at fifteen. I didn't want to want any life but the one I was living.

"No," I said to my mother. "He hasn't."

Once, in my father's eyes, I'd been special. Once, I'd been paraded around his office and brought to his company softball games. Our mutual adoration had expounded, a reflection bounced off another reflection, an infinite vacillation of light. But then he left my mother crying in the driveway, left me and Annie watching at the top of the stairs.

So no, Dad had not called or come by to see the baby. My stepmother sent an email from their joint account—no text, just a little animation of a stork turning his head first left, then right. The subject line: CONGRATULATONS!!

"Well, you let him know it's unconscionable." My mother sniffed. "Not visiting his grandbaby. Not visiting his daughters."

"I will," I said, knowing I wouldn't.

"Fuck him," said Annie when she came to bring back Solly. Clara was now five days old—or maybe six. Time was syrupy and difficult to measure. "Seriously, fuck him."

"Fuck him," Ben agreed.

"Can you just stop?" I said. "It's fine. It doesn't matter." I knew that they were looking at each other over my head, performing concern. "Of all the things for us to worry about, this doesn't even make the list."

"It must stir up some sort of feelings," said Ben, scratching Solly, who kept rubbing up against him. She hadn't come to say hello to me yet. She was wary of Clara.

"Don't you think we should at least talk about it?" Annie touched the tender spot at the top of Clara's skull where the bones hadn't yet fused. Clara burped, and Solly startled.

I knew my father well enough to have no expectations. I couldn't understand why everyone thought that a baby would change him, when it wasn't his baby, when he lived thirty minutes away from us in traffic, when he had my half siblings.

Now the upstairs sound was someone scattering nails on tin,

tipping a big bucket of nails and sending them clattering against the steps and against the floor and against the puckered metal landing. I winced, and Annie leaned forward with her fist under her chin. Solly ventured closer to sniff Clara's feet.

"Well?" said Annie.

"So?" said Ben.

"Can you all just stop whining about Dad and do something about that banging?"

BEN CAME FROM a nuclear family, the younger child of Linda and Seth. Seth was a stamp collector, a gardener, a man who watched birds. He'd retired at sixty and now sat on the board of his synagogue and read thousand-page histories of World War II. Linda volunteered. I did not know what this meant about the way she spent her days. She had a perfectly shaped blond bob and, although she knew that my mother was Jewish, liked to ask me when I planned to convert. She doted on both her sons, but Ben was her favorite. I had to work very hard to convince her I was not by any means trying to take him away.

Linda and Seth had been in Palm Springs with Ben's brother when I went into labor. We told them not to rush back on our account, yet here they were, the trip cut short, Clara one week old and Ben's paternity leave mostly spent and my hair still unwashed. I felt Linda eyeing my roots. She put a finger to the dust on the bookshelf, bent down to the bassinet. I could tell that Clara was too bald for her taste. She smiled without teeth and then said, "There's a good baby."

Ben told me the judgment was all in my head—I just didn't understand his mother. In truth, I understood her too well—we were too alike, which in retrospect must be why Ben had married me. Two simmerers, as my mother, a boiler, liked to call me. What I wanted: to be vibrant and mercurial, to have the highest of highs and the lowest of lows and enough faith in myself to ride them through; to be a happier, stronger version of my mother. What I was: a Linda—ruminating, nitpicking. Waiting for compliments to deflect, waiting for offers to turn down. Cleaning the salt-water splatter off the stovetop because otherwise who else would.

"What books have you been reading her?" asked Linda.

"She's eight days old, Mom," Ben said. "She isn't reading any books."

"And I hope you aren't letting her watch television." Linda drew the word out, adding additional syllables. I stood up.

"I need some air. I'm going to the roof."

"Bring a jacket," said Seth. "It's gotten chilly."

THE LAST TIME I'd climbed up to the roof, I was eight months pregnant. From the living room couch I'd watched clouds roll in and rain fall in sheets, knocking a potted plant from the balcony across the way. The darkness passed quickly but the rain continued, and I'd been struck with the urge to get out into it. The streets were empty and the alley was empty and my hair frizzed and my ankles swelled while Clara swam relays inside me. I only went back inside when my tank top soaked through. Since then I'd been too sore or too frightened or too tired to go upstairs again. I'd not yet been so badly in need of escape.

Now I was still sore and tired, but I made it to the top and I drew my coat around my new body. I sat down on a patio chair and listened to the faraway hum of the el on its track. Arthur had left a crumpled beer can on a ledge—or maybe it was Ben, who was now worried about breastfeeding and alcohol and trying to be thoughtful with his own consumption. But Ben wasn't forgetful. Ben hated the sound of scrunched aluminum.

A seagull flew high overhead, incongruous but common, its shadow a gliding blur. And then the banging.

This time it was coming from below me, which didn't make any sense, because below me was the furnace, and my bedroom, and the nursery. The sound was different when I heard it from up here, more like hammering, more like the crash of toppling plywood. A dog barked, lower-pitched than Solly, who didn't respond. She'd spent the morning conversing with the dog across the alley, so it was unsettling to now hear nothing from her, like shouting into a cave and receiving no echo. Perhaps she was frightened of Ben's parents.

Logically, the banging was coming from the insulation in between the roof deck and our upstairs ceiling—somewhere within the beams, hidden in the poisonous pink cotton candy. This seemed appropriate: a bit of commissioned construction between old life and new.

I was immensely, unspeakably tired.

What were they building? Where was the foreman? Who had Arthur hired? A mouse, I thought. A termite? A frantic rabbit burrowing—did rabbits burrow? Did they live in burrows? A yawn cracked my jaw. I would go down from the roof and catch the rabbit, remove its safety vest and helmet, release it into the park. I could take Solly with me. Though if I took Solly with me, she would likely try to play with the rabbit, and when that didn't work she might eat it. I didn't mind when in the past she'd brought us dead things—a bird crushed by a car tire, a rat. Ben didn't like it, but I didn't mind. I'd rather know what was out there. Still, now with Clara . . .

I heaved myself out of the chair, launching back toward my life. Shuffling across the deck. Grimacing.

And there it was, halfway down the stairs. An unusual door.

The rest of the building's entrances were uniform: heavy whitewashed wood, brass hinges, triple locks. Modern for the mid-2000s, when they were built, if simplistic. This door was intricately carved, its paint a peeling turquoise. I'd never seen it before.

What was behind it? I couldn't help myself. I knocked.

I heard, "Come in."

Come derives from the Old English *cuman*—to move with the purpose of reaching. I reached for the doorknob. I twisted. The door swung open.

Inside was a woman, and her medium-sized dog, which was dark and curly with a long face and a little sort of beard, and triangular ears that folded over. It was growling, but due to the heat of the room its tongue was lolling, dispelling the menace. The woman behind the dog had a long face and a straight nose, cheeks like apples. Her straw-colored hair was pinned back in 1940s victory rolls, her lipstick bright red and recently applied. She wore a brown tweed jacket with elbow patches atop a pair of wide-legged pants, and a brooch in the shape of a sharp-pointed star with an intricate swirl at the center. She seemed familiar, although I couldn't place her. Someone I'd seen, perhaps at Arthur's door, or the neighborhood bar. She stood on the third step of a ladder, looking down at me, a cigarette tucked into her mouth. Her feet were bare.

Fur rugs stretched across the floor, under the ladder: a bearskin with the bear's face still attached, but oddly flattened; some tawny thing that looked like different pelts all sewn together. No chic faux here—I could feel the animal heat still steaming off them. An array of paint-splattered tools and drop cloths sat in a corner—this woman was clearly responsible for the noise, though given the elegant finish of this particular room, her main construction site must have been elsewhere. On one wall hung a picture frame outlining a gaping hole through which I could see our back alley: an overflowing dumpster, weeds needling through concrete. Next to it was a second turquoise door, which, given the view through its adjacent window, had to open on a sheer drop down to concrete. The room should have been cold—it was early November and, as Seth had warned me, chilly. But the air coming in through the picture frame was mild, and smelled marshy, like the sea.

I said, "What are you doing?"

The woman laughed a low, raspy laugh, and took out her cigarette. Her eyes first welcomed me in on the joke, then softened and fell back to something painful before glazing over with a levity into which I was no longer invited.

"Why," she said, smiling, "I'm building a house for Michael."

"ARTHUR!" I WAS banging on his door, but I didn't feel guilty, not with his friend upstairs hammering away. Ben had handled the paperwork when we signed for the condo, but I was sure there was a clause about notifying neighbors before beginning any major construction. Behind my own door, Clara waited. I found myself equally frustrated and thrilled to have a project that was not just her survival.

"Arthur!" His car was in the garage, and his muddy shoes were sitting in the hall. Was he ignoring me? No, he'd just been in the shower. He answered the door while pulling on a T-shirt, and I resisted the urge to peer around him for a good look at his home. I'd always felt I could only know a person once I understood the places that had made them, the objects that they kept or threw away. The art on their walls. How recently they'd steam-cleaned their floors.

"Is something the matter?" Water dripped from Arthur's hair, down an earlobe, darkening his shirt. "Can I get you something? Maybe some coffee?"

This seemed like a strange offer. The circles under my eyes must have been particularly brutal in the glare of the bare hallway bulbs. He must have heard Clara in the early morning, crying.

"Sorry that the baby's been so loud," I found myself saying. "I try to get to her in time, but I'm still figuring out what I'm doing."

Why confess this? I was losing focus. What had happened to the rage that had propelled me here, caused me to slam the door on Arthur's upstairs friend?

"Oh, gosh," said Arthur, "don't even think about it."

"I do wonder," I said, chewing on a chapped lip, mumbling, "if you can ask your friend upstairs to be quieter."

"What?"

"I mean, I don't claim to know the building codes, and I don't even really care what she's doing. If you want to add a room or whatever. It's just the noise. It's pretty constant."

"On the roof? I didn't let anyone up."

"No," I said, "in the stairwell."

"A woman in the stairwell? You think somebody broke in?"

"No," I said. "The woman hammering."

"I'm sorry, Mrs. Weiler," said Arthur, "I don't know what you're talking about."

I started to cry. Not because of his denial, not because of the way the woman upstairs had sized me up and found me wanting with my dirty pajamas and my flabby arms, the fact that her dog didn't like me. Not even because I felt myself leaking, again, although I'd already dispelled what felt like twelve gallons of watery pee that morning. It was the Mrs. Weiler—the formality—when I knew him as Arthur.

"Oh gosh, Mrs. Weiler," he said. His earnestness made me cry harder. "It'll be okay. Here, let me get some shoes on and we'll take a look together." He was talking to me as if I were old. He was talking to me the way I talked to my mother.

I let him guide me by the elbow past our landing—where Seth's and Linda's shoes sat primly on the welcome mat—and up to the door to the roof.

"You said this lady's out there?" Arthur asked me.

"No, she's through the door on the stairs." I pointed at the turquoise door, exasperated. I only had another twenty minutes until

Clara had to eat, and I didn't want to spend them illustrating the obvious. Arthur scratched the back of his neck.

"Okay, I'll head up and look for her." He wasn't listening. Jesus Christ, why wouldn't anyone listen?

Arthur went through to the roof, and I put my hand on the turquoise door, feeling for a sign of life behind it. I didn't want to turn the knob without Arthur, to show up again without some plan of action. The door itself smelled like the ocean, brackish and burnt. Behind it I felt a vibration that was most easily reconciled as an electric drill. A hot-blooded chain saw. And suddenly the door was hot, the paint sticky and melting. Something behind it or within it was now angry, boiling. I yanked my hand away, afraid I might stick. Afraid this sudden anger, which was not my own, would seep in and consume me.

Why not let it consume me? Maybe surrender would be beautiful: a free fall, in which I'd bear no more weight, in which I'd find the distance to laugh at my futility—a little speck of nothing, making nothing, meaning nothing. Responsible for nothing.

"There was a time," whispered the woman behind the door, "I felt well loved by you, and it was the warmest, happiest time in my life." She wasn't talking to me but to the anger, the heat that even now was blistering the wood. I reached toward the door, but before I could touch it, Arthur slammed in from the roof, yelling down that he hadn't seen anyone.

"Everything seems totally normal." He took the stairs two at a time. *Normal*—from the Latin *normalis*: made according to the carpenter's square.

"Not up there," I said. "Right here." The door seemed cooler in his presence, the anger hiding itself.

"Like, in the wall?" Arthur frowned.

"Okay," I said, "so she isn't someone you invited." I was well past the point of regretting my decision to involve him, not least because I sensed another gush of fluid coming. No, not coming, already here, with nothing I could do to prevent it. There was a prickling at the back of my neck that felt like the anger, laughing at me. "Excuse me," I said, trying to push past him. But Arthur was adamant.

"If you saw a strange lady in the stairwell, we should call the police. And let the condo association know."

"Yes, we can definitely do that. Let's make sure to do that later. Can I please just get . . ." But it was too late. I had no pelvic floor, so it was silly to think that I'd have been able to make it down the stairs, through our front door, into the bathroom. My pants were soaked, rivers of clear fluid running down my legs into lakes on the pocked iron stair. Arthur looked as if he'd walked in on me naked. I could see his throat visibly tighten, his Adam's apple lifting.

"It isn't urine," I said, as if that made things any better. "It's just . . . stuff from my uterus." He was trying to smile, but it was a transparent mask that couldn't hide what his eyes were practically screaming: *Why would you do this? Why would you think this is okay?*

"Of course I'll clean it up," I said. I took a step down and stopped, bracing myself against the door, which had returned to a comfortable temperature. I felt my pelvis splitting, all the climbing I'd done earlier catching up to me. I didn't want to ask anything of Arthur, let alone ask him to carry me. I didn't want to drown him in this deluge of motherhood—this young man who I'd watched kissing the bartender from the bougie restaurant down the street, the two of them pressed against the far garage, Arthur's hands on the other man's cheeks. He'd never have to know the sagging and the full weight of the body after hurling out a child; here I was now, inconveniencing him.

I didn't want to ask anything of anyone. I wanted to carry myself through the turquoise door and lock it tight behind me, smoke a pipe with the woman in her wide-legged pants, take up her hammer. I would replace her, on that ladder, and lean out the picture window into the gray day, announcing myself. I would bang until Clara cried her throat raw, until Ben called the condo association, demanding consequences. But I wouldn't go back down. I would stay with the woman. I'd build whatever house she wanted.

Instead I said, "Can you go get my husband?"

Table of Contents

4

There was a door in the stairwell. There was a turquoise door in the stairwell, and nobody was talking about it.

"Get some rest," Ben had said after coming to collect me, his mother behind him with a pinched face, certain she had never expelled week-old afterbirth onto a neighbor, that she'd never expelled anything unpleasant, just two perfect pink children who'd come out clean and easy, her stomach still smooth.

I didn't care what Linda thought of me. Truly, I didn't. I didn't crave Ben's family's approval. I knew that he would choose me over them, whether in matters of religion or vacation destination or style of home. I knew, and took the sort of pride in knowing that comes from a petty victory—being first to a parking space or winning a board game that I hadn't even wanted to play. The feeling was shallow, and I liked not feeling deeply. I cultivated not feeling too deeply when it came to Ben. That was the whole point of him, of being married to him in particular, of choosing him over somebody I'd picked out for passion, not companionship, not ease. Somebody who could hurt me. Being married to Ben was nice. From the Old French *nice*: stupid, senseless; from the Latin *nescius*: unaware.

I couldn't help but feel deeply about the woman and her door. In no state to perform my usual dissection of the things that I wanted too much—dismantling and divesting until I'd pulled apart the essence of them, whittled them down into indifference—I spent nursing sessions watching HGTV with my eyes glazed over, thinking of her. Did she belong to me? Had I been specially chosen as the only one to see her? No surprise that Arthur was oblivious: he was a single man with no need to be watchful. Arthur didn't deserve her, and anyway she wouldn't want him. Ben was different. Ben was—as my sister said—a catch. Ben's response was more deliberate. I'd see him startle at a loud noise, then settle as if it had been nothing, because he wanted it to be nothing. He'd built his career on examining problems and deciding which were worth his attention. Ben was adept at setting aside minor concerns, and he'd decided these concerns were minor. They were not minor to me.

She was building a house, which to me made perfect sense. How nice to build a house, with a true picture window, and furs on the floors. Real furs on the floors and draped across the chairs, which had adult-sized seats but had been cut off at the legs so that they looked like they were meant for obese children. This wasn't the house she was building. This was the house she lived in, the house she already had—a house that looked out over the ocean. A fishing boat would come at dawn and a grizzled man would raise an arm in greeting, and the frothy swimmerets of the lobsters would tickle her toes when she went barefoot in the sand. At night the sky would swirl with stars, and her life would stretch wide across the water. Nearby, she would build the house for Michael.

On the television, a chirpy couple covered an old woman's kitchen in subway tile. Ben sat reading a book about the history of the stock market, one socked foot resting on Solly. In my arms, Clara made her newborn dolphin sputter. She sneezed, butting her head against my breast.

"Have you ever been to Maine?" I asked Ben.

"Vermont," he said, not looking up.

"Yeah," I said, "Me neither." For some reason this caught his attention. He put a gum wrapper down to mark his page.

"Should we take a trip?" he asked me, and I laughed, because I hadn't showered in three days and was pretty sure it would be years before I fit into my bathing suits. But I liked the idea of a trip. I liked the idea of feeling the swimmerets on my feet, of putting Clara in a little blow-up boat and sending her off to see the ocean.

BEN GOT UP with Clara on the morning he was leaving for Houston so that I could sleep in. I woke up too, of course, since she'd been sleeping right next to me, and I heard him run the water to heat her bottle and heard her whimpering, impatient to eat. He was good with her, so steady. She liked him. She only liked me when she was gorging on me—I couldn't have her in my arms without her nose questing my chest, her head surveying back and forth like a metal detector. She'd sit there with her lips latched, not even sucking, and then when I slipped her off the breast, she would howl. The habit made it difficult to love her. I lay in bed for a while, thinking about this.

"Don't bother Arthur," Ben said as he was leaving. He said more than that, to give him credit—talked about how sorry he was to be leaving, how he'd never have gone were it not the firm's highest-paying client, how he'd make it up to me when he got back. I nodded along, because what else was I supposed to do? I didn't necessarily want him around, but I didn't really want him gone either. I didn't want to be alone with Clara. Ideally he could just take her with him, and I'd stay here with Solly, watching bad TV in bed. Getting some work done. Actually sleeping.

Not ten minutes after he'd gone Annie called to check in on me. I knew that Ben had texted her, but she played it cool: *Just thinking of you, maybe I'll stop by.*

"No," I said, "don't stop by." Clara was sprawled in her bouncer. When people took professional photos of their newborns, the babies were scrunched up to fit into a cocoon or a bucket, or the shape of a heart with their hands on their chin and their tiny diapered buttocks stuck straight in the air. My baby didn't scrunch—she elbowed out of her swaddle, she rolled and she spread. She was a baby, not some strange fleshy doll. I had a doll once whose eyes only opened when you held her completely upright. When Clara's eyes opened, she looked at me suspiciously.

"It's gross here," I said. "Everything's dirty and I'm dirty and the baby isn't even cute yet."

"Oh, come on."

"She's still all yellow. She's smushy."

"Megan, you're not supposed to say that about your own kid. You're supposed to give her vitamins or something."

"Well, it isn't her fault," I said. "How's work? Did you meet up with that dude from the coffee shop?" I had always lived vicariously through Annie, her bucolic romantic entanglements, her therapy sessions, her good taste in clothes.

"He didn't call," she said. Normally I'd say something stupid like "More fish in the sea," but I said nothing. *One fish, two fish, red fish, blue fish.* Why hadn't coffee-shop guy called my sister? Annie was pretty, she was smart. I felt a void I thought was sadness swirling deeper in my chest. Burrowing. I pictured bunnies burrowing. Bunnies running in a field, chased by hounds, chased by humans. Boots and a breeze and a horn to start the hunt. Pet bunnies with ears that flopped down. Wild hares with mange, their ears erect. Good dogs lining up their kills, tongues out, *Look at me, praise me.*

"He still could," said Annie, her voice rising at the end, making it a question.

"Yes, he could," I agreed.

IN THE LAST months of my pregnancy, I had effectively abandoned my dissertation. We use *abandon* to mean leave, but what it actually means is surrender. In thirteenth-century France: *mettre sa forest à bandon*, a phrase from feudal law that meant the public opening of a forest or pasture for all who needed to come cut wood or graze. My work was open to the elements, available. By leaving it alone, I'd rendered it no longer solely mine.

There'd been an expectation of progress while I was carrying Clara, but I'd blithely missed the last check-in phone call with my advisor, telling him I was having "complications" and instead eating a carton of rocky road ice cream in my underwear, some stupid teen soap opera streaming on TV. The next morning I opened a Word document, flipped a comma back and forth for twenty minutes, and then closed it.

Now I was officially on maternity leave, saddled with a tiny, actual, human complication and too tired to do much of anything. Somehow I was not too tired to feel guilty about feeling tired. I dreamed that the rest of my graduate school cohort had shared a massive hotel suite at a conference in Bruges. I hadn't been invited. I had no need to go to Bruges, but in this dream the need had not been the determining factor in my lack of invitation, rather my breast pump, which they told me couldn't fit on the plane. In this dream my cohort called me from the hotel bathroom, Skyping me from the whirlpool tub where they all sat, sipping champagne.

I woke up and fed Clara, thinking about all the conferences I would be missing, the classes I would not be asked to teach, the parties and the networking dinners I wouldn't attend, the deferred tenure-track jobs. I didn't especially like my cohort—the two actual friends I'd made were casualties of attrition—but I still wanted them to like me. I still wanted to be relevant, for people to think of me, to google myself and find praise. It was hard enough being tied to Ben's job. We had to live by his office. No research sabbaticals or postdocs abroad for me. The best I could hope for was a part-time position at a school in Chicago, or a dissertation interesting enough to turn into a book. Neither would happen, unless I kept writing.

Clara was ten days old, and time felt both inconsequential and absolutely vital. She was pretty much a blob, and I still wasn't sure if I loved her, but I knew that at one point I'd loved my work, I knew my work was still there, waiting. What would my obituary look like, what would they write on my tombstone, were I to go up through the turquoise door and free-fall out the picture window? *Megan Weiler, survived by sixty unwritten pages and a round or two of revision. Also a baby.* That wouldn't do.

With Clara in her bouncer, I opened my laptop at the kitchen table, a suction attached to either breast. I was still trying to up my milk supply, and when Clara wasn't eating, I was pumping. I hadn't wanted to spend money on the bras that let you pump hands-free, which seemed silly now that I thought about the other gadgets I'd bought without question. Did I imagine there was shame in not holding the nozzle to the breast myself? Did I need to be involved in my own milking, the surprisingly arousing tug of nipple, the splat of fluid in the cloudy plastic cup? I sliced holes in an old sports bra and leaned forward, pressing the back of what the manual called "the pump parts" against the edge of the table. If I was careful, if I didn't move, this jerry-rig worked.

I was ready, yet I found myself uncertain. How would I find my way back in? I had to make my work accessible. My advisor said he wasn't "convinced" by my latest draft. I wasn't sure what that meant.

Scrolling through my document, I landed on a chapter about the Bureau of Educational Experiments, the Greenwich Village bastion of progressive education I was using to support my central ideas about modernist literature and early childhood education.

"Colloquially known as Bank Street School for Children, the bureau championed the notion that children develop language to communicate not with people but with the sensory world around them," I read aloud to Clara. I looked at her. She gave me nothing. "Well, put it that way, and who wouldn't be convinced?" Clara sniffled, then yawned.

For years I had been reading about how children should be taught to communicate, and for years I had been struggling to make other people care. I'd always had a love for words, but I had never been a very good communicator. I hoped this would be different for my daughter.

"Language," I said slowly to Clara. "Sensation."

Bank Street's founder, Lucy Sprague Mitchell, claimed that young children experimented with language regardless of meaning, that when meaning did come, it was in service to their own insular experience. I liked this: language as selfishness, language as categorization. An intangible sound making the tangible world real.

Clara whimpered. The little line at the front of her diaper that indicated urine had turned from yellow to blue. "You peed yourself," I said to Clara. "Your own insular experience." Her nose twitched.

I could put down the pump and change her. She was wet. Ben would want me to change her. But the number of diapers I'd already used that morning was unconscionable. Ben wouldn't want me to waste resources. And my milk was really coming now, finally splurging through the valves.

I kept reading. Clara kept whining.

At the end of the chapter I had copy-pasted my images, as if including them brought me closer to a finished draft. "Here," I said, using an elbow to angle my laptop screen downward. "I'll show you the pictures. Let's find out if you've learned how to see."

I showed Clara a few screenshots of original pages from the books I'd described, an imposing gray building, the New York Public Library lions, a snapshot of two Bank Street School teachers walking through the West Village. Two young Bank Street School teachers, one in a fur coat, one in a trench. One with a beret, one hatless and looking remarkably like someone I had recently seen smoking a cigarette.

I pushed my chair back. The shields fell off my breasts, sending the little collection bottles to the floor and immediately contaminating my freshly pumped milk. I didn't care. I pulled up the search bar on my computer, and while drops fell from my goose-pimpled nipples, googled Margaret Wise Brown.

There she was—the woman from upstairs, who I had not seen at the corner coffee shop or on a friend's Facebook feed or riding the bus. There she was on my computer, grinning out at me. Holding a black dog. Wearing a brooch. Cheeks like apples.

Margaret Wise Brown had moved in upstairs.

Solly came over to sniff around the breast pump. I'd have to boil everything before I could use it again.

Clara's cries were strengthening. I rocked her bouncer with my foot, which made my pelvis hurt but didn't calm her.

Someone who looked remarkably like Margaret Wise Brown had moved in upstairs. Someone who, like the real Margaret Wise Brown, had a close friend named Michael. Had a fluffy black dog. Had fluffy hair and fancy period clothing.

"Hush," I said to Clara. "Mommy's thinking."

A Margaret Wise Brown impersonator, hired for kids' parties. An actress, filming for a TV show—just the other day a camera crew had blocked our street. That didn't make any sense. That didn't explain the turquoise door.

Margaret Wise Brown lived upstairs.

And why shouldn't she be the real Margaret? Sleep was a distant memory, and I was a cow, and a human had come out of my vagina. Why shouldn't Margaret Wise Brown live upstairs?

Clara, still howling.

Life was nothing like it had been, nothing like I'd ever thought it could be. Why the hell not add Margaret?

Introduction

In 1934 the children's author Margaret Wise Brown wrote a letter to her mentor about Gertrude Stein's metafictional novel *The Making of Americans*: "In this book I am given new solutions," said Brown, "brand new ideas. . . . There is a rhythm of American day to day existence and relationship that is as certain as the rhthm [*sic*] of the ocean and as binding as the relationship of the ocean to the little waves that crash on our shore."[1] This brand new rhythm of day-to-day existence marked not only a shift in Brown's own thinking but a shift between the golden age of children's literature of the Romantic period, and the modern here-and-now school. Instead of allegory and fantasy, Brown and her colleagues in post–World War I children's publishing would focus on the realities of sensory experience, the sounds of language, and the particular worldviews and communicative abilities of the very young.

Historians have argued that the cultural shift away from fairy tales in popular children's literature reflected both the growing threat to the concept of idyllic childhood posed by World War I, and the influence of early childhood education reformers like Lucy Sprague Mitchell

---

1 Margaret Wise Brown to Marguerite C. Hearsey, undated (November 1934), Letter 15. Fishburn Library Archives, Hollins College, Roanoke, Virginia.

and Bank Street School.[2] But few have focused on the impact of literary modernism on those writing for children in the postwar years. What I propose to call the modern age of children's literature (1926–1945) was not, as most often described, a direct contradiction to the whimsy of the prior golden age, but a dialectic between golden-age thinking and new theories of education and literacy that remodeled the burgeoning modernism of writers like Virginia Woolf and Gertrude Stein for elementary audiences.

In the following pages, I will argue that authors like Alvin Tresselt, Margaret Wise Brown, and Dorothy Kunhardt combined modernist aesthetics and new educational philosophies with an updated brand of whimsy, resulting in—

---

2 For examples of this trend in historiography, see George Mitchell, *The End of All That: On Childhood After the Great War* (New York: Redmond & Company, 1990) and Allison Somogyi, *New Lands of Fantasy* (Toronto: Duchess University Press, 1976).

5

Margaret Wise Brown lived upstairs.

I found my house keys in Solly's water bowl, my sneakers in the shower. I said to myself, *I am tired.* I watched a documentary about mid-century American clothiers. I said to myself, *I am having lucid dreams that reshape my reality.* I heard someone sawing wood; I smelled cigarette smoke through our air vents. I considered climbing back up to the door, and felt afraid. I said to myself, *This is your life.*

"You will miss these days," said the message-board mothers, the baby books, the women who'd been through it all, who knew. These days and endless nights with Clara at my breast, the three a.m. television glow, the fuzzy bathroom fan and lullabies—supposedly someday I'd miss them as I now missed long afternoons drinking beers on the patio, dinner dates, and cab rides. People had told me that the first weeks of motherhood would be hard, but they hadn't told me how hard: how difficult it would be to contort myself into what Clara needed, how much she would need, how much time I would spend sleepless and thirsty and tied to the couch, nipples aching. How she would grunt and snort and sniffle in her bassinet, tongue dancing as she smelled my milk. How she would cry, and I would not always be able to console her—how deeply I would feel this as my failure. I watched the furrow of her dreaming brow while she slept on my chest. As I sank into my own sleep, I tried not to feel it as a free fall but an open pair of arms. *Don't wish the time away*, they said. *Don't ever wish the time away.*

I'd thought things might be easier with Ben gone: no one to snipe at, no one to begrudge for sleeping soundly on the futon in the living room while I pinched myself awake at four a.m., no one to roll his eyes when I mentioned the noises upstairs. Of course it was harder without him. I had only myself to talk to, I had to be up whenever Clara was, I had to take Solly for all of her walks.

"Maybe you'll be nicer to him when he gets back, now you've realized that you need him," said Annie over the phone. It was the end of my second full day solo, and I hadn't gotten my umbrella or Clara's stroller cover ready in time for a sudden downpour. I'd been soaking wet, with Clara soaking wet, and a soaking wet Solly shaking herself dry in the front hall. Who was to blame here? I blamed Clara. Without her, I could have run inside. Solly and I never got caught in the rain, before.

"I *am* nice to him," I said. I'd very nicely FaceTimed Ben twice that day so Clara could see him, so she wouldn't forget him. I dreaded night, when I knew Ben was asleep and wouldn't hear his phone. I could handle Clara's round-the-clock nursing in the day-time, in the sunlight. I could handle the exhaustion if I had a ready tether to the world. Alone in the dark, the weight was impossible. Just thinking about night made my throat swell.

"Mom said she would stay with you," Annie reminded me. "At this point maybe take her up on it. Or at least let me do a night shift."

But as harrowing as the thought of those midnight feeds was, even worse was the idea that someone else would take them over. That Clara would wake up and whimper and not find Mommy there. That she would realize she'd be just fine with Grandma, or

Aunt Annie. That I was extraneous. Already, my daughter didn't need me.

"It's fine," I said to Annie. "I've got it."

TIME OPENED UP, minutes bleeding into hours, day and night both the same gaping wound. I had never been so tired, and Clara seemed always awake. I walked her around our condo, singing softly. Once or twice I took her out into the hallway, contemplated bringing her upstairs for a change of scene, for another look at Margaret. I didn't, because it all felt too intimate. It was too early to introduce Clara to such raw emotion. I was afraid to expose her to that melting door, that heat.

When she wouldn't sleep, I drove her through adjacent neighborhoods, remarking to myself that such and such house was a nice one, that those window trims were pretty, wondering how I would feel if that semitruck one lane over lost control and smashed into our SUV. Would the guilt be of a different texture if the accident were not while on our way to the pediatrician, or even the store, rather on one such joyride? When the ambulance got to the scene and the EMTs asked me why I had my newborn baby in the car on such an icy day, I wasn't sure what I would tell them. I imagined them whispering together and wagging a literal finger, and I thought perhaps I was more worried about being judged as a bad mother than actually being one. At fourteen years old, Annie went through a phase in which she judged the Prius owners and the fair-trade coffee drinkers far more harshly than she did those driving Hummers. She said that it was better to love a bad thing well than to love a good thing badly.

"It's performative," she said.

But wasn't everything performative? What were we if not constantly refashioning ourselves into what we wanted the world to see? The interactive archives of an October car crash: the tortured metal frame, the drive-through Taco Bell wrappers, the pacifier sewn into the plush monkey. Attendees would stroll through and wonder if all three Crunchwrap Supremes had been eaten in one sitting.

This is what I considered while looking back at Clara, reflected infinitely between the rearview and car seat mirrors. She was asleep, the pacifier fallen from her mouth, her small nose twitching. I decided I should probably seek out some more serious adult company.

One of the reasons I'd given Ben for wanting to move to the city instead of the suburbs was the classes I could take with Clara—the mommy-and-me's and the music and the yoga—where I'd find her friends and meet other new moms. I scrolled through the listings for something appealing, something that would make me feel like a person and not just a mother. An exercise class where you brought your own jogging stroller, a meetup at a place known for its decaf, a session of soft lights and early movement targeting the under-six-month crowd. I didn't think I'd done any of these things as a baby—no playgroups or toddler art or jogs on the lake—but perhaps if my mother had tried harder, had given me just such a community, I'd have turned out better. I feared that parenting was a cycle in which your aptitude depended entirely on how much work your own parents had put in for you, which meant that I was predisposed to be lackluster and distant, and Ben was predisposed to be overly involved. I bet he'd been to all the classes. I bet Linda had hosted all the classes in her home and cooked gourmet lunches and never once turned on the television.

It had never been easier to feel both small and indispensable at once.

I picked a stroller workout class, doubled up my sports bras, pulled back my hair. I drove to the field house and parked the car, and then I sat nursing Clara in the back seat for forty-three minutes, at which point the class was over, so I buckled her into her car seat and drove home.

■ ■ ■

WHENEVER CLARA CRIED, my whole body needed her to stop, my shoulders tightening, stomach dropping. I wasn't sure if it was my need or her need affecting me, if it was her unhappiness or mine. I didn't want to be caught up in her need, I didn't want to be entangled. To be beholden to anything but myself, to be beholden to even myself.

I could pick Clara up and smash her. I could drop her on the bathroom tile. What would happen then? Solly might come to clean her up. I pictured rabbits being eaten by dogs. Splotchy hounds in a line, noses to the ground, finding prey and bursting bodies open. A rabbit with an open wound, a little kitten lapping up its leaking brain.

Milk from my right breast let down, staining my T-shirt. The thing to do was to feed Clara. I did, and she stopped crying.

The Visionaries and Their Mentors

Over the course of her life, Margaret Wise Brown was greatly impacted by relationships with women in positions of authority. Biographers have suggested that this deference to women who "knew more" stemmed from her tumultuous relationship with her mother, Maude Johnson Brown.[1] At Hollins College in Roanoke, which Brown attended from 1928 to 1932, she relied on her English professor, Marguerite Hearsey, for philosophical advice. By the time Brown began work at the Bank Street College of Education, she had surpassed her college mentor and was ripe for Lucy Sprague Mitchell's influence.

Mitchell found Brown's natural inclinations too "precious," and hoped to guide her toward a more practical approach to writing for children. But Brown subscribed to T. S. Eliot's explanation of the new "mythical method" of art creation that bypassed traditional narrative as "a way . . . of giving a shape and a significance to the immense

---

1 Maude Johnson and Robert Brown had a strained marriage, with Robert often on the road for his job as vice president and treasurer of the American Manufacturing Company. By 1942, Robert was living at his yacht club on the occasions that he was "at home," and Maude had filled the void left by the ruined marriage with a brand of American spiritualism called Theosophy. The demands of the religion, combined with often debilitating high blood pressure, left her little energy for her children. Leonard Marcus, *Margaret Wise Brown: Awakened by the Moon* (Boston: Beacon Press, 1992).

panorama of futility and anarchy which is contemporary history."[2] She was also deeply influenced by the actress and poet Michael Strange, whose mentorship began in 1940 and led her to develop a more spiritual approach to her work.

Born Blanche Marie Louise Oelrichs in Newport, Rhode Island, in 1890, Michael Strange spent her youth as a Gilded Age socialite before coming to literature. She published several books of poetry and plays between 1916 and 1928, and gained notoriety for her second marriage to the actor John Barrymore. During her third marriage to prominent lawyer Harrison Tweed, Strange released an autobiography, to limited success. She was introduced to Margaret by mutual friends and immediately took to the younger woman, acting first as writing mentor and then lover.

As Brown's career flourished, Strange's was waning, and biographers have noted the insidious influence the women had upon each other's work. Brown's most commercially and critically unsuccessful picture book, *The Dark Wood of the Golden Birds*, a purported allegory of the artistic process, was dedicated to Michael Strange. Its illustrator, Leonard Weisgard, confessed he never understood the book's conceit, and a *Kirkus* review said it had "gone too far into the rarefied atmosphere remote from child interest" (June 1, 1950). The book exemplifies the difficulties of combining theory and narrative, and serves to highlight the success Brown found when distilling theory, rather than obscuring it.[3]

The book begins—

---

2 T. S. Eliot, "Ulysses, Order, and Myth," *Dial* 75 (November 1923): 480–83.

3 Harper & Row, Brown's publisher, also recognized the faults in the manuscript. A reader for Harper editor Ursula Nordstrom called the book "an overripe tomato" and advised against publishing it. Nordstrom appears to have gone ahead not because of the book's merit but due to her close relationship with Brown, to whom the manuscript was vastly important; Marcus.

6

thought, If I could only take my body back. If I could just find some space between myself and my child, then I could find my way out of this *between* where I was always attached, constantly ravished. The books called that back-and-forth Clara did when she sought my breasts "rooting." The word came from the Old Norse *rut:* the origin. I was the cause of Clara, the seed and the soil, she the plant draining nutrients, rearranging my established composition. Using me to push up and up and up.

She was two weeks old, and still so desperate. If I just had some space, could just stretch out, even a little. If I didn't have to lean forward, crook my neck, squeeze my nipple, every time Clara wanted to eat. I kept ruining my pumped milk—germ-ridden Solly coming to investigate whenever I turned on the machine, my hands too full to shoo her. But each of the major formula brands had sent samples in the mail after we moved, their new baby tracking system honing in on Clara's approach. Since I planned to nurse, we were going to donate them; the boxes were still sitting on a shelf in the garage. Surely no one would know if I skipped one breastfeeding session, if I mixed Clara some formula and sat her in her bouncer and held her bottle away from my body for just twenty minutes to feel something close to free.

I put her in the baby wrap to go down to the garage. After a few false starts I managed to knock the nearest box down from storage.

Then I brought the powder back upstairs and mixed it. I knew I wasn't supposed to use the microwave, that Ben never microwaved my pumped milk—always ran the bottle under hot water and then tested the milk on his wrist. But it was frigid outside and our water heater was finicky; it would take forever for the pipes to run hot. Clara was crying.

I moved the warmed bottle from the microwave to the counter, slammed the microwave door shut, heard it click. And then the suction swish of the door opening. I frowned, slammed it again. *Swish*, again. Slam.

The bottle smelled funny, felt like maybe the plastic was melting. The milk was too hot. I shook it. Clara wrinkled her nose, judging me. Another *swish*. The condo, fucking judging me. I stuck the bottle in the freezer and closed the microwave, went over to replace Clara's sock, which had slipped. When I went back to check on the bottle, it fell out of the freezer and onto the floor, formula splattering everywhere. Solly padded over to lap up the spill. I took Clara to the armchair and unfastened my bra.

Swish. When open, the microwave emitted a weak orange light. From where we sat in the living room, it looked like an alien ship had landed in the kitchen, dark but for that glow. I'd never been one to buy into extraterrestrials. I'd spent several drunken evenings debating the issue with Ben, who was certain not only that life was sustainable on Mars but that somewhere out there in some galaxy was a world of creatures more advanced than humans: an equal consciousness not as petty, more rational, better equipped to handle crises. It was enough for me to know that I existed in a world of other people, as a point in a line of human consciousness that might not be infinite but stretched centuries forward and back. I didn't need nebulae and solar systems and extra dimensions. Thinking about other galaxies made me dizzy, made me think too hard about how much our own planet was spinning, how impossible it was to ever hold on or stay put.

Clara was latched now, but the television remote was all the way across the room. I leaned over for my phone and immediately noticed an alert from Mrs. What-to-Expect's message board. I had never been alerted before—I only scrolled through, an observer, leaving no trace of myself but the thumbprint on the screen of my phone.

Throughout my pregnancy I'd dabbled with several apps and online communities, evaluating each on interface and how often it crashed. They were all similar in content. Women posted *Is it normal to be growing hair on my nipples* or *Pls take a look at this discharge and let me know if its rly my bloody show.* Mrs. What-to-Expect's app was my favorite, both because of its lavender titles and for the validity afforded by its association with her best-selling book. The October board was a group of over ten thousand women, all over the world, our only commonality the window of time in which sperm met our eggs. I didn't track everyone— that would have been impossible, and besides some of the women spelled *love* L-U-V or had handles like GunPacknMama or wrote lengthy posts complaining about their night nannies. These were clearly not my people. Nor were the women who commented with photos of themselves with tired eyes and neon lipstick, posing with their swaddled, smush-faced babies. The whole point of the message board was anonymity—I didn't want these actual women, but their avatars. I wanted them the way the audience of a Greek play wants its chorus, masked and hovering, commentating on the action, passing judgment on the players on the stage, not on me, safe in my seat.

Ah, Megan, silly Megan. The audience and players are one and the same.

I opened the app, clicked on the little speech bubble. The heading of the post I was tagged in: MICROWAVE.

Megan, it began. I didn't use my name anywhere on the app. *Megan, did you mean to put the bottle in the microwave?*

"What the fuck."

Clara whimpered. She was falling asleep still attached to me, her mouth a vise on my left nipple. She had a small bit of dried snot stuck to her nostril that fluttered with each breath.

Had Ben set up a nanny cam to keep an eye on me? Had Annie? My head swiveled toward the curtains: all shut. We hadn't yet installed the baby monitor. My laptop was closed. How were they watching me? Who were they, and why did they care? And what was with the passive aggression?

The author was Anon987, and Mrs. What-to-Expect didn't let you click to see what else she had posted on the site. I could, however, follow the thread to get alerts whenever somebody responded. Clara made one of her high-pitched dolphin sleep sounds. My finger hovered.

Before I could smear my thumb across the screen, the app refreshed itself, and three responses followed.

Anon987: She came because she was called.

The message read like a horoscope, the perfect ratio of particular to vague. Of course there was a she—there was Margaret. There was Clara. There was the anger emanating from the turquoise door, the heat.

Anon988: Don't let her in, and don't upset her. You wouldn't want to upset her. You wouldn't want her to come in.

Some other message-board mother had heard the hammering, smelled the smoke. They knew about the upstairs house and Margaret's dog; they knew my microwave was broken. They knew I was drowning.

Anon989: Megan, don't upset her.

The situation with Margaret hadn't yet been frightening. Strange, unexpected, frustrating in its opacity, but never yet frightening. This warning was frightening.

And then:

Clara363: It hurts.

My twinge of fear became full-body terror. Clara was fully asleep now, her mouth slack, a little blister forming on her top lip from the friction between our two bodies. I thought I might vomit. I thought I might scream. My stomach swirled, my vision invaded by dark, dilating stars. Moving Clara to her bouncer, I went to the bathroom to dry-heave over the toilet, then doused my face in cold sink water when I realized it was to no effect. My whole body itched with heat—with the knowledge that something was coming—and I knew I couldn't face it, couldn't stand it, whatever it might be. I ran out the sliding doors onto the balcony, to face instead the thrilling cold of November predawn.

Frozen concrete. Quiet street. City-dark, with dim-lit streetlamps. I was vastly underdressed, and the temperature was bordering on freezing, but at least I'd put some distance between myself and Clara, between myself and that message board, the house. At least I could breathe.

Beyond the alley, the boulevards were silent. A light was on in the house across the way, and I could see a television flicker and the shadow of a woman standing at the shadow of her kitchen island. My breasts hurt from the cold, from Clara leaving neither empty. There was a blanket just inside, but I couldn't bring myself to step beyond the threshold of protection, the glass door keeping me outside my own life, maintaining my status as passerby, observer.

My panic had crested, and now it began to recede. Time to take stock. I was sleep-deprived. Hormonal. We hadn't focused on the condo since Clara was born, but it was an *it*, a place and not a consciousness, could foster no resentment. The microwave was broken, I was tired and anxious; in my exhaustion I'd imagined Margaret. Somebody out there was playing some stupid, sick joke. I'd be fine if I took a step to the left, toward the glass, if I just turned the handle. Better than fine: I would be warm and indoors with my child. Glass was glass, and the internet was just a mess of radio waves and wires. My toes had turned to ice.

I braced myself and peeked beyond the brick. Clara asleep. One hand stretched above her head, as if she'd found her church and was testifying. She was two weeks old, and in between the times she'd be able to hurt me. My baby. My girl.

I put my hand on the door handle. It wouldn't turn. The door was locked.

Impossible. I jiggled again, refusing to let it be true. It could not be true. It was four in the morning, and my phone was on the couch, and Ben was in Houston, and only Annie or the cops could let me in. Annie, who would tell me she'd told me so, or the cops, who would tell me I was an unfit mother. Once I froze to death, they'd come take my baby away—but how would they find her? How would they know to come look for her? Days would go by, and Ben would come up the stairs, and a smell would waft out when he unlocked the—

Stop it. Get a grip and call for help.

"Help!" I slammed my hands onto the balcony railing, branding them bloodless white. Nothing changed—the alley indifferent, the world as still as if I hadn't said a thing. "Somebody help us!"

Was Clara moving? Was she stretching toward that electrical outlet? Could the system short-circuit, with that creep using our Wi-Fi, with her diaper wet, my laptop plugged in?

Could Margaret hear me from her upstairs room? Would she come down? I needed someone to call Annie.

"*Help!*" Why was my voice still so quiet? Why had I spent so much time training myself to be quiet? "*Help me, please!*"

I had no way and nowhere to climb—too high up, nothing to shimmy down or use for a foothold. At least Clara was asleep.

Had she wanted me gone? Had the condo wanted me gone? Clara was mad about the microwaved milk, which even as I was heating I had known was a mistake. Clara was mad about my apathy, mad at my resentment. She knew that I preferred Margaret's fur-lined room—the silver tea set and the old-fashioned telephone, the green glass hurricane lamp with the dangling copper cord—to her own sterile nursery. She was trying to get back at me.

All rationality abandoned, I readied myself to wail, to pound the thick cement of the balcony, to sacrifice my next-born child to the spirit of the building in exchange for a way in. And then I heard the revving of an engine, and smelled the heady rot of garbage. A blinking orange beacon appeared out of the morning fog, the lighthouse coming slowly toward me.

"Hey," I yelled down, leaning so far over the balcony that my feet lifted up off the concrete. "Hey, guy with the truck!"

He had on thick headphones, the band glimmering in the streetlights. If he just turned his head, he would see me. Three dumpsters sat spaced across the alley at about twenty-foot intervals; ours was the last. I watched him hook the first onto the back of his truck, the growl of the motor drowning out my cries for his attention. Inside, Clara was stirring. It would be hours before the neighbors woke up, and then who knew how long before they noticed me. In that time Clara might have learned how to roll and fallen out of the bouncer. Solly might have peed on the floor. I might have frostbite.

I was wearing ripped pajama bottoms and one of Ben's old T-shirts. In just a minute, my only chance at rescue would be standing right under me, but I had nothing to get his attention. We'd meant to get planters, and hadn't. A planter would be difficult to lift, but also difficult to miss. A planter would rain potting soil and seeds down onto the alley, would land with a resounding and declarative crash. But I didn't have a planter, so I pulled off Ben's shirt and dropped it down, where by the kindness of some fate it fell onto the garbage man's shoulder. He looked up at me leaning out over the railing, one hand flailing madly and the other not quite hiding my nipples. He took off his headphones.

"You stuck up there?"

"I have a baby locked inside!" Saying it out loud made it truer. I started to cry.

"Whoa! Okay, lady. We're gonna fix this, okay? I'm calling nine-one-one now."

"No! Can you please just call my sister? I don't want to make a scene." Already I could sense the neighbors stirring. Why did I care? If not now, when would ever be the moment to demand everyone listen, to claim space for myself and my child? But I didn't want Arthur to see me naked, or the girl across the way. I didn't want them to see the soft flab of my stomach, or my greasy, unwashed hair.

"I'm calling nine-one-one, and I'll stay with you till they get here, okay? They're gonna send the fire squad. Your kid will be fine."

"Please . . ." I whispered.

"What's that?"

My teeth were chattering.

"Can I give you my sister's number? Can you call her, too?"

"Don't worry, lady. The fire squad's on their way."

"Six-three-zero-two-four-one-one-four-nine-seven."

"What?"

"Six-three-zero . . ." The way he looked up at me, squinting; the way my mouth sharpened the words so much that I almost could taste them. I shook my head. "Never mind." Inside I could see Solly standing guard over Clara. She blinked out at me, mournful and waiting. My breath fogged the glass and obscured them both from my view.

Sirens approached, the full-on fire brigade clanging down the silent street. Lights turned on in the condo across the way.

Of course Clara woke up when they hammered down the dead-bolted front door, tracking mud onto our hardwoods. Of course Solly started barking. But the worst of it was how easily the men turned the lock to bring me inside from the patio, how calm and ordinary and even deferential they were as they walked me to the couch and wrapped me in a silver heat blanket. I was too cold to pick up Clara—I could feel the cold radiating off me, and even Solly sniffed me with uncharacteristic disdain.

"She can't smile yet," I said to the man bending down to wiggle his gloved fingers a few feet from the bouncer. I don't know why I thought I needed an excuse. He hadn't asked for any; he was trying to be kind. But I felt a frightening bitterness toward his heavily clothed body, his calm, easy way of wooing my daughter. The ease with which his body broadcast *man*. His partner took my blood pressure, and the band around my arm gave me something to push back against. There was comfort in being contained.

It took three calls to wake up Annie, and then several minutes of sleep-addled confusion before she understood my plight. The garbage-truck driver was gone, as was Ben's T-shirt, and while I figured I'd see neither again, I was sure that the driver would see me when he looked up at our balcony each time he passed through on his run. He would remember my body, spilling.

Annie arrived in sweatpants, which made me feel a bit better. Our dead bolt needed replacing; the hallway was littered with debris. She used a rag to wipe the muddy footprints from the floor. She told me we would talk about this later, but for now to go lie down, and I did, and for the first time in what felt like several decades I was alone in my bedroom, with the door shut.

It was only as I drifted off to sleep that I remembered the message board: *Don't let her in.*

It hurts.

The Major Impact of a Minor Publisher

While exceedingly simple, the new genre of the "tactile book" put into practice many of the prominent modernist literary theories of its day. Just as Stephen Dedalus gave adult readers a world of sensory impressions in Joyce's *Portrait of the Artist as a Young Man*, Dorothy Kunhardt's *Pat the Bunny* offered a fully immersive sensory experience to her young devotees—children could fluff a rabbit, feel the itch of a man's beard, and flip through a full miniature book within its pages.

Pat the Bunny was a runaway best seller for publisher Simon & Schuster, but it was not the first of its kind. Two years earlier, in 1938, the small independent publisher W. R. Scott put out Ethel McCullough's *Cottontails*, a "feely" book that featured rabbits with real cotton-ball tails, and apple trees adorned with red glass buttons. The books were meant to be handled by children as young as eighteen months old, and were printed with nontoxic dyes on untreated cloth. Because of a lack of resources and shoddy production—editor Margaret Wise Brown and publisher Bill Scott sewed all the sensory details into each book themselves—the majority of *Cottontails* stock fell apart in the mail or at the warehouse.[1] The idea, however, was groundbreaking.

---

1 Marcus, 101.

And the small company's innovation didn't stop there. Bill Scott, a letterpress printer with family money and a child enrolled at Bank Street School, had formed W. R. Scott in 1937, operating partially from his home, and partially from a school projection closet. His goal was to tap into the nursery school market, at the time largely untouched by major publishers. While the progressive early education movement had grown swiftly over the past decade, no one had solely dedicated their list to experimentally tested here-and-now children's books.

Margaret Wise Brown proved an excellent choice to serve as W. R. Scott's chief editor and spokesperson, soliciting manuscripts from her wide range of acquaintances and suggesting and supporting a variety of avant-garde styles of book. Under her supervision, W. R. Scott pioneered the board book (using cardboard and spiral bindings rather than traditional materials), the tactile book, and the first-person history genre.[2] In allowing the children's book to go beyond its traditional form, Brown paid homage to her literary idols, who were experimenting with form in their own work—

---

2   W. R. Scott began this run with a book for middle-grade children written by Lucy Sprague Mitchell, from the first-person perspective of one of Christopher Columbus's sailors.

finally called my mother, and when she arrived, I felt saner, mostly because it was hard not to feel like the most logical one in the room next to my mother, in her deep-V cashmere sweater, mascara tracked under her eyes. She had on a gold Magen David necklace, and the lowest point of the star pierced her right in the sun-freckled fold of her cleavage.

The first thing that she said: "You look a mess."

"It's harder than I thought, not having Ben here," I said, and immediately she gave me the look I should have anticipated, the look of *Try raising two girls without a father, try dating with two daughters at home, and by the way, has Dad been by to see the baby?* I chose not to respond; Annie's therapist had told her that the only way to stem my mother's passive aggression was to force her to express herself overtly. We weren't going to give her crumbs.

It was nice that Annie had a therapist. It was like having one of my own, only for free and without having to schedule appointments.

I watched my mother pull the headband she had bought for Clara out of a little pink gift bag, her French-tipped nails grating against the excess tissue paper. Why wrap something for a two-week-old? It seemed like such a waste.

My mother positioned the headband on Clara, who frowned at her. The little flower screaming *girl girl girl* and we wonder where we get the complex, the feeling that we're supposed to fit into some schema. That we, the whole messy humanity of us, are supposed to fit neatly inside the elastic of a tiny pink headband.

"We should take her somewhere," said my mother. "Where can we take her?

"We should take her to the beach," said my mother. "We should take her to the zoo."

The thought of either was unbearable. Sand gritting Clara's diaper, a mouthy tiger watching me nurse. My mother had two daughters. She had done this twice, and she knew. But that was who she was, a woman in denial, a woman convinced that the truth of things was putty she could mold at will. This hadn't served her well.

THE FIRST FEW months after my father left, my mother behaved as if he'd be back any second. She cooked enough for him to join us at dinner, waiting to set the table until well after the food had gotten cold, *Let's just see if Dad is walking through the door.* There was no conversation, no explanation as to why Dad no longer lived with us. Annie and I placed bets on when Mom would sit us down and say "divorce," how she would do it. Annie thought it would be solemn, the two of us squished onto the plaid basement couch, Mom on her knees on the carpet, a hand of ours in each of her own. I thought she'd just start feeding us at a more appropriate time, that she'd stop waiting to see if Dad would be home to give us baths or tuck us in. We still got baths, at that point. We still had bedtime. As the weeks went on, routine dissolved into a slow, fibrous stretching of time, a thinning scrim of what was acceptable. Because she was my mother, I didn't think that this could hurt us. The whole point of your parents, to my childhood understanding, was to be pillars that would hold you up, bedrock you could return to if you crumbled. The family was an object, and subject to object permanence. When my mother got flickery, I had total confidence she'd come back into focus.

We found out Dad was back in town because one of Mom's friends saw him at a grocery store. We came home from school one day to find Shelly Moretti sitting at the kitchen table with Mom, drinking a beer. My mother was pinch-faced and silent, and Shelly flurried us back into the yard, where we sat on the front stoop with our book bags, hungry and chewing our fingernails.

Thank god I had Annie. After Shelly, the stretched putty got progressively thinner, and then finally snapped through. Mom didn't set her alarm, or set it for three in the morning, when she'd get up to clean the house top to bottom, including our bedroom.

"The vacuum waits for no man!" she would say, crashing the machine against our bed frames. Once she sucked up Annie's spelling worksheet, had to paw through the clog port to get it back.

One night, after we were asleep, she set the china out for two and made spaghetti and molten chocolate cakes. She put out the tablecloth, cloth napkins, week-old flowers in a vase, long phallic candles. She lit the candles and passed out on the couch, and then woke up at two a.m. to suffocating smoke after a candle tipped over and the flame caught a napkin. She was calm when she came to wake us, which made me calm, despite the smoke wafting in when she opened our door. I rescued my math textbook. We slipped out of the house through the back and stood waiting in our bare feet for the fire trucks, Annie still wearing her headgear. She pulled it out when the neighbors came nosing, but had nowhere to put it, and I remember shying away from her hand, fearful of orthodontic slime.

Mom had been looking at her wedding album, and it, too, burned that night—the kind of metaphor you'd scoff at if you saw it at the movies. When we came back to the house in the morning, Annie and I pierced the chocolate cakes, and instead of spilling out, the liquid centers sat gelatinous and trembling. Annie said it was a shame Mom had never gotten good at cooking; maybe we should get her a recipe book for her birthday.

My mother went away for a bit, after that. We stayed with Dad, first in the apartment he was sharing with Claudia, his twenty-year-old girlfriend, and then the three of us moved back into the house once it was cleaned. We went to school, we came home, we ate boxed macaroni and cheese. I had a class field trip to the planetarium, and when I brought Dad my permission slip, he seemed very proud to sign it, almost possessive, though he wouldn't volunteer to be a chaperone. Some days he'd offer to play catch in the front yard. Some mornings we'd be pouring our cereal, and he'd slip in the front door with a wink and a Styrofoam coffee.

"Don't tell anyone," he'd say, and we'd know that he had spent the night with Claudia. He spent the night with Claudia more and more often.

The doctors let Mom come home once the life that she wanted came closer to the life that she had, the Venn diagram no longer two completely separate circles.

Mom didn't get electroshocks to kick-start this new era. She didn't get cold-water baths. They gave her CBT and pills, they talked her down from the delusions. Like my father, Mom was back three months later, standing there at throwing distance, hugging us, holding our hands. But also, like my father, she was never really back.

"LET'S TAKE CLARA to the zoo," said my mother.

It was the next day, not yet twenty-four hours after I'd explained how futile the journey would be—how hard it always was to find parking, how Clara couldn't see anything, how she'd have to be breastfed, how she'd mostly be asleep. "I'll pay to put the car in the lot."

I'd always liked the zoo. As a kid Annie had a vendetta against it, talked about the brutality of keeping animals in cages, how they should all be roaming free. Typical bleeding-heart teenager stuff. But the animals had indoor space, and outdoor. They had ready food and an audience and a purpose. My only issue with the zoo was the smell of the primate house.

"Okay," I said, because I knew that as long as Mom was with me, she'd keep pushing it, because I knew that otherwise I might never get out of the neighborhood. *Go out into society*, said Mrs. What-to-Expect's SouthernMamma613. Lately I was obsessed with the What-to-Expects. I checked the message board religiously, emotionally invested in both OHbaby243's failing marriage and SierraX-Grace5's pregnancy scare. There was a perversity to my attraction, a quiet shame; each time I typed out a response, I'd get embarrassed and immediately delete it. I couldn't find Clara's message. The moderators had probably deleted the thread; they probably didn't want any other October Moms feeling threatened. But the message board was obviously a conduit to Clara, and I liked the idea of her as more than just a thing I had to tend to, the idea of her having a mind. I couldn't figure out how she connected, but I thought if I just kept refreshing the feed, I'd come across some sort of clue. Meanwhile, I scrolled through, collecting wisdom. *Don't dress your boy in yellow clothes unless you want him to have sexual performance issues later. Buy a wipe warmer. Go out into society.* I wouldn't mind seeing some tourists for one afternoon. I said, "Let me walk Solly while you get Clara ready."

Solly was thrilled to have my full attention, to be stroller and bunting and carrier-free. She peed freely and often, rediscovering each fence post and tree. On our way back up, she bounded past our landing, heading up the stairs to the roof. Heading toward the turquoise door. Sitting patiently outside it.

I hadn't been to see the door since Ben left. I was afraid to show it to Clara—afraid she'd respond to the fur room with its adult child-sized chairs and its proliferation of flowers. Afraid she'd be her same impassive self. Afraid I was wrong about who it was inside; afraid I was right. I did wonder if Margaret had finished building Michael's house, how her terrier was doing. I knocked.

"Yes?" Her voice was raspy, with a mid-century pretension. "The door is open, just come in."

Inside, I saw no sign of the heat or the anger. Nothing was melting.

Nothing was forcing its way in. The dog was asleep, and he stirred a bit upon hearing us enter, but did not acknowledge Solly. Margaret was seated at a desk, wearing an elegant green blazer, writing with an ink-dipped quill.

"Oh, you good girl," she said, and Solly went right to her, stubbed tail wagging. "What a sweet, good little girl." She leaned down to cup Solly's chin, and her wide-linked gold bracelet slipped down over the back of her hand. I stood in the doorway. In the corner of the room a small round table had been set for two: long candlesticks, champagne flutes, folded napkins. A chaise longue with a cigarette burn was piled with cashmere blankets. A calendar with paintings of dogs hung by the picture window: two red setters in profile, February 1944. Without looking up from Solly, Margaret chastised me: "You're letting in the cold."

I closed the door, and Solly settled at her feet.

"I only have a minute," I said. "We're going to the zoo."

"With the dog?" she said. "How silly."

"No, with the baby." Also silly.

"Oh, the baby," she said in her low, gravelly voice. "Why didn't you say?" And all at once I was nervous to be in this room that was not a room, in this house that was not a house. There was a smell to it that I couldn't quite place, a combination of the sea smell from before and something gamier. Margaret seemed amused. She cocked her head at me, her hair falling jaunty at her shoulders. She smiled, and then turned back to her work. Her dog was still sleeping.

"You've tired Crispian out," she said without looking up. "All of that screaming."

"What?"

"He's very excitable."

Are you actually her? I wanted to ask. *Are you Margaret? What are you doing here, why have you chosen me?* Instead I picked at a scab on my elbow. How do you ask a breathing body if she's actually a ghost? How do you say, *You are a secondary figure in my*

*graduate school dissertation, I'm sorry that I've abandoned you,
I did just have a baby, to be fair. Is life easier, here in the 1940s?
Where did you find dahlias out of season? What are you doing in
my home?*

"How's the house?" I asked. "Is it coming along?"

"The house?"

"The one for . . . Michael?"

"Ah," she said. "We'll have to see. I'm hoping to persuade her it's
worthwhile. She'd rather summer in Bar Harbor. She has very good
taste, very expensive, and won't suffer inconvenience. It's always a
challenge to win her completely, which is why it's so satisfying when
one does."

"It seems like a lot of work for someone who might not even be
grateful," I said.

"Well, she won't show the gratitude," said Margaret. "That
doesn't mean it won't be there."

"Of course," I said. Margaret frowned and brushed the feather
end of the quill against her cheek. I put my hand to my own cheek
in sympathy. There was a fire in the hearth. Polished brass bars
supporting the whispering logs, a brass basket holding the logs not
yet burned. A collection of fire tools, leaned against a curved brass
sculpture. A blue clock on the mantel. *Goodnight, goodnight.* I
wasn't reading to Clara yet, although we had books. At my baby
shower we'd been gifted some obscure Curious George books,
Count to Sleep Chicago, Sandra Boynton. Everyone assumed I'd already bought the classics. I hadn't.

This room was small. It was not green. It seemed as if the fire
was flickering in stop-motion, not fluid in the usual way of fire but
moving in segments, like tissue-paper flames blown by fans on a
stage. My life was moving in segments, shifting in front of me. My
eyes were forever peeled open, and still I was missing the meat of
things. When I moved closer, the fire was hot, the blaze translucent.
I thought about Clara grown up, and I started to cry.

"You wouldn't want to be late for the zoo," said Margaret, and I knew that she was sending me away. I took a breath and wiped my nose on my sleeve, and by the time Solly and I were back downstairs, my eyes were dry.

MY MOTHER HAD said she'd pay for the lot, but when I turned in to the entrance, she balked.

"It's so expensive," she said. "I'm sure there's something free and closer."

"There won't be," I said.

"Let's just check."

So we circled the free spots along the park three times, checking, me clenching my jaw, my mother *ooh*-ing and *oh look*–ing and pretending to be useful.

"There's a family up ahead just leaving." With a sharp manicured fingernail she pointed at a couple pulling a stroller from the trunk of their car. "Or maybe this group here?"

I was frustrated, but mostly just tired. My mother showed me who she was twenty years ago, had shown me every day since. I knew better than to think I could depend on her. I used my credit card to pay for the lot and then my mother stood tapping her foot as I hefted the stroller from the trunk of the car, detached Clara's car seat from its base and snapped it onto the stroller. "What a process," she said as I unfolded the handles and unlocked the brake. "When you were little I did things the normal way."

Mom wanted to push our stroller, and kept telling me that people passing by probably thought she was the mother, not the grandma. I let her have this illusion.

"Look at the seals," she said to Clara. "Look at the leopard."

"It's a cheetah," I said.

"No need for sass."

Mostly Clara slept, or stared up at the sky with those blue eyes that kept darkening. I hunched over on a plastic bench to feed her, cold despite the nursing cover, cold from the way my mother kept waving her scarf in an attempt to provide "modesty" that actually attracted more attention. The hot chocolate that we bought from a cart was cool.

When Clara cried, my mother picked her up and rocked her, wrapped in the scarf, holding her up to the fabricated savannah to look at the lions' half-eaten lunch. The zookeepers served the bloody carcass in a large cardboard box, folded up like a container of Chinese takeout.

I had the feeling someone was watching us, that something dangerous was coming. I pushed the empty stroller along the enclosure, and kept whipping around to catch the owner of the eyes that I felt on my back. Was it because my pants were too loose in the waist? I was fifteen pounds of child and water weight down, but still carrying twenty. I wasn't going to spend money on clothes until I knew where my body would land.

Mom was holding Clara up to the lions, out over the rail. The zookeeper was standing nearby, watching them. Wet leaves decoupaged the stroller wheels, which felt like the zoo laying its claim on us. I couldn't decide if this meant we'd been fated to come here. Across the concrete expanse, by the seal pool, a toddler in an unzipped coat hung from her nanny's leg, hysterical because the seals were underwater.

"No!" she kept wailing, "I need them on top."

"It hurts," Clara had written on the message board. Or had she? Had I dreamed Clara's first real communication? If it wasn't a dream, how wonderful that her thoughts could be so clearly transmitted, how awful that they'd be so much like mine.

About a hundred feet down the walkway toward the birds of prey, an old lady bought popcorn from a vendor. She had on an odd blue straw hat and a long trench coat. My mother still showing Clara, what? Her future? Her domain? *Anything the light touches.*

Or was it *everything* the light touches? Popcorn grease was dirtying the lady's white gloves, and when she turned, I could see that she was watching us through a veil draped across her wide hat brim. My mother held Clara farther out, palm supporting her neck. She was saying, "Can you see, little bird? Can you see?"

The lion tearing into the carcass, his mate sunning herself on the far hill.

"Little bird, can you see?"

WE GOT HOT dogs from another cart, and I ate mine one-handed, splattering mustard on my coat. Clouds amassed, the afternoon fading. I knew we should leave—Clara would have to eat again, Solly was waiting. But I felt that I was waiting for some cue. Nothing had happened, there'd been no splash to break the surface of our day.

Clara was back in her bunting. My mother's eyes wandered, flitting from visitor to visitor. The veiled lady had followed us to the café, and sat with a hot cup of something, looking down at her feet. A popcorn kernel had stuck in the veil's netting, hanging like a spider on a web. It must mean something. I half expected her to stand up with a big reveal and announce that she was what I had been waiting for: the warning sign, the storm. To stand up and announce that she was angry, and must be let in.

But she just sat there with her tea, and we threw away our silver wrappers and folded up the stroller and clicked the car seat back into its base. On the way home we got every green light. Maybe that was my sign.

8

The diaper bag was filled with pockets—for bottles and wet wipes and pacifiers, for cell phones and snack cups and extra pairs of socks, for credit cards and ChapSticks and rash creams—but even with a place for everything, I couldn't find my key ring.

"You drove the car home," said my mother, grimacing under the weight of Clara's car seat.

"Obviously. They're here somewhere. You can put Clara down."

"I'm getting a mark on my hand from holding her up here," said my mother, always a martyr.

I reached my hand into each crevice, each pouch. At least this time Clara and I were on the same side of the door.

"Just wait with her a minute while I run back down," I said. "They're probably in the car."

"You didn't leave them stuck in the ignition?" My mother winced, stretching her hand.

"That's not a thing anymore," I said. "You don't stick anything in, it's just a button."

Ours was the only car in the garage. I could have sworn I'd turned it off, but it was idling. The headlights were bright. The car was locked, which was a paradox: the car couldn't be on unless the keys were within range, and if the keys were within range, the car should unlock when I pressed the SmartKey button on the door handle. It didn't. They weren't.

I put my nose to the tinted rear window and quickly jumped back. The car felt as if it had been baking in an August sun, not sitting here in the garage on a cool November evening.

We'd bought this car just months ago—a totem of our new life in Chicago, our new life as a family of three. It was sleek, and I liked driving it, but it was a gas-guzzler. Every time I filled the tank, I thought about how I was burning up our planet, how we'd decided that cloth diapering was too difficult, how once Clara was on solids I'd probably forget to fill the reusable baby food pouches, the stroller was too heavy to carry up the steps to the train. *Don't think about it*, said Ben. *Nobody else does.*

If there was a disembodied anger—and I knew there was, I'd felt it at the turquoise door, I'd felt it on the stairs and read the warning on the message board—it stood to reason it would punish me for buying this car, for choosing comfort over the future of the planet. It also stood to reason that the car would be upset—it hadn't asked to be a massive metal guilt trip, it hadn't asked to meet the anger. People had made it, and sold it, and bought it, and now people hated it. I almost felt sorry.

I couldn't tell if the anger had locked itself inside the car, or if it was trying to get in. Either way, this seemed to me a battle of anger versus vehicle, and it was better for the anger to be focused on the car than on our condo. I didn't want to get stuck in the middle of things, so I went back upstairs.

"I STILL CAN'T find the keys."

"Well, I can't wait with you," said my mother. "I'm meeting Shelly."

Annie was on her way, again.

"When you have kids and you lock yourself out, I promise I'll come save you," I said to my sister over the phone, as if getting locked out was an inevitable consequence of childbirth. As if I didn't need her so desperately I almost couldn't breathe. Annie had just finished work, she had to come all the way from downtown. She said "I'm coming" in a tone that let me know this conversation wasn't over.

"That's fine," I told my mother. I was sitting with my back to the door, cradling Clara, who had started to sweat in her bunting.

"If I'd known you'd lose your key, I would've brought my copy. Really, Megan, now that you have a child, you've got to be more careful. Keep track of your things. Prioritize."

I hadn't told her I'd gotten the locks changed after the fire department broke down the door, that the key Annie was bringing was a new one. There wasn't anything good that would come of her knowing. *If I'd known you would lose your key.* If you'd known your marriage would fail. If you'd known that once your daughter was born, you would have to be a mother. I supposed I would have to, again, call the locksmith. It could wait until tomorrow.

"Go have fun," I told my mother, and she kissed Clara on the forehead and swung off with her cross-body purse.

Annie texted that the trains were running late. A mysterious object had been thrown on the track. I took off my boots to make sitting cross-legged on the floor a bit more comfortable. Ben had talked about getting a bench or a table with some flowers to liven the place up—so far we just had a taupe doormat. A scuff on the wall from when we'd moved in. A little 3B, hanging crooked. The zipper on my left boot was broken, the pull-tab snapped, jagged and sharp, and I nestled Clara in the crook of one arm while my other hand cosseted the metal.

It was boring, sitting on the floor, waiting for Annie to come let us in. It was dirty. If I kept messing around on my phone, it would die. And so I told myself I'd walk up to the roof, just check in on the door. Clara didn't belong behind it—I knew that in the same way I knew rain was coming when the sky was steeped gray, when the waves on the lake battered and spat against the boats tied up onshore. But I was already the type of mother who'd sit with a cup of tea and listen to her child cry, who'd justify with *Well, this once.*

I stood, still cradling Clara. I climbed up the stairs.

I'D BEEN LIVING in New York, where for a while it was easy to take the subway to a different self, easy to put on a new dress and try out a new restaurant and feel for just a moment you'd become a new person. But the illusion faded. I'd been in New York for three years, and I was tired. I was dating a guy who drove stick shift. We talked every day, and when we didn't, I got antsy.

A neighboring building was getting reroofed, and the insistent crash of hammers was abrasive until I recast it as a drum circle, a ritual. One afternoon, aching for distance, I took a pill that stick-shift guy had left in my bathroom—he was always taking pills, always ribbing me to take them. I told myself it was part of the ritual, the way up out of the rabbit hole, into a different sort of life. But all that happened was the sunlight glinting off the parked cars got even brighter. My mouth got very dry. My disposable razor blade shone deliciously sharp when I pressed it into the meat of my thigh.

The hammering stopped, and my blood pulse took up the beat. I walked myself to the ER—tied an old T-shirt around my thigh and went to get stitched up at New York Presbyterian. At the hospital they gave me to an old guy and his intern, who was disappointed to find that I hadn't sliced an artery. Was it on purpose? they asked, and I said no. Do you think about self-harm? they asked, and I said doesn't everyone? And then I laughed and said no and they sent me home with some pamphlets and a bandage that I could have bought at Rite Aid and a thousand-dollar hospital bill to fight about with my insurance company and eventually pay most of myself.

It was time for a new way of living, I decided then. Time to be more in control, to take a step back from the edge. I'd go back to school, like I'd been telling my sister I wanted to. I broke up with stick-shift guy the next day, and my coworkers took me out for martinis, where I let them set me up a profile to meet someone online. I hadn't really changed, outwardly. But in piercing the skin, I'd sliced something inside. I was too chicken to cut in and find it again, to push past the indentation, to tickle a paper clip under my thumbnail until it was suddenly real, a flyspeck of blood bruising beneath pearlescent polish.

"What's this from?" Ben asked once after sex, early on enough that it was still exciting, late enough that we'd spun ourselves intimacy. He touched the gummy layers of scar, and I didn't mind because it felt like the scars weren't really my skin, like he wasn't actually touching me.

"My inability to commit," I said. Ben didn't push me, just smiled and licked my thigh and pulled me closer. He was good with his tongue.

I WAS TELLING this to the woman upstairs, who was now nodding and not at all shocked by my descriptions, though she'd come straight from the 1940s, all pin-curled bob and brooches and that mink coat draped over her chair. Nobody wore mink anymore, not real mink. PETA wouldn't have it.

"But the point is, it's embarrassing," I said, "Being a half-assed cutter. Not having the drive."

"Like being a writer of children's stories," she said, "instead of a true poet." I wasn't sure if that was quite what I'd meant—Margaret was very good at children's stories, while I had no comparable achievement—but it felt close enough in sentiment. I was comforted to know that we shared a deficiency. This felt like something we could help each other out with, a shared goal that might foster a more symbiotic relationship than me just barging in whenever I needed time away from my own life. A possible clue as to why she was here. A possible beginning of a friendship.

Margaret hadn't been surprised to see us. She'd opened the door before I could knock, and now I was bouncing Clara in my arms, the two of us perched at the edge of the cigarette-burned chaise. The wall calendar read July 1947, a watercolor Dalmatian sniffing a daisy. Clara drooled onto my sleeve, and I considered using one of Margaret's throw pillows to mop it. Her head lolled. I shifted myself awkwardly.

"Would you like me to hold the baby?" asked Margaret. My first thought was to say no, not because she hadn't yet made any effort to explain who she was, but because she was smoking. The message-board mothers reminded me regularly that secondhand smoke would increase the risk of SIDS, that even thirdhand smoke was dangerous. But in the 1940s, I assumed people smoked around their kids all the time, and for better or worse we had a whole generation of baby boomers who'd made out just fine. *Well, this once.*

Crispian started barking once Margaret had Clara in her arms, jumping up and nipping her heels. His jealousy confirmed my suspicion that Margaret was choosing me.

As long as I don't feed Clara here, we'll be okay, I told myself as Margaret swayed with her in front of the fire. I didn't have any factual evidence to tell me this, just the story of Persephone eating the fruit that bound her to Hades, just instinct. Being a mother was all about instinct. *Instinct*: from the Latin for excited, but the aroused kind of excited, not the celebratory kind. A bunny ensnared in a trap, with an instinct to escape. *Arousal*: a tickling of the cunt.

Once, when I was twelve, my mother called me a cunt. I was mad at her, and toasted all her mail in the open gas grill in the backyard. "You're a cunt," she'd said. Or maybe she said, "You're acting like a cunt." I could never really distinguish between "you are" and "you're being," and though I knew they were different in kind, it was the brusqueness of the word—the click at the back of my mother's throat, the juicy tongue-to-roof *n*, the full-stop *t*—that truly mattered. *Cunt*: from the Latin for hollow, or wedge. From the Latin for woman.

I admired Margaret's brand of womanhood—carefree and individual, exciting and glamorous. It would be nice to have a strong female influence in Clara's life, once Margaret and I solidified our friendship. In a few months Clara would presumably start paying attention, and I should consider what I wanted her to pay attention to. Obviously not my mother. At the moment, I, myself, was iffy. Annie might have been a strong female influence at one point, but she'd abandoned her commitment to adventure. Annie was getting overprotective, too parental, no fun. I felt like I could make myself adventurous, with some assistance. I could be free-spirited and glamorous—the kind of woman I'd have wanted as a mentor in my youth—if I just had some time to get myself together. If I just had a bit of space, somebody else to care for Clara.

Before she was my father's twenty-year-old girlfriend, Claudia Reid had been my babysitter. She let me use her lip gloss, and smelled like Boone's Farm Apple Blossom, and drove a Jeep. She taught me how to pretend not to care when boys made fun of me. She taught me about Kurt Cobain. She didn't like me very much, and I found that appealing. I needed someone like Claudia to take care of Clara while I figured myself out.

"Do you babysit?" I asked.

"I won't let anybody get away with anything just because he's little," said Margaret.

"That makes sense. Having rules for kids is good. So you'd be interested?"

"I'm interested in people, and children are people. I don't know that I like children, but I do understand them."

"What about babies?"

"Babies are sweet."

I decided I would take this as a yes. This was a step in a desirable direction, both in my effort to matter to Margaret, and my effort not to matter quite so vitally to Clara. It could help both relationships to flourish.

"I'd pay fifteen dollars an hour," I said. The going rate was higher, but up here in the 1940s, fifteen dollars would get you much farther than it would downstairs in 2017. "I'd leave you milk in a bottle. You'd just have to be careful with the heat."

"The heat?"

"The anger," I said. "We can't let it inside the house. This message board I follow says be careful. It's already gotten into the garage, into the car, but we have to make sure that it stays there. It can't come inside the apartment."

"Oh, the anger," Margaret said. "That would be Michael. She can come off that way, you see. She likes to think of herself as a tempest, but she doesn't really mean it."

"She doesn't have to be so forceful."

"But she isn't truly angry," said Margaret. "She's afraid. She's sad. Her poetry has been neglected."

"It feels like anger to me."

MY PHONE BUZZED, and Clara and I said goodbye to Margaret and went down to meet Annie.

"I thought you'd be here waiting for me," she said, digging the new iteration of our spare key from her purse. "The car seat's here, where were you?"

"I was upstairs with the new neighbor." I let Annie take Clara, unlocked the door, and held my hand out to Solly, who took one sniff and started skittering around the front hall. We must have still smelled like the zoo.

"I didn't know you had a new neighbor."

"Yeah," I said, "I don't know much about her. I don't even know her name."

"Which unit is she in?"

I paused. There was no unit. Margaret would never condescend to a condo. A bohemian apartment, yes, a penthouse, an offbeat cabin, but no paint-by-numbers *unit*. *Unit*: from the Latin *unitatem*, sameness or agreement; a unit, a sole entity comprising part of a larger whole. Margaret was no group member. Margaret was unique. She stood up for what she wanted, which was why she could be Clara's good influence. Margaret would have reminded her mother about the agreement to pay for zoo lot parking. She would have been proud to share news of herself to Annie, not afraid—as I was—that if I introduced her to Annie, she'd like Annie more than me.

"Megan?" Annie was waiting for my answer. "Which unit?"

"Upstairs," I said. "Before the roof."

"What does that mean?"

"I'm not sure."

"You're not sure?"

"It's unclear."

"Megan," said Annie, "sweetie."

My younger sister did not call me sweetie. Surely nobody had called anybody sweetie in the past fifteen years. The word made me think of sour Valentine's Day candies, of lollipops that turned my lips blue. *Have a sweetie. Be a dear.* A deer in headlights. A rabbit in a trap.

"Megan, have you been eating?"

It was impossible to eat with a newborn—or at least to enjoy eating. I'd have Clara in one hand and a forkful of cold lasagna in the other. I spilled noodles on her swaddle, baptized her with marinara.

"Maybe you should go out," said Annie. "Get your nails done, get a massage. Do something for yourself."

"We could get drinks," I said. A tequila bar had opened down the street, and in my last month of pregnancy I'd lurched myself past trendy haircuts and bicycle chains and little fake-flamed candles. Distressed wooden stools lined the bar, and a massive wagon wheel hung over the entrance, reminding me of a Catherine wheel. One of my cataloging jobs at the New York Public Library had been a video of a dance performance from the 1980s, a Twyla Tharp piece called *The Catherine Wheel*. It wasn't really my sort of thing, but not everything could be when you were archiving. I'd had the music in my head for weeks, and when I closed my eyes I'd picture this one strange, screaming dancer dressed up as a maid. I wasn't really sure what the piece was about, but I had responded to Catherine as an icon. What was she the saint of, again? Education? One of my favorite parts of art history in college had been identifying saints based on their attributes. You could always find Catherine, carrying her wheel. Yoked.

"Ben gets home on Sunday night. That's not so long from now. I can be okay on my own tonight, if we do something tomorrow. If there's tomorrow, and then Sunday to look forward to." The implication, which I realized only after I'd spoken, was that I was depressed.

"You have a sitter who you trust?" I could tell Annie thought this was a bad idea, and she was asking the question because she thought the answer was that I didn't.

"Yes," I said, "a good one. She understands children."

Book Sales and the Zeitgeist

O ver the course of Margaret Wise Brown's fifteen-year career, she published over one hundred books with dozens of publishers. She worked with almost every prominent illustrator of the day, and her accomplishments as an editor were paralleled only by those of Ursula Nordstrom, head of Harper's Department of Books for Boys and Girls from 1940 to 1973. At the time of her premature death in 1952, Brown was involved in a number of projects, including a collaboration with Alvin Tresselt, and a foray into songwriting.[1] Today, her most popular book remains one of children's literature's best sellers. An estimated 49 million copies of *Goodnight Moon* have been sold worldwide since its first publication in 1947, with 13.5 million copies published just in the last ten years. *The Runaway Bunny*, Brown's second most popular book, has sold 7.5 million copies.[2] Brown's impact on modern children knows no—

---

1 Brown was determined to write simple songs for children whose melodies and lyrics inspired them to come up with their own. Marcus, 258.

2 Nielsen BookScan, accessed 17 May 2016.

9

Clara was asleep when Margaret came downstairs. She knocked on the door, just like anyone else would. She walked in, but didn't take off her shoes. I had just gotten out of the shower and was trying to choose between a maternity dress that hung like extra skin, and a pre-baby dress that clung too tight.

"This one is nice," said Margaret, pointing to the tight dress. It was a nice dress, one of my favorites, which meant I'd only worn it twice—once to a wedding, another time to dinner for my own wedding anniversary. An occasion-marking dress, which was why I'd laid it out. Leaving Clara was an occasion. But I didn't want to feel fat in front of all the emaciated twenty-year-olds at the bar in their short skirts despite the weather, in front of the bartenders who'd probably seen me glassy-eyed and wandering with the stroller, in front of the Catherine wheel. The goal for the next two hours was to be Megan, not Mother. Funny how the things that had once made me feel like myself now did the opposite—the dress I could barely squeeze into, the curling iron, the patterned clutch. I'd been untethered from the objects of my former self, and this explained why I was flailing. Until I found some other stake to tie myself to, I'd be floating high on the helium, stuck in the space between who I'd been and who I would become. I had the makings of the new self: the bassinet, the diaper bag, the bottles, the pump. I just didn't want to claim them.

I put on the maternity dress, which at least still somewhat fit me, covered with a sweater that was possibly still in style. I braided my hair and finished my makeup in the downstairs bathroom while Margaret tried to bond with Solly, who ignored her, padding around to whine at me.

"We don't really have a schedule yet for Clara," I said. "But I've written out when you should give her a bottle. And she usually poops while she's eating."

"How endearing," said Margaret. This was probably sarcasm, but I couldn't be sure. I faked a laugh.

"There's just not much to do with them at this age," I said, as if I knew.

"At this age they see books as living objects," said Margaret. She crouched down to assess Clara, in her bouncer.

"You can read to her, if you want," I said. "Or tell her stories." I tried to imagine Margaret sitting with her skirt spread around her, pointing out primary colors. That wasn't her style. She was more the sort to take Clara for a walk in the woods, tell her about the secret life of acorns or renegade bunnies. That could work, too, although for safety's sake I hoped they would stay in our condo. "Any sort of educational *indoor* activity, really," I said, and then I worried I was taking advantage. Margaret wouldn't want to be my friend if I kept taking advantage. "I mean, you definitely don't have to. You can also just watch TV."

I walked Margaret over to the fridge, showed her the bottles of pumped milk and how to warm them. "Here's my cell phone number, and my sister's number if I don't pick up, and the number for the pediatrician. Can you leave me with some contact information? So if I need to, I can reach you? I'll be just around the corner, but still."

She smiled. "Margaret Wise Brown," she said. "New York City, sometimes Maine. You can reach me through my editor, Ursula Nordstrom."

■ ■ ■

ANNIE WAS WAITING at a high-top, twisting the toothpick garnish on her drink, scrolling through her phone. Although she was framed in the front window, I felt I was spying, seeing her before she saw me. She looked up when I dropped my purse next to her.

"How was it leaving Clara with the babysitter?"

"Like walking out the door without my heart," I said, because I knew that was what I was supposed to say. I wasn't supposed to say that it felt like a relief. "Like someone carved my heart out of my chest and then gave it to the babysitter."

"That's a weird thing to say." Annie scrunched her nose.

I shrugged. "I don't want to talk about the baby tonight," I said. "Let's talk about everything but the baby."

"Okay," said Annie. We sat there in silence. The bar was playing the original John Prine version of "Angel from Montgomery," which would have been a strange choice for a cocktail bar on a Saturday evening anywhere but here, in Logan Square, where what had been old and ugly was now new and beautiful.

Annie sucked down the last of her mixed drink, and the slurp reminded me of being fourteen and sharing a waxy McDonald's soda.

"Easy there," I said, and then immediately regretted it.

Across the bar a man was looking at us, probably at Annie, but maybe at me. I twisted my wedding ring around so that the diamond was hidden against my palm, and when he held his hand up in a static hello, I gave him what I thought was a mysterious half smile. Of course I wasn't going to cheat on Ben, of course this wasn't going to go anywhere. But it was nice to feel like somebody was seeing me. Like I'd done myself up for a reason.

When Annie went to get herself a second drink and me a first, the man slid off his bar stool and walked over to me. I couldn't remember if I had brushed my teeth, though I supposed it didn't matter. Even showered and perfumed, I smelled like milk.

"I think I know you," the guy said, holding up an index finger the way people do when they try to discern the direction of the wind. Was I North or South, a breeze or gusting? I didn't recognize him.

"You live down the block, in the condos by the 7-Eleven, right?"

I nodded, attempting to place him. "Have we met? Sorry, my memory's shot. I just had a baby."

"I know," he said, "I saw you last week. Early morning."

"Sorry?"

He mimed driving, and then taking off his shirt. When I still didn't follow, he smiled. "You locked yourself out. I called the police."

"Mr. Garbage," I said.

"Ouch." He grimaced, but didn't seem offended.

Annie came back with a mixed drink for herself and a glass of wine for me.

"Mr. Garbage," I said, "this is my sister." Annie swatted at my hand under the table. I was being rude. "Mr. Garbage saved me from myself the other day," I explained. "He's the one who saved Clara."

"The guy who called the cops?" Annie held up her glass in a solo toast. "You're a hero. Let us buy you a drink."

"I don't want to interrupt," he said. "Just thought I'd come and say hello, see how you're doing."

I didn't like how Annie was smiling at him. He was attractive enough, if you liked stubbly and tattooed. I didn't. His teeth weren't straight, and he had buttons on the collar of his shirt, and he drove a garbage truck for a living. Was I being too judgmental? He'd seen me without a shirt, and now he was flirting with my sister.

Annie introduced herself to Mr. Garbage, and I turned away, lightheaded after only a sip of wine. More wheels hung from the ceiling, dotted with lamplight. How did you die on a Catherine wheel, anyway? Did they pin you to the rim, or lace you in through the axle?

"Megan," said Annie, "Greg is talking to you."

"Who?" *You're a cunt. You're acting like a cunt.*

"It's fine," said Mr. Garbage. "I should get going anyway. Good to see you."

I took another sip, and blinked.

"I'm so, so sorry," said Annie, slipping off the stool and walking with him back to his seat. She leaned in to him, explaining something. An infinitesimal feeling of loss, an urge to go to them, apologize. Annie was holding his phone, typing something into it. Mr. Garbage sat back down on his stool, and Annie made her way back to me.

"We should probably just have one drink," she said. "You seem . . . tired." That was charitable.

"I'm no fun," I said flatly.

"You're not," Annie agreed.

"This was a good experiment," I said. "This was a good thing to check off the list. We can do it again when Ben is home and I'll feel better." Probably this was true. Hopefully.

"Okay." Annie glanced over at Mr. Garbage, starting in on a beer. He wasn't leaving. He'd lied to us. "Do you need me to walk back with you?"

I knew that she wanted to stay with him, to maybe go home and fuck him in the house that garbage built, to get naked and put on his orange hat and massive silver headphones.

"Yes," I said. "I do."

ALL THE WAY down the alley I was shaky, the alcohol and sleep deprivation combining for a tenuous high. I'd asked Annie to come with me out of spite, but it turned out that I did, actually, need her.

"Shit," I said when we got to my front door. I could hear Clara through the wall, an unintelligible scream. *Hungry* was whiny, had a glottal burst at the beginning of each wail. *Wet* was sharper, more hysterical. This was neither.

"Sounds like the babysitter has her hands full," said Annie.

We walked in and saw Clara, buckled into her bouncer. Annie went to her at once.

"Margaret?" I said, scanning the room. The television remote was where it had been, the door to the downstairs bathroom cracked just as it had been when I left. No used glasses on the kitchen counter, no frozen pizza cardboard in the trash. Other than Clara and a desperate Solly whining in the kitchen, the condo was empty. "Jesus Christ," I said, my throat a cinch pulled tight, and swooped Clara out of Annie's arms. She was howling, pulsing and contorted, a blazing purple flame. I wriggled half out of my sweater and sat down on the floor, giving Clara a breast. It had been an hour or so since I'd left her. Where had Margaret gone? Had there been some sort of emergency? Why hadn't she called?

I realized that I was crying along with Clara, hiccupping, heaving sobs. Annie sat down next to me, the garbage episode forgotten.

"Meg—" She nuzzled my cheek with hers, like we were children. "Everything's okay. Nothing bad happened. It's going to be all right."

We sat, the three of us, while Clara fed, huddled together on the area rug. It felt good to have their bodies against mine—Clara hot at first, but cooling as she sated herself; Annie chilled from walking outside. The living room felt colder than I thought it should, but it was hard to know if that was the actual temperature or the icy enmity I felt for everyone but Clara. The icy enmity that I felt for myself. The world was harsh and cruel and cold, and I'd done nothing to protect my own child. I hadn't asked if Margaret knew CPR. I hadn't checked her references. I hadn't made sure she was real.

"I'm a terrible mother," I whispered. I didn't need to say it out loud to know it was true.

"It's going to be okay," said Annie, squeezing closer.

I fed Clara, and changed her heavy diaper. We examined her all over, lifting eyelids to check for popped blood vessels, swabbing the folds behind her knees with a warm washcloth, feeling her stomach for hernias, her forehead for fever. She seemed untouched, and now content. Instead of putting her back down, I maneuvered her into the baby wrap, our heartbeats gentling together. All the bottles were still in the fridge. The pajamas I'd laid out across the bassinet still hanging there. Annie put on the electric kettle and brought me a blanket to drape across my shoulders. I swayed until Clara was asleep.

"We have to talk about this," Annie said, once it was clear that Clara wouldn't be disturbed, once I was somewhat calm and settled.

"I fucked up," I said. "I picked the wrong babysitter."

"Mmm," said Annie, in agreement.

"I'm lost," I said. "It's so much harder than I thought it would be."

"Mmmm."

"Annie," I said, suddenly frighteningly lucid. "You can't tell anyone. I'm just tired. I made a mistake, and I'm tired. If you tell anyone, they will make me go away, and for my whole life Clara will look at me the way we look at Mom."

"That's ridiculous."

"It isn't. Annie, please." I gripped her hand, pressing bone against bone, her knuckles cracking. "Annie, you have to promise."

I felt this with an intensity I hadn't known since before Clara's birth, before the move, before pregnancy. A desperation that reminded me of childhood—the intense vulnerability of utter dependence. Annie had been there with me, in childhood, adolescence. She knew what it was like to eat canned corn and stale potato chips for dinner, to watch our mother eat nothing. She knew what it was like to know that Mom had gone away, to talk to her over the phone on Sunday nights through sophistry and static, what it was like to sit on the front stoop on the day she came home, the five pounds she'd finally put back on after losing more than twenty hanging foreign on her upper arms, her jawline. And then to walk on tenterhooks, to tiptoe, to help her comb her hair, to see the streaks of gray and realize that she was older. That she was brittle now, and any slammed door or backtalk might shatter her.

"I won't tell anyone," said Annie. "I'm not going to call the cops on you or anything. But Megan, you have to tell Ben. And you have to find somebody to talk to. You guys have good insurance. It's normal to feel messed up after having a baby. Get a referral for somebody who can help you. It'll help Clara, too."

I nodded. She was right. I knew she was right. But I wasn't the only one who'd messed up—there'd been Margaret. How could Margaret have done this to me? I'd trusted her with my child, which meant I'd trusted her with my whole life. Was it my fault for feeling like I knew her? For thinking that a few hours of mostly one-sided conversation and a bit of biographical reading was enough to warrant confidence?

Margaret wrote stories by the fire with an old-fashioned quill pen; she cut windows out of imaginary walls. Of course this was not someone to whom I should give my child. Just because Margaret held Clara, touched the fur coat to her cheek. Just because Margaret had stylish taste in clothes. Just because Margaret said she understood children. What had I been thinking? I hadn't been thinking. I'd been thinking too much.

At the beginning of the hunt, the rabbit knows the dogs are coming. It springs up on its haunches; it trembles.

"I'll stay the night on the futon," said Annie. She went to take a shower in the guest bathroom.

Opening the fridge, I counted the lined-up bottles of breast milk. I wasn't ready to take Clara out of the carrier, to let go of her. Was this love? This combination of self-hatred and refusal to remove her skin from my skin?

Even with Clara attached to me, it was still so cold. In the living room, the ceiling fan was on, but the chill continued after I had gone and switched it off. The tag on Clara's nursing pillow fluttered. When I went over to examine it, I realized the living room window was cracked open, about an inch and a half of naked screen exhaling night. I slammed the window shut, and locked it.

But the balcony door was also cracked open. So was the window in the kitchen. I peeked into the guest bathroom, muggy with Annie's shower, and saw that the tiny window there was lifted up an inch as well. I felt lightheaded, as if I might fall forward just from Clara's negligible weight. I put my head down to nuzzle the velvety top of her head.

In the master bedroom upstairs, the windows were pushed fully up, the frames like raised eyebrows above massive, whiteless eyes—a flicker of a pupil from someone's television flashing across the dark alley. I yanked them closed, swept shut the curtains, and then sat down on the bed, trying to steady my breathing.

A subtle creak came from the other side of the room, a gear winding, a handle turning. The bassinet was next to my side of the bed—just a thin mattress and tight fitted sheet, see-through mesh sides so that Clara wouldn't suffocate if she showed herself a prodigy and suddenly rolled over. Ben had set up a mobile of plush stars at the head. As I watched, it started spinning, tinkling out the first few notes of "Twinkle, Twinkle Little Star." The motor settled in, and the song strengthened, getting faster.

I knew that I hadn't turned it on, that Annie couldn't have touched it.

Margaret had let the anger in.

Margaret had let Michael in.

Part II

In her own opinion, she is greatly influenced by the opinions of those she respects.

—Charles Shaw on Michael Strange, December 1927

November 1941

The night is too cold for the terrace, but Margaret, in her dark green dress, has tried. She has escaped the inside of Harrison Tweed's celestial penthouse—New York's velveteen elite clinking martini glasses, plinking out piano ditties, gossiping about bankruptcy and cuckolds and divorce—and now stands shivering on the balcony. Below her the East River sits serene, Welfare Island barely visible through fog. Margaret leans out over the wrought-iron barrier and finishes her drink, leaving the tumbler balanced where the railing meets the building.

Ostensibly, this party is for nineteen-year-old Diana, who is leaving for Hollywood in the morning, despite her mother's efforts to keep her in New York. But Diana made her exit early. Most of her cohort is also gone, as are all Margaret's close acquaintances. Michael, Margaret's mentor, has become her dearest confidante, yet even after two years of these soirées, the others still are not her friends. Especially not Michael's husband Harry's crowd—didactic and judgmental, talking finance and legal justice, puffing their cigars and letting themselves be charmed by Harry's wife, but never her pupil. Harry himself tolerating Margaret, as he tolerates most of Michael's whims—the poetry he doesn't read, the radio program to which he doesn't listen, Michael's expensive tastes and dilettantism. Margaret is distinctly aware of herself as being tolerated, which makes her uncomfortable, and timid in the company of Michael's high society.

What she sees now in the vast drawing room: a small group of lawyers in a corner by the tall stalks of delphinium, Harry at their helm—his flat, pleasant face nodding along to the man next to him, only the reddening tips of his wide ears betraying any sort of humor—and a conclave of Michael's devotees strewn about in armchairs by the fire. Michael stands by the painting of herself that hangs over the mantel, which, for better or worse, serves to highlight the difference between the debutante who sat for the portrait thirty years ago and the woman who holds court below it now. Both display the same thick eyebrows, the same narrow nose. An expression of defiant haughtiness that dares one to doubt her. But now Michael is fleshier. Her cheeks are fuller, her jewels more expensive. She wears silk trousers and a long string of pearls, and as she gestures toward the man next to her—a college friend of her son Leonard's—she keeps getting her cocktail ring tangled in the fringe of her shawl.

"She'll have a chaperone, of course," Michael is saying as Margaret approaches, "and I made her promise never to stay overnight with her father. God only knows what goes on there after dark. Still, my poor Diana"—Michael's voice sits on the middle vowel, her eyes cast down—"the press are going to eat her alive."

"But the film studio offered the contract?" asks the college friend, whose name Margaret cannot remember.

"Of course the studio offered, they want her, everyone *wants* her—but only to have a Barrymore up on the marquee. They wouldn't sign her under any other name." Michael's stage whisper carries to the group of lawyers, several of whom now turn toward her. Harry, looking up, offers a bland and thin-lipped smile.

A member of the household staff appears at Margaret's side with a tray of old-fashioneds. Margaret considers her waistline, then the palpable tension between her two hosts. She takes the drink.

"We all know Diana's pretty enough," Michael continues, opening her inner circle to include her husband's colleagues, no longer any pretense of secrecy or tact. "And with time she could develop some talent. But the girl won't take the time. She's too impatient. When the public sees her act, they'll tear her to pieces."

"You worry for her," says Harry, with a dryness that tells Margaret he has heard this all before.

"I do." Michael ignores his tone and sighs. "And it's exhausting. I can barely focus on my own work."

"Your work," says Harry, blank-faced, blinking.

Margaret wishes she were back out on the terrace. She sends Michael a silent prayer of strength. But the explosion does not come—instead of taking Harry's bait, Michael laughs heartily and lifts her glass, crosses the room to give her husband a kiss on the cheek. And now Harry is smiling and raising a hand to the smudge of dark lipstick on his jowl. Now the businessmen are chuckling, and the young people who've hung on to every word Michael has spoken this evening about European nationalism and contemporary art are letting their shoulders relax ever so slightly and sloshing their drinks. Relief makes them sloppy. One young woman—someone's date—lets a pump slip off her foot, revealing a small tear in her stocking. Somebody elbows a tumbler of whiskey, and the others around him titter, ignoring the help sidling in to sop up the liquor that has splashed onto the opulent mauve carpet and mahogany floor.

"One must always prepare for criticism," Michael says with practiced gaiety. "Such is the burden of the Poet. Readers are dull and reviewers are bastards, and it is up to the Poet to remain true to her art." The way Michael says *poet*, with her wet lips rounded—the final *t* suspended by her exhalation, the brief flash of her tongue—makes Margaret's breath shallow, her desire a beached dolphin refusing defeat. She blinks and cracks an ice cube with her teeth.

"And how is the biography selling?" asks a man in Harry's cadre, dinner jacket abandoned and sweat dark under his arms. Michael's book is an autobiography, and it is not selling well. She pretends not to have heard him.

"There is a necessary tenacity that dear Diana lacks," she continues, "an artistic vision." The sudden edge to her voice slices the room's bonhomie, and Margaret sees where Michael's energies are headed. Having fully lamented Diana, Michael will find another target; Margaret's career is ever in her sights. She tries to back quickly into the library, but bumps against a gilded floor-length mirror. The disruption catches Michael's attention. "Take Margaret," says Michael, and the whole room turns to look at Margaret, and consequently at themselves. Margaret sees Michael make eye contact with her own reflection. "She writes those kiddie books, but if she had more self-discipline, she too might be a poet."

"You like her poetry?" The same man who'd asked about book sales is looking at Margaret. He's lost a cuff link, and one sleeve flaps when he fondles his mustache. Silence, as all try to discern to whom he's referring, and to whom he's tried to speak. Michael wears a benevolent expression: nose upturned, brows creased in anticipatory amusement. She says nothing.

"I do," Margaret says finally. "I like her poetry very much."

Michael nods. She turns slowly to look at her husband. "And you," Michael says. "You, my darling. What do you think of my work?" The *darling* is a dagger, the question a dare.

Harry will not meet Michael on the field of battle, not directly, not in front of their guests. Michael's second husband, John Barrymore, would have yanked the knife from his chest and thrown it back at her, but Harry, her third, is urbane, careful. Not for Harry, John's theatrics—the locked bathroom doors and suicide threats, the smashed antiques. Harry takes Michael's hand and pets it.

"As I've told you before, I don't have an opinion," says Harry, "because I have not read it." In Harry's eyes Margaret believes that she can read a sudden hatred, followed by remorse toward that hatred. Perhaps the memory of love, then the determined, unchanged mind.

A silence. An awkward dispersal as all find their coats and bid their adieus. The sense that as Michael discharges her guests, she is simmering, then boiling.

And now Margaret follows her through hallways of mirrors and flower arrangements the size of small front gardens, past blue and gold brocades and Baroque armoires. Michael kicks off her shoes and leaves them in a corner of her bedroom, begins unbuttoning her wide-legged silk trousers before the door is fully closed. Margaret perches at the edge of the bed.

"He's having an affair," says Michael, removing her earrings. "He's too smart to leave me proof, but I can tell." Michael's last drink is just now hitting her—she stumbles a bit as she slides out of the pants, and braces herself on Margaret's knee. "Twelve years of marriage," she continues, fingernails digging into Margaret's stocking, "and he treats me like a child." Margaret opens her mouth to speak, but Michael isn't finished. "I loved him once," she says, "though not like you.

"I've begun to feel very close to you," says Michael.

10

Annie was downstairs on the futon. Clara in her bassinet. Me, in bed, covered by just a sheet—the condo warmer than it should have been, given the recently opened windows. One curtain peeking open, a brume of city midnight cast across Clara. Her pacifier had fallen, though her lips didn't recognize the loss: still pursed, they quivered like a trembling fish. A ribbon woven through the crown of her mobile fluttered in a nonexistent breeze.

I was nearing the heaviness of sleep. I felt a stirring at the foot of the bed, and assumed it was Solly. She liked to join me sometimes, when Ben was gone. But the breath was soft and dry under the sheet, and when it moved up the bed to my thigh, I knew it couldn't be Solly. Ben, then, come home to surprise me? Of course it wasn't Ben. Ben wasn't the type to surprise me. Besides, we hadn't broached the topic of sex since Clara was born, which felt appropriate. I wasn't one of those women who needed to feel physically desired after giving birth, I didn't measure my worth by the erectness of his dick.

But this. This apparition at the foot of my bed, the sheet tented by my curling leg, nobody visible, and yet someone beside me. The sudden intimacy shocked me. It was frightening at first, but so deliberate and gentle I relaxed into the joy of it. The someone took such care of me. It had been so long since I, myself, felt taken care of. A brush of hair, a tapered finger, exploring. A tongue that found the fulcrum of my pleasure, the skid of a silk negligee against my bare skin. A confidence that was not the straight-shouldered bluster of a man who has studied his craft, but something deeper. Someone who knew.

I gripped the side of the mattress, I lengthened my neck. When I finally cried out, the phantasm receded. It hadn't expected me. In the night, in this house. Who had it thought would cry out? Who did I taste like?

I knew this must be Michael. Margaret had promised that she wasn't truly angry, which must be why she wasn't giving off the heat. She was inside now, and in need. She had expected someone else.

THE NEXT MORNING Annie was still over, though she'd have to leave soon to go move her car—it was street-cleaning day in Uptown, and she was parked on the wrong side. She made an espresso on Ben's machine and sat cross-legged while Clara writhed on her baby gym mat. Every so often Annie would jostle the padded poles that held the dangling animals, and little bells would ring inside their plush stomachs. Clara looked skeptical, because she always looked skeptical. Her eyes widened with each reverberation, but her mouth remained consistently turned down.

"I think she likes it," said Annie, jostling the play gym in a familiar rhythm that I couldn't quite place. "You go do your thing. Go take a shower, we'll be fine."

I ran the shower steaming, letting the mirror fog, half expecting Michael to write a message in the condensation. It made intrinsic sense to me that Margaret had a body—she had a body of work, she had a readership. Michael, on the other hand, had fallen into obscurity. No one was reading her, or buying her, and so she was reduced to an incorporeal self. Michael always craved the spotlight, and her obscurity must have been fuel for her anger. She clearly wanted to announce herself. She might leave a ghostly fingerprint, a ragged lipstick HERE I AM.

But when I stepped out, the glass was just glass. I hadn't cleaned the master bathroom since Clara was born, and there was a streak of toothpaste globbed at the side of the sink, an upside-down bottle of baby shampoo leaking on the counter. The imperfections were grounding: this was my life and this was real, because why would anybody have delusions of a hard-water-stained toilet? What message would my subconscious be sending with egregious shower mold? *Clean up your life.* Or: *Ben will probably fix all of it once he gets home.*

The exhaust fan made a clicking sound that seemed dangerous. Was having Margaret upstairs dangerous? What about the water I'd spilled getting out of the shower, the fact that I'd skipped last night's dinner, the fact that Clara had been alone here with Margaret and Michael? What if Margaret had hurt Clara? What if Clara had cried herself sick? What if she'd stopped breathing? What if the car couldn't be fixed, what if the windows couldn't be closed, what if the upstairs dog bit Solly?

Other than the reality of grime, I couldn't place what was balanced and what was off-center. So much about my life had changed so quickly, and I couldn't sort the shifts. Was it unusual that Clara slept at most only four hours at a time? Was it normal to discover a window that couldn't be seen from the outside of a building? Was my hair supposed to be falling out like this? My breasts, when full, were ridged and veiny, foreign.

I sat on my bed and started a new thread on Mrs. What-to-Expect's message board under a string of is-this-normal-can-you-helps. I wasn't sure what to title it, wasn't sure what time of day was best to post to ensure that the mothers whose expertise I needed would read and respond. I'd been obsessed with the message board ever since I was hacked, but I still hadn't contributed. *Is anyone else feeling weird about new neighbors,* I began, before deleting this line of thought entirely. *Do you feel like your dreams have been more lucid since the birth of your child?* Wrong again. Too academic, and besides, it was my waking life that was the matter. Sleep was dreamless these days, dark. *Does anyone else feel like someone they can't see is watching them?* I pressed post and left my phone plugged in on my nightstand to charge.

I WANTED TO get to Margaret before Annie left, to tell her how disappointed I was by her behavior. I'd thought we had an understanding, and it was going to take a lot for her to regain my trust.

I used Solly as my excuse, asking if Annie could stay another minute so I could run her out to pee without having to bring Clara in the cold. Then I went down and opened the door to the alley, tying Solly's leash to the bottom of the dumpster and leaving her to do her business while I ran back inside. I entered through the garage, where the car was now dead. Ben would have to get someone to jump it.

Racing up the stairs so quickly that I felt my bladder sinking, I made it to the turquoise door. I turned the handle, and for the first time, it was locked.

"Margaret!" I only had a moment before Annie had to leave, before I had to retrieve Solly. "Margaret, it's me!"

She didn't answer, but I thought I heard movement: the shuffle of a chair across the floor. I put my ear to the door and caught the low murmur of someone's conversation—Margaret, most likely, and a man. Something that sounded like a champagne bottle popping. Stifled laughter.

I knocked again, although I knew that she was lost to me. I slid my back down the turquoise door, mad at myself for caring. Trying to listen.

When I went downstairs and checked my phone, no one had commented on my What-to-Expect question—apparently it had become lost in a sea of other questions, a drop in an ocean of drops.

Put on your own life vest first, I supposed. Lock your own turquoise door and drink champagne.

BEN LANDED DURING rush hour, and took the el instead of a car to get home to us faster. I heard his key scraping the lock, which I hadn't yet told him I'd changed. Clara was begrudgingly doing her tummy time—rather than lifting her head or even turning her cheek to the mat, she was facedown in rainbow quilting, protesting silently, and this was just one of the reasons I was hesitant to leave her in the living room while I ducked down the hall. I sat listening to Ben try and fail for a full minute until Solly started whimpering, unable to withstand the anticipation.

I'd known he was coming, but I wasn't prepared. What face would I wear? Annie had helped me clean the first floor, and I had a frozen casserole already in the oven: I could be happy homemaker. It was impossible to hide the bags beneath my eyes with concealer, my breasts were hard and heavy, and it seemed futile to try to make the bed: I could be the exhausted, self-sacrificing wife. After a week without consistent adult company, I cared more about Ben's business dealings than I ever had before: I could be the willing confidante. I'd spent an hour this afternoon picking up Clara's jingle-bell rattle and putting it on one side of the room, only to watch it, of its own volition, roll across the floor: I wasn't sure what archetype that would make me. Hysterical? Insane? Eventually I had just let it stay under the couch, where Michael apparently needed it to be.

Cupping Clara in an arm, I got up to receive Ben, still not sure who I would be, not sure who Clara would become. He was wet; it had been raining. His carry-on suitcase had repelled the rain in fat drops that pooled onto the floor. Solly slid through them, careening into Ben. Instead of calming her, he came toward me and Clara.

"My girls"—he grinned—"all three of you." An awkward dance ensued as I decided whether or not he was too wet to hold Clara, made the ultimate decision that he wasn't. The energy was different, having him here and not on FaceTime—a charged particle hovering between pleasure and pain, relief and dissatisfaction. I reminded myself he wasn't permanent. He would still go to work in the morning.

"How was the flight?" I asked him. "How was Houston?"

I thought I cared to know the answers, but as soon as Ben began to speak, I realized that I didn't. Luckily the oven timer would go off soon.

"Hold on," I said. "I've got dinner."

Ben followed me into the kitchen, still wearing his shoes. Solly followed Ben.

"Look at you," he said, "getting everything together. Holding down the fort."

"Since when do you say 'holding down the fort'?" I asked, but I basked in the compliment. Happy homemaker it was, then, and happy homemaker did not get locked out of her house, or run the car battery out, or make friends with the garbageman after throwing her shirt on his head. Happy homemaker had no time to talk about her recent faux pas with choice of babysitter. Happy homemaker called what had happened a faux pas—a false step. That could all wait. That could wait until later. Or never.

"It's one of the freezer meals I made before Clara was born," I said, leaning down to the oven. Steam came in a great wave. In Ben's arms, Clara twisted toward the heat.

"She's cold," I said.

Ben said, "She wants her mother."

My shoulders straightened. I let out a gasp. Had no one said this yet? *Clara wants her mother?* I'd been afraid, and I was still afraid, but with a sudden streak of joy run thickly through. Need is an albatross. To be needed is to wear the weight of stones across your chest. To be wanted, that is different. To be wanted by a child is the cleanest of desires—to still be wanted once the child is fed and rested, once the diaper is fresh and the snot has been siphoned from the nostril and the gas has passed through. To be recognized not just as a body, but a person, a comfort. To be loved.

Not that Clara, in that moment, really saw me as a person. Until she was at least five, Clara would know me as an extension of herself, to be climbed over and drooled on, to send out as a scout to find what foods were safe to eat, what paths were safe to travel. How lovely, I thought suddenly, to be such an integral part of another person's selfhood. To be a piece of Mommy-Clara, Clara-Mommy, to be a tree that she'd come home to. How stifling, of course, and what a vast responsibility, but also, in a certain light, how nice.

From an outsider's perspective, there was no way that I'd made Clara safer in her brief time out of utero. However you hung it, I had not been good for Clara. And had Ben known, if Ben ever were to know—

Yet Clara wanted me, her mother. Clara felt safe with me. I traded Ben oven mitt for infant, and she leaned into me and sighed, content. She trusted me, and that trust was the most precious intangible thing I could imagine. It would take more than fifteen years of consistent disappointment to really break that trust—I knew because I'd kept coming back to my own mother, cord frayed but intact, for almost that long. Clara was new, and we could still be new together. I hadn't yet lost her.

The oven timer beeped, and Ben turned it off and took out the casserole. All it took was the press of a button to make the sound stop. Solly knocked into us, still slaphappy at Ben's arrival, and Ben's smile was back to that ridiculous frown as he swept us all together in his arms. In his wet, squeaking shoes he danced us around the kitchen, my hip banging into the island, Clara's head wobbling.

The whole time she'd really just wanted to suck on my tit, but even knowing didn't matter. I loved my daughter. Finally it all felt right.

"I WAS WORRIED," Ben said later, "you might have postpartum depression." The night had been good, my joy continued. Nursing hurt less, Ben changed diapers, dinner wasn't freezer-burned, and Clara's bath was cozy, and now we were lying in bed, our daughter in the depths of sleep that made her impervious. I didn't say anything, just rubbed Ben's back in a way I hoped was comforting. "I thought," he said, "something was really wrong."

My throat tightened, and I kept rubbing his back. He should have noticed the focus, the consistency of my hand, the symmetry of each circle. He should have known that we were on the cusp of something really wrong, that we were teetering. He didn't.

"Baby blues," said Ben, "extremely common." He was slurring his words in the way that meant he was almost asleep, his brain struggling to spark nerves, his left cheek slack.

The ceiling fan began to spin. I knew for a fact that the main power switch was off—I had checked it. I knew for a fact that we three were in bed and bassinet, that Solly was splayed atop Ben's foot. I knew for a fact.

The week I'd taken the stick-shift guy's pills, when I'd peeled the plastic off my cheap razor, finagling until I was left with just a blade, I had, for a moment, thought it better to be nothing. I hadn't wanted to die, per se, but I had wanted to be nothing. When the razor dug in, the pain of it had throttled me: *be something*. It had all been a mistake, but in the end, it had hardly cost me.

I was lucky. Clara was lucky. Sometimes it's too late, even if you've changed your mind, and you're punished for the one stupid decision, the split-second rogue emotion. The impulse ruins you. You end up with life in prison. You end up losing somebody you love. You end up nothing.

"Thank God," muttered Ben, "I was wrong."

February 1942

Margaret leaves her car in a mess of cars by the stables, her fur coat on the passenger seat. The wind whips hair across her cheek as it blusters its way around Long Island mansions. No one has stayed behind to meet her, and the hunt crosses ten miles of contiguous estates, but she can hear the clamor of the hounds sniffing the rabbit, the beaglers trailing the hounds. The group has not gotten far.

Monty Hare has come to run with her today—he's in town putting up a new production of some off-Broadway show or another, and though he isn't a natural hunter, his long legs will serve him well.

"No promises," Margaret said last night when she invited him to join the Buckram Beaglers. "But after eating, the dogs look like the grooms in Macbeth. As a man of the theater, I think you'll be impressed."

They were at Michael's apartment, waiting for Michael, who was meant to be hosting a meeting of Margaret's worlds. It was not yet seven thirty, with the entire dinner party left ahead of them, but Michael hadn't shown, and Clem was already close-mouthed, Bruce antsy, and Bill overpouring the martinis. Michael was supposed to help make the potatoes, and there they were, unpeeled. Margaret was used to Michael making a fabulous entrance; she'd swoop in unconscionably late with an expensive bottle of wine and no excuse. Probably the night would go well. Still, she felt she had better recruit Monty to discuss things the next day.

She follows the call of the hunt around precisely pruned hedges, through beach plum trees and down along the Sound, to spot him now at the edge of a manicured lawn, just before the plants turn native. Not as fast as the hounds, which yip ahead, spread twelve across, already chasing the hare's scent, but in good showing—somewhere near the middle of the clunkier human pack. Even with the ten pounds she's put on during the holiday season, the run to join the group is no trouble to Margaret.

This is their fifth afternoon in pursuit of Flora the jackrabbit, recognizable by a particular notch in the ear, and so named by a boy in the field. At this point the whole club has developed an attachment to the old girl. The hounds can only hunt with their noses, and about a month ago had lost her scent—she'd been in plain sight but the dogs searched in vain, and finally Morgan Wing called "Go it, Flora!" and off she'd gone. The Beaglers will be sorry to lose her. The scent is stronger now, the pack gaining speed.

"So," says Margaret, darting up and whomping Monty on the back. He mimes exhaustion, then grins. "Already tuckered?"

"Already drunk. Or rather still drunk. You can throw one, Brownie."

"Michael can throw one."

Silence, which can be interpreted as Monty just catching his breath, until it can no longer be interpreted as Monty just catching his breath.

"I felt it all went well," says Margaret finally. "Bruce seemed to like her."

"Bruce likes anyone who'll talk to him about his instruments."

"But?" Margaret has a nagging sense she has to prove herself. By all means she knows the dinner went well—although Clem barely spoke all evening, and Posey had seemed close to tears. But this might have been because of the war. Besides, Clem is so different from

Michael, what were they to talk about? And Posey always does follow his lead. Still, there'd been the remark about Margaret's new book, the one she'd done with Clem and had pulled out to show the party—*The Runaway Bunny*. The others complimented the watercolor, the cleverness of the language, the whimsy of the rabbits' transformations. Michael sat down at the head of the table and read quickly, sniffing as she flipped through the proofs.

"Have a carrot!" she scoffed. "How distinctly like Margaret to treat someone who loves her with such disregard."

The room was silent, until Margaret forced a laugh. Then Bruce mentioned an article he'd been assigned. Bill complimented Michael on her arrival, how she'd swept in an hour late—a massive basket of caviar and gourmet meats and cheeses in hand—and dropped her furs to the floor to reveal a sumptuous off-the-shoulder evening gown. Posey was wearing plaid flannel. The chicken that Margaret had been basting went straight into the fridge.

"You know we went to school with Leonard Thomas," says Monty now, carefully, jumping a downed tree branch and keeping his voice low. Leonard, Michael's son from her first marriage, is married to a painter and by all accounts a bore. "He used to talk about his mother. Tell us stories."

"And you think that's why Clem was uncomfortable?"

Monty allows himself a breath. When the hunt is done, there will be tea with their host and talk of rabbits and society. This conversation has no place there; best to finish it out now. Margaret pulls him out of the crowd, letting the field surge on ahead of them.

"Leonard didn't always have the nicest things to say," Monty concedes as his steps slow. "And the way that she picks at you, belittles your career—"

"She's right. I'm going to graduate to writing for adults any day now," says Margaret.

"I'm just saying that we want her to respect you. We want to see you treated well."

"In that case, you've nothing to worry about."

"Did I say that I was worried?" Monty squeezes Margaret's hand.

"When Michael walks in a room, it lights up," Margaret looks at him with uncharacteristic sincerity. "She's teaching me to be a serious writer, so that I can do the same."

Monty opens his mouth to tell her that she already does, or that she doesn't need to, or that he believes her, or that he is tired. Margaret doesn't wait to find out which. She's said her piece and takes off running, at first toward the field, then past it. She imagines watching herself from high above, a smear of straw-colored hair against the deep green of the trees against the breadth of the sky. Here, and then gone.

11

With Ben back at home, things fell into an easier pattern. I could shower in the mornings, while he sat by Clara's play mat, and in the evenings he could hold her while I ate. When I woke to her hunger mewls at two a.m., I still felt dredged from the warm deep, it still felt like a Sisyphean task to yank my boob out of my nursing shirt and get Clara to latch, but there was a current of tenderness toward her that had previously been missing. I was better about remembering to keep protein bars by Ben's pillow—after the first night he'd moved back onto the futon so that I could watch TV without waking him up while I nursed. Several times I climbed the stairs to go ask Margaret about the night she'd been with Clara, to ask her about what to do with Michael. Each time I did, the turquoise door was locked.

Clara was gaining weight, filling out her onesies in a way that made her look more like a human baby than an alien creature. Her cradle cap was disappearing, and her umbilical stump had finally fallen off. She seemed to enjoy classic '80s arena rock: we listened to "We Built This City" and "Can't Fight This Feeling" on repeat, and she'd perk up at the swell of a syncopated chorus. I paid $5.99 a month for a music app on my phone that would let me stream practically anything. Once whatever song I selected was done, it was supposed to recommend similar music—from Foreigner to Whitesnake, from Natalie Merchant to Norah Jones. But sometimes midway through a Pat Benatar hit the music would stop, and Bing Crosby or Rudy Vallée would come on.

Sometimes the overhead lights would turn off, and a side lamp would turn on in their stead. Sometimes the curtains would fill with hot air and bellow out, although the vents were all above them and the windows were closed. Sometimes I felt that I wasn't the only adult in the room.

I knew this must be Michael, asserting herself. She didn't want to be forgotten. But none of it seemed threatening. None of it felt especially malicious. I didn't feel unsafe.

OUR HALF SISTER Kelsey had been spending lots of time with Annie while our stepmother was visiting her sister in Switzerland. It was Kelsey's junior year of high school, and she could no longer justifiably miss school for an extended pre-Thanksgiving vacation, so while her older brother Sam went skiing, she was stuck at home with Dad. She hadn't come to see Clara yet—our relationship was too caught up in my father for her to come over without him, and he'd only popped by for a minute one evening on his way home from work. Clara was sleeping, so he'd ducked in and quickly out, not accepting Ben's offered beer, not even taking off his coat. A nonevent; Dad in our home for less than ten minutes.

I felt the lack of relationship with Kelsey was my fault, since I was older. Annie tried hard, but I hadn't made the effort. It would be good for Clara to start fresh, to know her family, and I brought this up with Annie over the phone when she mentioned that Kelsey was at her apartment.

"If I bring her over, will you act normal?" Annie asked. I'd promised her I was seeing a therapist, that I'd discussed all my issues with Ben. I wasn't, and I hadn't.

"I don't know what you mean, 'act normal,'" I said. "I have a three-week-old baby attached to my tit and I'm covered in puke."

"Yes, you do," said Annie. "Don't be mean to her. Don't talk to her about that weird babysitter, or new neighbors, or how often you have to pee."

"She's practically an adult, I don't know why you have to baby her," I said.

"Don't be mean to her," Annie repeated. "She's just a kid."

"I haven't been mean to anybody since Ben got home," I said. This was true. I'd somehow found reserves of patience for the neighbor who'd blocked our car into the garage, for the shrieking teenagers in the alley. I even had patience for Michael, who, three days into her tenure, had taken to playing with the gas valves on the stove. Earlier that day I'd caught a whiff of nitrogen and turned to watch the front left burner sputter, then enflame. The others followed, sparking on and off in a code I couldn't decipher. I turned each knob firmly off and stood in front of the stove, wearing the same look of disappointment that I'd use when Solly misbehaved.

"That's inappropriate," I said. "We've been kind enough to share this space with you, now please do me the favor of being a good houseguest."

The tension melting from my shoulders as if someone was massaging them, I took to be contrition.

She just wanted attention; they all wanted attention. I guess I'd wanted attention too, but now I had it and so I was magnanimous and gentle, putting in my earplugs when the teenagers yelled and feeling above it all. Maybe it was because Ben was taking the early-morning feed. Maybe it was because I was more comfortable with Clara.

I'D NEVER BEEN mean to Kelsey in the way that Annie thought I had. I just didn't think of her as my sister—she was sixteen years younger than I was, and we didn't have any shared history. My father was a different man by the time he was her father, and I'd gone east to college before she'd even turned three.

The last time I'd seen Kelsey was just after Ben and I moved back to Chicago. She showed up with Jeanie and my father. We had drinks on the roof—Kelsey had lemonade, and my beer was nonalcoholic—and Dad complimented the clear view of downtown. They'd parked in a metered spot, and when the timer on Jeanie's phone went off we all smiled with relief. After they left, I let myself have half a glass of good red wine.

Now here Kelsey was, on my couch next to Annie, wearing a Ninja Turtles T-shirt and a Cubs hat. The knickknack holder on the back of her phone read "Hufflepuff." It all felt very branded, very messy, especially considering her impeccably applied dark-purple lipstick and the glasses that I wasn't sure she needed. The general sartorial oeuvre was one I found severely wanting.

I wasn't sure what to say to her, so I did what I'd seen lots of mothers do and talked to my infant instead.

"Are you hungry? Are you so happy that Aunt Annie and Kelsey are here? Did you have another poop?"

Act normal. I could feel Annie's eyes on me, the pressure of the four of us together in the room. Clara wasn't hungry. She hadn't pooped. She seemed indifferent to our visitors.

I turned to Kelsey. "That's a neat shirt," I offered. *Neat. Shirt.* Translation: Please leave so I can keep watching HGTV, so I can take a nap, so I can wash spit cloths.

"You know that sleep deprivation is a form of torture," she said then, apropos of nothing. Annie looked at Kelsey in the way she'd lately been looking at me. "The CIA use it at Guantanamo," she continued. "They keep the prisoners awake so long that they get loopy, and then let them have like forty minutes, and instead of feeling refreshed they just get loopier."

"Who's teaching you this?" said Annie. "Are you learning this in school?"

"Wikipedia," said Kelsey.

The whole conversation felt very of-a-moment. Very here-and-now, in the same way that the room behind the turquoise door felt very 1940s. And now I was warming to the whole thing, this capsule of late 2017—my mainstream counterculture half sister who'd criticize decades-old torture techniques but was so inured to the sitting president's theatrics that they weren't worth mentioning. Who was wearing a T-shirt of a TV show that was on its way out even when I was a kid, who'd been able to read all the Harry Potter books over a single summer.

It was snowing outside—nearly invisible flakes that would soon turn to mist or to rain—and the afternoon dark was approaching. Our across-the-alley neighbor had already put up her Christmas lights, and soon she'd plug them into the outlet on her patio; hard-candy colors would blur into the living room. There would never be another of this moment. Nor this one. Nor this.

The room smelled like gas.

"You left the stove on," said Kelsey, standing up to see the kitchen. "Did you mean to?" I shook my head, and she went around the island, bending down to turn it off. "My mother would *kill* me if I just forgot the burner like that," she muttered.

Annie looked at me. She widened her eyes and wrinkled her forehead, but I wasn't in the mood so I just said, "What?"

"We'll talk about it later." But she couldn't control herself, and before Kelsey came back to us, Annie whispered, "You aren't lying to me, are you? About the help?"

"No."

I wasn't sure why she suspected I was lying. Of course I was lying, but I'd never lied to Annie before—not when I snuck out of the house in high school, or when I hated her boyfriend, or when I'd been out of work right after college but told Mom that I was fine. I knew I wasn't a bad liar, either. Ben always believed me, and I lied to him all the time.

THINGS WITH BEN were as good as they had ever been, as good as I could imagine them. He wasn't on a specific client project, so he only had to work out of the office a few days a week. On the days he could work from home he'd tried to set up at the kitchen table, but got distracted by Clara—not her crying but the magnetic pull of her lying on her play mat, blinking up at us, learning the movement of her limbs. He couldn't focus, and with him watching her, I felt I should also be watching as she jerked her hand a little to the left, or turned her head toward the sour sunlight streaming through the window. Apparently I was missing something vital, some innate parental pride, but if I followed Ben's lead, I thought that maybe I'd unearth it. Clara was just lying there. I told myself to do better.

Once he realized he wasn't getting anything done mooning around the condo, Ben started posting up at a nearby coffee shop. If it wasn't too cold, I could walk Clara to come see him. At five thirty exactly he'd sign out and come home to either make or order dinner, and he'd sit while I marathon-nursed and watch crappy TV with me until we were both ready to fall asleep.

While he was home, nothing happened.

Nothing notable happened.

Which is to say, he didn't notice anything.

June 1942

Michael notices everything. The sharp edge of a stone poking out of the wet sand, the evening habits of the gulls, a slant rhyme that doesn't quite fit. Margaret has given her the draft, and now she sits on a divan, a pencil hanging from the side of her mouth, the afternoon light skimming off the water, lacing through the slats of the porch railing. Every so often Michael's hand clenches when the words she reads move her; the sun has turned her forearm's dark hairs gold, even her ankles are bronzing. Margaret pretends to read Whitman, but can't help but look up at each murmur of approval or disdain. Finally Michael sets down the article, sighs, and holds her hand to her forehead to gaze out toward the Sound.

"It's good," she says. "Though it isn't literature."

"But it's for grown-ups," says Margaret.

"Yes, it is. And I can see it in a place like *Vogue* or *Harper's*, but you have to somehow reference the war." The war feels very far away, both physically and in its relevance to Margaret. To mention the war here, while the tide laps the edges of the long wooden dock and the rum cherry stretches over the swimming pool; where everywhere one turns, the world is quiet, blue-green, glorious—

"I'm not interested in politics," says Margaret.

"Yes, my dear, that is one of your flaws." Michael stands. She makes her way to the stone path that leads down to the seawall, rolling her shoulders back and unbuttoning her shirt.

Margaret trips after her, barefoot.

"It's fine to propose that New York is 'a melting pot of wonder-ful cuisine,'" says Michael, "and the maps truly are darling. But the timing isn't right. We can't be celebrating unity when Europe's in such turmoil. I don't see anybody running this piece now."

"Still—" Margaret grins. "It *is* for grown-ups."

"Indeed."

A small wave slaps the dock, startling a piping plover. The dogs take off, and Michael laughs. She sheds her button-down and leaves it on the rock wall. Margaret watches her slip out of her shorts—her thighs luscious and freckled, her stomach loose after three chil-dren. She doesn't remove her drop pearl earrings; the risk excites Margaret.

No experiment in living has ever proven so fruitful. No man has such depths, can push Margaret so far.

So much of life is solitude—so much misunderstood. But with Michael, language is more capable, focus more attainable. Joy more deliberate. Margaret is stripped and seen and orbiting. She curls her toes in the sand and feels her soul swimming with Michael, slapping each stroke even before she's left the beach.

ALONE AT THE rented house on Long Island Sound, they are free from the demands of Michael's lecture tours and vast social engage-ments. But their solitude has an expiration—for here is Harry's be-hemoth of a Lincoln crunching up the gravel drive, announcing the weekend arrival of himself and his guests. Margaret and Michael freshly bathed, but Harry recognizing the briny musk of intercourse as soon as they greet him. Michael designates rooms, and Harry glares at Margaret, taking Michael's elbow as they go upstairs to dress for dinner.

Supper is glazed vegetables and a ham the size of a small child. Harry carves at the head of the table, stuttering over the bone. Next to him, Michael tells a district judge about the house she plans to purchase in Connecticut.

"I'll have a bedroom overlooking the ocean," she says. "And a space in which to write. I won't be far from my son, Robin—he'll be the only person I'll see on any regular basis. The solitude will be good for me. I'm quite ready to be alone." Harry's bad ear faces Michael, and though she will not look at him, her voice rises so that he's sure to hear. He simply smiles and offers the serving platter around the table. When he gets to Margaret, he does not offer, instead overpiles her plate.

"Wine, I see." Harry squints at her glass. "I suppose you wouldn't have the stomach for scotch. Or the taste."

"Kiddie books and kiddie drinks, I'm afraid," says Margaret, swallowing contempt with her expensive cabernet. Still kiddie books, but grown-up literature soon.

After eating, Harry goes immediately to bed, while Michael ushers their guests to the porch. The temperature has dropped, any residual warmth hiding in pockets, with a breeze that forecasts rain ruffling the post oak. Margaret laughs when the storm finally comes, stays out longer than the others, tries to smell the lightning.

"How could you?" hisses Michael once the last of the party have gone to their rooms. "You know I'm afraid of storms. I don't understand how you can be so insensitive." Margaret reaches for Michael's hand, but she snaps it away.

"I didn't mean to upset you," says Margaret. "If I had you worried—"

"You didn't 'have me worried.' What does that even mean? No wonder you'll never write anything but nonsense."

Michael sniffs. Margaret again offers a hand. She cannot stay the night in Michael's bedroom, not with the house full of guests, but Michael might come now to Margaret's room, slip out to the beach at first light. They need not change everything because of Harry. Michael brushes past Margaret, stomping up the stairs. From where she stands on the landing, Margaret watches Michael open Harry's door.

12

Michael Strange had barely factored into my dissertation, which meant I was even less equipped to handle her than I was Margaret. So far it felt innocuous—this houseguest, this haunting—but I supposed that things could easily turn toxic. I'd read enough about Margaret to know how difficult her lover could be—Michael's anger could reignite at any moment, hotter than before. To further arm myself, I ordered her autobiography from interlibrary loan. I read what little there was about her online.

She'd been the spoiled youngest daughter of a rich Rhode Island family, connected to European royalty, a Gilded Age elite. I'd thought at first that in choosing the name Michael, she was asserting her gender identity, but the more I read, the more it seemed to me she just enjoyed the glamour of the Michael Strange mystique. It did seem that when she was married to John Barrymore, they'd played with gender roles—she feminizing men's suit cuts, he lowering his necklines—but so much of that relationship was performance art: two large personalities fighting for air. By the time she settled in with her third husband, Harrison Tweed—by the time she met Margaret—Michael had turned her energies elsewhere.

She wasn't a very talented poet, but she was an early suffragette. That was one good thing about her. That was something I could respect.

She was often in the society columns, and she liked it. Though always wealthy, she was never as famous or respected as she felt she should be. Michael was charming; she was difficult. In photographs she seemed coy, stylish, self-possessed. It made sense that she would show up for an afterlife, that she'd plan for a resurgence. I just had to figure out why that resurgence was through me.

Ben was excited to see me so excited, proud that I seemed to have a goal. And this research was a welcome distraction, as Annie kept calling and texting, kept wanting to talk about how I was feeling, kept asking me about the stove. "I'm in the middle of a project," I replied.

BEN WAS ALSO working. He held court at the coffee shop, with two laptops that he set up at a communal worktable, a headset, a large water bottle, an extra-large black coffee, a plate with some sort of muffin or its crumbs, a yellow legal pad, a Bluetooth keyboard, a mouse and a mouse pad. I noticed a younger woman side-eyeing his makeshift office as soon as I got to the door, and while I'd probably have done the same if I were her, I was resentful. She didn't know him. He was trying to provide for his family. He was sweet. But he was oblivious in the way that straight, white men are oblivious; comfortable in the way only men can be comfortable. He had on a button-down and a Patagonia vest.

As soon as he saw me struggling with the stroller, he ran over to hold the door, letting in a gust of peppery air. The woman rolled her eyes, and when she saw that I'd brought Clara, she almost physically shuddered. It's not like we were on an airplane. Clara wasn't crying. The woman could easily get up and move. In a remote corner of my mind I knew we were treating this coffee shop like our living room. But what was I supposed to do? Just go to Gymboree and preschools?

Ben didn't notice. Ben beamed. He took Clara out of her bunting and held her up for all the denizens of Espresso House to see. He was such a delivery-room dad that I thought he would start passing out cigars. A few people smiled, but most turned away. They didn't need a baby in a coffee shop on a Thursday afternoon, this same baby that many of them had seen in this same coffee shop on Tuesday afternoon. Why did I feel such a sadness for Clara?

She barely seemed to recognize that we were no longer at home; the bagel slicer behind the counter was just as intriguing as the ceiling fan as the bathroom tile as the hand Ben was now waving in her face. She yawned, and sort of hiccupped.

I ordered a tea, but didn't have time to drink it. Clara started turning her face back and forth, the way she did when she'd be hungry soon, the way she did when she was seeking out a breast. I got Clara bundled up to leave again, and put the tea in the stroller caddy. I forgot it in the garage, left it atop the car, still steeping.

The next afternoon I walked by the coffee shop to visit Ben and saw Mr. Garbage paying for something at the counter. Too risky. I turned around. It was too cold for a walk, so I went back home through the alley, saying, "Crunch, crunch, crunch," as the stroller wheels ran over fallen leaves, as if Clara understood me.

I could hear Solly barking from inside our unit as I hefted the car seat up the stairs, the clip of her paws on the hardwood as she skittered back and forth in front of the door. Something was wrong.

"Careful," I said, as I walked in, lifting Clara at an awkward angle—all angles were awkward—so that Solly wouldn't slather her with kisses. She must have been excited we'd come back so soon, I thought, although that didn't quite make sense.

Solly's feet were wet. She ushered us toward the master bathroom, yipping.

Music was playing, but I couldn't trace its origin. A tinny sound; a woman's voice spun out like treacle. Birdsong? There couldn't have been birdsong.

I'd set up candles in the master bathroom while I was pregnant, but never lit them. I didn't like baths—couldn't get past the thought of marinating in my own dirt—but they were supposed to help with the contractions once labor began. These candles were lit now: one on top of the toilet, two on the ledge by the bath. The tap was on, the water overflowing. A tenderness to the grout—the water would seep down through the ceiling to the kitchen.

If Ben had walked in on such a scene he would have panicked, called the police and maybe the plumber. I couldn't bring myself to feel anything more than a resigned recognition. This made sense. This was just Michael, asserting herself.

"What do you want?" I asked out loud, over the splurge of the tap. I put Clara on the middle of the bed and went back to turn off the water. Michael had it on the highest setting, scalding. Too hot for me to reach in and lift the drain. The kind of hot that forced you into your body, overwhelmed all other feeling. Was she looking for a body? Trying to come back to herself—the physical self that portrait artists had lauded "the most beautiful woman in America," that performed Shaw's *Saint Joan*, crossed the country giving lectures, had her own radio program. A dilettante. Always needing a platform. Always needing a stage. I thought about how it must feel to be seen, to be so beautiful, and then to be nothing. But first, to be old.

There are two kinds of legacies to leave—the things that you build and the things that you conjure. Michael had left both: she'd written poems, she'd birthed children.

"She didn't like her children much," Margaret had said, "but she did love them."

"And did she love her poems?"

Margaret hadn't answered. She'd been watching me put on my lipstick, that night that I left her with Clara. Why had we been talking about Michael? Because Margaret always wanted to talk about Michael—what she wore, the way she spoke. There was something oedipal in her obsession, her need for Michael's affirmation. But Michael didn't want to be needed—she wanted to exist in a place where she was idolized but not asked to do anything, where when she offered her opinion everyone would stop and listen, but no one would ever ask her for it, and it would mean more for the lack of asking, and she would mean more for the mystery. Or maybe that was me.

Did Michael love Margaret? I wondered this as I finally stuck my hand into the tub, the tile firm against my knees, my arm immersed to the shoulder, my entire body prickling with the heat. If there was no love, then why was Michael here? The baby bunny tries to run away, and the mother will always run after it. Margaret had based *The Runaway Bunny* on an old French love song about a man chasing a woman. It wasn't romantic, it was threatening: *I don't want to be yours, yet you refuse to let me go.* Margaret had co-opted it, shifting the narrative in the process: the mother and her child, the cord stretched tight but never broken. The lover and beloved. Poor Margaret, I thought to myself. Poor Michael.

I was facing the tub from above. There was no reflection. Why was it that in films there was always a reflection? There should be my face in the bath, and then another face behind me, or my face rippling to morph into another face, the reflection of it laughing at me. Visions in the fire were always signs of things to come, but visions in the water showed what already had happened.

I felt around for the drain, but couldn't find it. Instead, something slippery and grasping was blocking its spot. Up on my haunches to remove it, I was elbow-deep, digging blindly. In candlelight, the water seemed opaque. Was this a fingernail? A knuckle. Then a hand rising to meet me, an impossible arm stretched thin through the pipes, slithering out through the drain.

How ridiculous, I thought, but then the hand grasped my wrist, pulling itself up by pulling me down, and now my arm was completely in the water, now my chest. My nose skimming the surface of the floral-scented bath, those fingers clawing at my shoulder.

Then I was under.

There were two hands now, ten fingers, and they were holding my face, stroking my cheeks. My back, already sore from the constant curl of breastfeeding, was shot through with fire, and my lungs shot through with fire, and I tried to pull up, but Michael was strong. My every instinct screamed freedom, my body bucking for breath—still she held on. What was I to do? Even as it was happening, I knew that it couldn't be happening. I was deeper than the depths of the tub, I was burning. An airless giddiness overtook me. I thought I tasted salt. I opened my eyes and saw a lobster sputter by.

And suddenly the hands were not only letting me go but forcibly pushing me out of the bath. As soon as I realized what they were doing, I yanked myself up and the drain cleared and the water began swirling down. Water rained from my hair as I watched it chug shallower, and then I was coughing, and then I was crying—the two compounded until I couldn't untangle them, one egging on the other until I was snotty and hoarse. From the bedroom, I heard Clara's faint babbling, and this normalcy was calming. My breathing slowed, my sobs less frequent. I wiped my nose. The candles flickered against the dark walls. The foreign music was still playing, and I heard the dripping of the tap, the thrum of the heat heaving down through the air vents. Then the candles snuffed out, each releasing a sooty wisp of loss, and I waited for these wisps to come together, for Michael to materialize.

She didn't. What did she want with me? I had laughed at her narcissism. I'd thought her poetry pretentious. I'd belittled her, disliked her, because Margaret's biographers disliked her, because they claimed she'd encouraged Margaret to dislike herself. Maybe now she disliked me. Had I already made her angry? The message-board mothers had warned me not to make her angry. Clara had warned me. Clara was out there, alone.

Clara lay on the bed, on her back, and from the angle of the floor it looked like she was laid out on an altar, wrapped up in her bunting as a sacrificial lamb. The ceiling fan *click-clicked* above her, hypnotic. The shadow of each blade cutting through and across, waves of light and dark exploring her face. I'd hit a wall of exhaustion, and was unable to climb it. I sat against the bedframe, trying to steel myself, trying to force myself closer, trying to breathe. Clara up on the bed, enraptured. Me on the carpet, shivering in my nursing bra and yoga pants, grasping at the bedspread, trying to protect her from someone I couldn't see. Someone who wanted to be seen.

My phone was flashing—a series of notifications, one after the other, sliding down the screen like beads threaded on a string. The phone was at the edge of the bed, and I yanked the sheet to slide it down so I could reach it.

Someone had responded to my message-board question, reviving my thread from so many days back. *Does anyone else feel like someone they can't see is watching them?* The answers flooded in now:

Anon654: Yes. Pay attention.

Anon655: Get back to work, Megan. Start writing. She's waiting.

StrwbryLvrTx97: My motherinlaw is around all the time and shes really nice but sometimes I can't stand it. Also she gibes my baby water even though I've asked so many times for her not to. I don't know what t do.

I shuddered. Michael was watching me. Michael was waiting. But Michael was telling me exactly what she wanted. Michael needed me alive, because then I could write about her. This knowledge was a comfort.

I hiccupped. Swallowed. Whispered, "Clara?"

Although she didn't yet know her own name, Clara turned her head toward me. She was fine. She was just a normal baby, safely positioned at the center of the bed, discovering small and lovely truths about the world. The magic of the ceiling fan. The safety of a mother. She cooed; the sound was steadying. I took a breath, and clicked out of the What-to-Expect app to find a text from Ben waiting: *Hi babe, I miss my girls.* The little emoji with x's for eyes.

(What did that mean? I'd always thought that one meant *dead*.) *I'll head back early and we can take C out for dinner tonight?*

I rubbed my eyes with the heels of my palms. I wrung out my wet hair.

This could all make sense, if I tackled it with logic. Ben wanted to get dinner. Michael wanted me to write. These were basic desires, and I could fulfill them both. Ben could text me to let me know what he wanted, but Michael didn't have a smartphone; she had to resort to other methods. But now I knew. She'd made herself clear, and now I understood, and since I understood, I could take action, and since I could take action, it wouldn't happen again.

I just had to reply to Ben. I just had to write about Michael.

I straightened my shoulders, rubbed my eyes with my wrists.

I texted back: *Sure.*

13

Ben had to go back to Houston—this time just for a few days. He was going to miss Clara's one-month birthday, but would be home for Thanksgiving.

"I'd rather you be here for her birthday," I said. "I don't even care about Thanksgiving." For the past two years we'd flown out to Ben's brother's place in Utah for a week—Linda and Seth, too—a whole Weiler reunion with awkward small talk and too much wine and attempts at flag football that went nowhere. We'd suggested that this year we have Thanksgiving in Chicago, given that we'd have a newborn baby and were in no shape to fly, but Linda had balked. That was not how things were done. We could stay at home, but she and Seth absolutely must fly to Utah. She hosted Hanukkah. She hosted the High Holidays. She did not host Passover, and she did not host Thanksgiving. Ben was clearly disappointed about how it all played out—he wasn't used to hearing no from his mother—but he agreed it made no sense to fly with Clara.

"It's not a birthday every time she turns a month," he said now.

"You know what I mean."

He nodded and acted contrite. Clara was lying on the bed next to his suitcase while he packed, her special tummy-time mat with its raised pillow puffing up atop the comforter. Her forehead still loose and wrinkly, like elephant skin. When would she grow into her body? Ben tickled her stomach after folding his socks.

I was in the master bathroom, cleaning the infant tub insert that fit into the sink. My hands kept slipping: white vinegar pooling on the counters, weeping down onto the floor. I spilled or tripped or crashed a lot lately—from the elbow down, my arms would start to tingle the way they once had if I drank too much caffeine. The message-board mothers blamed hormones for the clumsiness, and for the night sweats, and for the difficult digestion. It gave me a sense I was no longer in control of my own body. I supposed this was appropriate, as my breasts were Clara's alarm clock, the crook of my neck was her pillow, and my hair was only there for her to gnaw on, as a place for her to spit. I'd wake up some mornings—a relative term—and my full left side would be numb, and I'd wonder if she'd finally sucked me dry, if this was it for me.

"You should exercise," said Annie when I told her about the feeling. She was calling to check in, since Ben was gone. After seven voice mails, I'd finally decided it was easiest to just pick up the phone.

"It doesn't happen when I'm holding the baby," I clarified. "Just when my arms are free. Maybe I pinched a nerve carrying the car seat."

In the kitchen, Michael jostled the icemaker. For the past week she'd only been around the house when Ben wasn't, and now that he'd left for Houston, she was making herself comfortable. She liked to remind me she was there by turning on the electric teakettle or rolling pens across the counter—things that either hinted at the heat of which she knew I knew she was capable, or things that prompted me to get back to my writing. She wasn't used to modern appliances. They frustrated her.

"Your fridge is loud," said Annie. "I can hear it through the phone."

Over on her play mat, Clara moved her foot so that her jingle-bell anklet sounded a tiny, tinny peal. Theoretically, Clara would associate the sound with the movement, and therefore recognize she had a body. I wasn't sure if this theory was a good one. After all, you didn't have to have a body to make noise. You merely had to move molecules. Make waves.

Another crash from the kitchen, the ice falling from the top of the freezer to the well in the door. I knew better than to say anything to Annie about Michael. She was mine—mine and Margaret's. And Clara's.

"Jeanie asked us to Thanksgiving," Annie said suddenly.

"Wait, what?" I coughed.

"Yeah, she emailed me the other day, said it was Dad's idea, he wants to see the baby. I guess Kelsey mentioned she'd come by."

"Why wouldn't she reach out to me herself?" I asked. I gave Clara her pacifier and stood up, cracker crumbs cascading off me.

"I don't know, Meg. Should we go, do you think?"

"I don't know," I said.

"I think we should. Rip off the Band-Aid. Introduce Clara to the rest of her family."

"Introduce Clara to her family," I repeated.

"Are you okay?"

I was thinking about rabbits. I was thinking about beagling. One of the many things to love about beagling was the clear delineation of predator and prey. Not once in its terrified existence did the rabbit think it was in charge—its little heart fluttering, its ears alert, its back legs propulsive, never fast enough, no such thing as fast enough. Speed was its only asset, which in a way made everything easier, closing off other possibilities, letting it focus on one thing. Sometimes the rabbit got away. Sometimes the dog would crack its neck but other times would mouth it, wet and matted, bloody, still alive.

With my father, I had never been in charge. But I was a parent myself now, and he and Jeanie wanted something from me. I had power.

"Okay," I said. "We'll go."

■ ■ ■

I FELL ASLEEP in Clara's glider, my neck slumped down, my arm perfectly still. I woke up to the panting of the garbage truck out in the alley, the scrape of the dumpster, the exhaust's distant trills. Clara dozed on my chest, a little baby bird asleep. Someone had covered her with a quilt. It hadn't been me.

MICHAEL WANTED ME to write. Research I did gladly, but for me writing had always been a painful bloodletting that had to be scheduled. I found it unfair that in order to be a doctor of history, you had to produce, you had to publish. Really what I wanted was to be a receptacle for knowledge, to hold the knowledge in my body and just pass it on to Clara through the enzymes and the vitamins and the minerals, let her suckle at the font of my knowledge, and do with it what she would.

I sat down at the kitchen table and pulled up my Word document, jumping through the tracked changes, which were mostly dated more than four months back. I pulled up a new, blank document and wrote "Michael." I could tell that she liked this, because the room got comfortably warm. My phone rang. Annie again. I ignored her.

"When Michael finally died," I wrote, "Margaret's old friends said, What a relief."

This Michael did not like. A lightbulb in the kitchen burst, spun sugar shattering everywhere. I had to lug the vacuum down from upstairs, had to wipe down the floorboards with a damp cloth to make sure Solly didn't step on any shards.

"Okay," I said when I was done, "I get the message."

I sat back down and I wrote:

It was summer, pavement steaming, and Margaret was working as an editor for W. R. Scott. She wrote three copies of a letter to send to Ernest Hemingway, John Steinbeck, and Gertrude Stein. *How would you like to write a children's book*, but cleverer, more persuasive. Only the publisher, John McCullough, put his name on the letters. Only Gertrude Stein responded.

(I knew Michael would like this, because it demonstrated Margaret's desperation. It justified what Michael always said about Margaret: that she was needy, that she cared too much about the opinions of others. Music began to play, soft trilling flutes. Clara was gurgling on her play mat. I continued.)

Everywhere was somewhere and everywhere there they were women children dogs cows wild pigs little rabbits cats and lizards and animals. That is the way it was.
                      —Gertrude Stein, *The World Is Round*

The World Is Round featured a little girl named Rose, and as such, Stein thought it should be printed on rose-colored paper. "We are having a terrific time locating a Rose colored paper," wrote John McCullough. "Next time we hope you will name your heroine Peach or preferably Snow White."

(Michael didn't appreciate Gertrude Stein in the way that Margaret did. Michael liked Whitman, and Byron. She liked passion and Romance and interesting verbs. But at least I wasn't writing about Margaret's work. At least I was getting a crack in at old Gertrude. She let me continue.)

Margaret sent Gertrude Stein the galleys for *The World Is Round* alongside forty single-spaced pages of minor editorial suggestions. Almost every revision involved the proper placement of the comma.

The word *comma* comes from the Greek—*komma*, a single coin, a cut-off piece. When Aristophanes of Byzantium proposed the idea, *komma* was a term for the clause itself, and not the mark that distinguished it.

How many clauses might you have in a sentence? How many beads on a string? How many days in a week in a year in a lifetime? How many mosaic tiles of fact to piece together a truth?

And what does a comma do a comma does nothing but make easy a thing that if you like it enough is easy enough without the comma. A long complicated sentence should force itself upon you make you know yourself knowing it and the comma well at the most the comma is a poor period that lets you stop and take a breath but if you want to take a breath you ought to know yourself that you want to take a breath.

—Gertrude Stein, *Lectures in America*

Gertrude Stein did not know about Margaret's involvement with *The World Is Round*—while Margaret bore the brunt of the work, John McCullough signed his name to every letter. In 1940 Margaret wrote to Stein off the record, a note praising her work, pulsating with desire for connection. No correspondence was established. A year later, Margaret wrote under her own name a second time, laying bare her literary aspirations, her foray into oil painting, her thoughts on fairy tales, her ideas for Stein's next work. At the end of the letter she sent her best to Stein's dog, and mentioned her own terrier's new puppies.

Stein responded this time—on a postcard. She congratulated Margaret on the birth of the dogs.

Margaret did not reach out again.

I sent this newest chapter to my dissertation advisor. Two days later, he wrote back: "Megan, I'm not sure how this integrates into the rest of your project. Perhaps you should take a bit more time. We'll speak in the spring."

Michael would have told him that a true poet is rarely understood. She was pleased, so I was pleased.

September 1942

New York in early autumn: grimy with residual summer not yet rinsed by rain. Too hot under the duvet, too cold with just the top sheet; the clock creeping toward midnight. Margaret starts when the phone rings. She hasn't heard from Michael since that week in late June on Long Island Sound—not even a note declining Margaret's invitation to come summer at The Only House, her cottage in Maine—yet she is not shocked to hear Michael's voice now:

"You must come get me."

Embarrassing, how quickly Margaret's resolve can melt at the sound of Michael's voice, at the idea that Michael needs her. At The Only House last month, Margaret thought that she had finally given up Michael. She wants children, and cannot have them with Michael. She wants reassurance, and will not get it from Michael. And though her former beau Bill Gaston—who has a home across the water—is still married, any day his divorce will come through. If Margaret can be patient, she can have him. She knows Bill's children, loves his dogs—no matter that he'll never be faithful. She has decided to move on from Michael, who wants Margaret not as she is, but in Michael's idealized form. Better to marry and let your husband's eye wander, knowing eventually it will wander back to you, than be a piece of coal forever failing as a diamond.

But now, Michael:

"You must come get me immediately. Harry found proof of us, and he's sent for his doctor."

Proof—most likely letters, or perhaps the household staff. Harry wouldn't have Michael arrested—he wouldn't risk such a scandal— but he would put her on medication. Margaret imagines Michael, bleary-eyed and drugged to dullness. Michael, forced into an institution. She sits up in bed, pressing the telephone closer to her ear.

"Lock yourself in your room and pack your things," Margaret says. "I'll bring a car."

Outside her apartment cabs crawl the street, waiting for the Café Society crowds to disperse for the evening. Cigarette smoke spirals down from fire escapes along with snippets of conversation about Camus and La Guardia, Sinatra and sex. Men gather under neon signs, the storefront canopies too small to contain their revolutionary fervor. When nightclub doors open, applause and alto saxophones waft through. Margaret barely notices. Walking down Sixth Avenue, she has the feeling she's forgotten something—the keys in the door, to turn off the oven. Whatever it is no longer matters. She's left behind the quotidian world, as she always does with Michael.

When the taxi reaches 10 Gracie Square—that pristine Upper East Side castle with its limestone rooftop loggias, its plush lobby and bay windows and quiet river view—Margaret has the driver honk. Michael appears not long after with a monogrammed suitcase. She has taken the back stairs, assisted by her maid, and slides in next to Margaret in a cloud of expensive perfume.

Margaret clasps Michael's shaking hand and says, "Go, go!"

"Where to?" the driver asks.

"Just drive," says Margaret. "Don't worry, we'll pay you."

Where to take refuge? The women huddle together, fingers laced. Margaret's apartment in the Village is too easy a target, and Michael's sons' homes both too far. Besides, they cannot know whether the boys will even welcome their mother. Robin takes men to his bed, but he is fickle. Leonard's wife is cold.

Margaret has never seen Michael so flustered, so clearly in need. Her eyes dart frantically. She grasps Margaret's hand with an unprecedented strength. She ignores the sudden stops and starts of traffic that usually afflict her; she sucks at her teeth, her breath unsteady. But as the taxi takes her farther from the prospect of the law or an asylum, Michael slowly comes back to her body.

"My back," she says, wincing when they reach Lexington.

"Can you drive slower?" Margaret asks the driver.

"More slowly," Michael says, but does not harp.

By the time Margaret has deposited Michael at the Colony Club—the exclusive Park Avenue social club of which she is a member, where men are forbidden, so they knew she will be safe—Michael is wearing the face that she so often wears, the face that makes her Michael: confident and glamorous and wronged, but forgiving. "I'll see you soon, my dear," she says to Margaret, and climbs out of the cab, sails through the clubhouse door—an avenging goddess framed by marble pediments and vast Corinthian columns.

IN THE MORNING, Michael calls her lawyer. One week later she is back at Gracie Square, her husband gone after issuing a formal apology. The separation is officially under way, and Margaret spends her nights in bed with Michael, planning a future together. She uses Diana's old bedroom as her office. She abandons Greenwich Village for Carl Schurz Park, bohemian literary gatherings for yacht moorings and doormen. Harry gets the Gracie Square penthouse in the divorce settlement, so Michael rents two neighboring East End Avenue apartments for herself and for Margaret, who gives up her downtown claims. They dine at a table set with silver, the candles melting.

14

When's the last time you had a really good cry?" Ben asked me on the drive over to my father's. It was Thanksgiving Day. He'd jump-started the car after it finally died in the garage, and ever since, it hiccupped whenever we went over a pothole. I kept checking back to make sure Clara hadn't split from us, that the back of the SUV hadn't broken off.

"I don't know," I said. "Maybe in labor?"

"Mmm, I don't think so." Ben turned left, headed north toward the highway. "I'm pretty sure you didn't cry. Just sort of yelled. Maybe that first week home from the hospital?"

"Why?" I didn't know what he looked like, in this moment. I couldn't look at him because I had to be looking at Clara—if I took my eyes off her, she might unbuckle herself from the car seat. We might hit ice. She might float away.

"I was wondering if you want to try to get it out now. Instead of while we're at your dad's place. Or just after."

"What?"

"I'm not making any judgment, just noticing a pattern of behavior," Ben said. "This isn't going to be a . . . cakewalk. And it's normal for you to still be balancing the hormones, getting back to equilibrium."

"A *cakewalk*? Like musical chairs where you win cake? Since when do you say cakewalk?" Clara was stirring, and I'd have to un-buckle my seat belt and reach over the headrest to get to her pacifier. Her crinkle toy had already fallen.

Ben ignored me. "I know you, babe. You like to act like it doesn't matter to you, but I know it does."

"This seems like a strange time to be having this conversation," I said. It was an easier critique than pointing out that I did not think Ben knew me. There was a ghost in our house with whom I was intimately involved, and he hadn't said a thing. I said, "I'll be fine."

Still, he was right that I never liked visiting my father. I al-ways went in with subconscious expectations; reminding myself he wouldn't have changed, still harboring hope that he had. Why was it so hard to harden myself against the inevitability of my father? Why, time after time, did I think that I would arrive in a parallel universe in which he was no longer himself, sixty-two and stolid and uninterested in me? At least I wasn't like Annie, forever disap-pointed that he hadn't called. At least it was only when we walked in the door that the unfairness of it hit me and I'd scoot off to the bathroom for a minute to collect myself, leaving Ben to small-talk alone. I'd cried into Jeanie's embroidered pink hand towels more than once.

I could look at his home and know exactly who my father was, exactly what my father valued. I could look at the books on his shelves and the art on his walls and the pillows on his couch and un-derstand the way he thought he'd be remembered. He read business books, the type that reaffirmed what he already thought of him-self, certain passages underlined with "YES!!" as marginalia, "keep doing what you're doing." He'd trained entry-level telephone sales representatives at a mid-level auto insurance company for the past twenty years. Every six months came a new crop of adoration, re-cent college graduates eager to learn how he'd risen in the company, how they themselves could make such good money. In truth, he'd come in as a sales trainer from an entirely different field, but he'd told the story of his ascendency from humble t-sales rep to demigod so often, I was sure he now believed it. Just as he believed that Mom had forced his hand in leaving us, that Annie and I didn't need him, that he'd been a good father. It isn't possible to reason with that level of delusion, that level of narcissism. When he died, he'd likely keep on like Michael—a machine so entirely comprised of ego, it wouldn't matter once the meat of it was gone.

On the walls in Dad and Jeanie's living room: their marriage license, Sam's graduation photo, a picture of my father as a seventeen-year-old swimmer. Kelsey's homecoming pictures, a framed poster of Klimt's *The Kiss* that could have come straight out of someone's freshman dorm room. All Jeanie's doing, I imagined, and also how I knew that their marriage was nearing its end. He didn't care enough to make the house his home. He was probably sleeping with somebody at work.

"SIT, SIT, SIT!" said Jeanie when we walked into the living room. No mention of the baby, who let out a massive burp and then smiled. At home, when Clara burped, Michael made her displeasure known to me—knocking over a candlestick, rattling a box of wooden blocks. Here, my twenty-two-year-old half brother Sam just laughed and offered her his finger.

"Cute kid," he said. I sat. Kelsey came in from the kitchen carrying a beer and a glass of red wine. She offered the beer to Ben, who took it, and then sipped the wine herself. A sidelong glance at Jeanie showed she either didn't care or hadn't noticed. I adjusted Clara on my shoulder and awkwardly cleared my throat.

"Oh!" Kelsey blinked at me. "I thought that because you were breastfeeding . . ."

"It's okay," I said.

Annie was sitting in the corner, her own glass almost empty. She said, "Megan doesn't need to be drinking." She was glaring at me, though I didn't think I'd done anything wrong.

"Where's Dad?" I asked, and no one answered.

Whenever we came over to Jeanie's, she acted as if we were strangers, international travelers she was hosting on some exchange program, incapable of helping cook or clean up, of finding the bathroom or comprehending basic requests. The first time I brought Ben to her house, she'd stared laser beams at his shoes until I finally asked if she wanted him to take them off, at which point she laughed nervously and said of course not and then continued to glare at the rubber soles until we were gone. She had a way of looking at you and blinking and cocking her head just enough to the side to make you feel like you were some sort of circus freak, some cabinet curiosity she neither approved of nor cared to understand. She'd never made any effort to mother us, which was just as well. In the past, she'd called our actual mother "that woman," even as Mom called Jeanie "that woman" in an ouroboros of passive aggression that made it clear why I'd felt I had to go away for college, why I'd felt I had to move to New York.

"Sit, sit, sit!"

At a certain point, I could sit no longer. My butt was numb, and Clara was squirming. Kelsey offered to hold the baby, but her teeth were red from merlot. Sam and Ben were having some stereotypical Thanksgiving football conversation—*half yard? full yard?*—and Kelsey kept trying to chime in and getting bulldozed. Eventually she refilled her glass and sank into the couch.

My dad, I imagined, was smoking cigarettes outside some bar, steeling himself to head home.

I walked Clara around the living room, past the blond wood piano and the business books and *The Kiss*, past the fireplace tools and the decorative empty birdcage and the basket of throw pillows and woven blankets. It wasn't a bad house. It felt lived in. Jeanie had done a decent job with it. She brought out the cheese and crackers and some sort of vegetable dip, sans vegetables, and while everyone else dove in I carried Clara down the hall, past the pictures of Sam and Kelsey as babies, past the pictures of Dad and Jeanie on vacation. We slipped through the glass doors of Dad's rarely used home office, and I spun Clara around on the desk chair. She didn't like it. I bounced her on my hip, and wiped a little web of drool from her chin.

The front door opened loudly, Dad arriving and greeting the group, I guessed, with spearmint on his breath, a spindly redness to his eyes. I could hear him briefly say hello to Annie, clomp in to Jeanie in the kitchen, come back out to join the men. Kelsey's voice was up an octave, whining. The television on, the crunch of chips. Something was overcooked, or burning. I licked my finger to wipe a film of dust off the top edge of the computer monitor and heard Annie behind me.

"We thought you were nursing," she said. I shook my head. "Or at least that Clara was asleep."

Clara would be asleep soon. She was going slack in my arms, nuzzling and then pulling back, making a sound like the creak of a body releasing its last breath.

Annie stood in the doorway, holding her wine. Blinking.

"Come in," I said. "Close the door."

Annie set her wineglass down so hard on the desk that some sloshed out the sides and onto the plastic blotter. She was watching me with hard eyes, eyes that didn't belong in her body. Animal eyes: brown and round and glassy, like something had taken off my Annie's skin and slipped into it like a dressing gown, tying her up around them. She was drunk.

"Careful," I said, which was a word spoken so often it had escaped its own meaning. From the Old English *cearful*, meaning mournful. *Careful bed* used to mean sick bed. I tried to use it in the way I would use a comma in a sentence, a way to acknowledge the clause that had passed, a way to ask for the next one. But *careful* was really a period, an acknowledgment of an ending. I only said "careful" once there was no going back, once the glass had already been broken, once the toe had been stubbed. Once I was mourning.

"This has gone too far," said Annie. She had closed the door, finally, her face so close to mine that I could feel the heat of the wine on her breath. I wanted to ask her what had gone too far, to be specific. I couldn't defend myself against something I couldn't see or understand. But the words got lost somewhere between my synapses and nerves, and I couldn't form them. Chilly, I held Clara close.

"I said something to Ben just now. I know you haven't talked to him. It's all still happening, isn't it?"

"What did you say to him?" I asked.

"It doesn't matter. Nothing major. Enough to know you're lying."

"You'll upset the baby," I said.

"Jesus, Megan, stop pretending you're this perfect virgin mother. I know that something's going on."

I was in my father's chair, Annie perched atop the desk, looking down on me. I felt like a misbehaving child called in for punishment.

"Megan, you're not taking this seriously." Annie slid down to kneel by the swivel chair, her hand on my knee. A new tactic. "I'm worried about you," she said.

"I thought you were mad."

"I'm worried, and I'm also mad."

"Everything's fine," I said. "You don't need to be worried about me. You can just be mad."

"Megan, Ben mentioned that your bathroom flooded. You keep locking yourself out. The other day your gas burners were all turned on."

Well, that had not been me. That had been Michael. If anything, Annie should be worried about her, how she was coping in her current state of incorporeality. How she felt about being dead.

"If you don't get help soon, you're going to hurt yourself," said Annie. "You're going to hurt somebody else. You could hurt Clara."

At this, Clara, who'd seemed sleep-adjacent for the past several minutes, let out a hell-raising shriek. Normally her frustrations began at a whimper, rising only as we idiot adults failed to determine her needs. This panic was immediate. She was squalling and stormy, red with rage. Annie put a tender finger to her cheek, but it did nothing. I tried to rock her, to coo to her, to bounce her up and down, but she continued to cry.

"It isn't fair, to put this all on me," said Annie, voiced raised to be heard over Clara. "Do you understand that it isn't just about you? You're putting me in a really tough position, and I want to be on your side, I *am* on your side, but I can't lie for you. If you don't tell Ben by the end of the weekend, I'll tell him myself."

Tell him what? What would I say? *Our home has been infested.* No, *infested* meant hostility, and I didn't think Michael was hostile, at least not as her resting state. *We've opened up our home to a visitor.* Yes, that was better. Like we were hosts of an adorable bed-and-breakfast, and provided little bottles of shampoo to our guests. I could make fancy brunch casseroles and large batches of fruit compote pancakes, if only Clara would stop crying long enough for me to get the house in order, long enough for me to gather the ingredients, long enough for me to think.

"Is she hungry?" asked Annie, and I opened my shirt, but Clara wasn't hungry. Her diaper was clean, I'd tried to burp her, I was *shoo-shoo-shoo*-ing rhythmically to mimic the beat of my own heart. "Maybe she's constipated," said Annie.

I didn't think Clara was constipated; it was just that she was living. She was staring the act of living in its impossible, cruel face, and all we could do until she'd conquered or forgotten it was try to give some comfort. I didn't know how to say this to Annie without worrying her further. I didn't know if this was something only children and their mothers knew, something I'd known once as a child and then forgotten, recollecting only with Clara's birth. Michael was a mother. She would understand. Margaret wasn't, and by this logic she wouldn't. But Margaret knew children, Margaret understood children, Margaret talked to children in their own language. Annie didn't. She wouldn't understand.

Clara was hiccupping, which I hoped meant she'd found some sort of temporary resolution. And then Ben was at the door, reliable Ben, helpful Ben, coming to check on us.

"You doing okay with her?" he asked me.

"She's just having a rough time," I said. "We'll be okay." Ben came to put his hand on my shoulder. He took Clara and started whispering to her, holding her with his big hands against his solid chest. Making her safe, or at least giving the illusion. I rubbed her back while he held her, and by some magic the sobs trailed into little whimpering ellipses.

"Ahhh," said Ben, "that's better. You're okay."

We were constantly telling Clara that she was okay, and most often it felt like a command. Like a *careful*. But now she truly was okay, nuzzling up against Ben, blinking, letting out a milky yawn. Instead of the jealousy I expected, I felt relief that he could calm her, that she knew him and settled into him in a way that I never would know him or be able to settle. At inception she'd been equal parts of both of us—sperm stitching into egg—but since it was my body that blanketed her, I'd thought it would be only my body that could soothe her. Sometimes it was. Sometimes it wasn't.

Ben took Clara out of the office and down the hall to where my father's second family was gathered. Annie followed. Before she turned at the end of the hall, she looked back at me and said, "Tell him."

DINNER WAS OVER quickly. I had to stand up and bounce Clara halfway through, and then I had to go into Kelsey's bedroom to nurse her. Dad talked about work and about Sam's fraternity. He gave a perfunctory glance at Clara, nodded to tell me she was acceptable, then shoveled in more mashed potatoes, flecking gravy onto the collar of his shirt. When we left at eight thirty, he was no more known to me than he had been when we arrived, no more known to me than he had been when I was a child after he'd moved to the suburbs, no more known to me than he had been when we lived eight hundred miles apart. He would always be either unknown or so categorically, conventionally knowable that I refused to accept that was all he had in him, that was all that there was.

ONCE WE WERE home and Clara was settled, Ben went out to get more beer. As a general rule he was either basically sober or twenty beers deep, and tonight he was drinking, which I didn't begrudge him. It was not, however, a good time to let him know about Michael. Instead, while he walked down the street to what in New York we had called a bodega but here we just called the corner store, I tried to summon Michael, to warn her.

She didn't come when called. She wasn't a pet. I wondered how I would know she was listening. Light as a feather, stiff as a board? The disembodied lighting of a candle? A tap on the wall? Knock three times on the ceiling if you want me?

Most appropriate, I finally decided, was to open all the living room windows, as Margaret had done the night Michael first came in. After all, I was trying to tell her goodbye. I was trying to tell her that it had been lovely having her, that she'd been decent company, but now it was time for her to go wherever Margaret had gone so they could work out their issues and I could get my sister off my back. The woman who lived across the alley watched television late into the night, which seemed like a nice and timely activity for Michael to interrupt. If her window happened to be open, Michael could just hop over. A smooth transition. Very easy.

"Thank you," I started, because Michael was the sort to respond best to praise. I had to make it seem like I needed her, but it would be better for her if she left me. Like she was vital somewhere else, but I was *désolée* to see her go. It would help if I said some of it in French; she was the sort to respond well to French or German. "It's been so wonderful having you here," I began. "I feel so lucky that you chose me to help you . . . return."

A gust of air across my neck made me feel like she was there, and she was pleased with me. This was good, because I only had minutes before Ben would be back.

"Still, it's unfair to keep you all to myself," I said.

The air took on a chill. I wasn't sure how to continue. Michael wasn't naturally patient, but she knew how to wait out a verbal gaffe, and I imagined her with brows raised, looking at me down her aquiline nose, anticipating her own displeasure.

"The lady who lives over there, I think, would love to have you . . . I mean, I think she needs help with her . . . it might be a good time to . . ." I paused, recalculating. "Look," I said finally. "Michael. I'm going to tell it to you straight, which is how I would want you to tell it to me. My sister's worried. I don't want my husband to be worried. I think it's a good time for the two of us to go our separate ways."

She prickled at that, which is to say I prickled, the hair rising on the back of my neck.

"I mean it in the best possible way," I tried. "I'm really not mad at you. It really isn't even my decision."

The windows slammed shut, and suddenly the kitchen countertops were steaming—across the divide of the kitchen island, I could see the stove knobs spinning, the gas a struggling blue light. I was a few feet from the kitchen, but I felt the heat rise up in a great squall, damp and thick against my throat and my chest. The anger was directed at me, and I was afraid of what would happen if the flame caught, what height it might reach, how it might spread. I was afraid it would inhabit me, that I would feed it to Clara.

Then the electric lights in the room all flickered at once, and this felt like such an obvious choice for Michael to make that I was no longer afraid, because she was predictable. She wanted me to re-write her story, and if I didn't, she would bully me into submission, the way she'd always bullied Margaret. But I had researched her. I could prepare for her. I might be irritated, or inconvenienced, but I could steel myself against her coming anger, reflect it back to her or bury it deep. I didn't have to worry that she would catch us un-awares, that she would hurt us. I could protect my daughter against anything I knew and understood. I simply had to name it.

"Michael," I said to the darkness.

And then she was gone, and Ben was walking in with a six-pack, asking me why I had turned off all the lights.

October 1947

If you don't learn to say what you mean, I'll go mad." Michael draws herself up as she speaks, a bullfrog full of its own voice. Margaret sits with her legs crossed underneath her on the bed, looking out on a bleak city morning—a flag hanging limpid on its pole in the park, a motorcade on its way back from Gracie Mansion. "Your language matters. You expect me to keep propping you up . . ." But Margaret isn't listening. Margaret is watching a balloon wisp out over the river. She was trying to find the right words to tell its story when Michael burst in from across the hall, irate.

These are Margaret's working hours, but with Margaret's career continually on the rise, any work done for the publisher is a perceived affront to Michael, whose own career is fading. She must have seen the messenger from Golden Books leaving with Margaret's paperwork, must have heard Margaret on the phone with Garth. She says that Margaret came home from dinner too late last night, disturbing her rest, and had visitors come much too early this morning. She says that Margaret is sucking the life out of her, making it impossible for her to do her own work. She says that Margaret doesn't speak clearly. Look, here, she's spelled *balloon* wrong, how can she call herself a writer, how can she call herself an artist, how can she—

Margaret climbs down from the bed and goes to Michael, holding her, finding her hips through the silk housecoat, nuzzling her neck. Michael's body sighs and submits. The two of them stand clutching each other. Then Michael pulls away and coughs and says she has to go rewrite a lecture, pack for London, choose a dress.

"I love you," Margaret says.

"I know you do," says Michael.

BY NOON TRAFFIC is heinous around Union Square, and while Margaret doesn't mind being late, she hates to be bored. This orchestra of horns and drums and protestors might once have excited her, but these days the spark of what might once have been excitement turns quickly to frustration.

"I know you do," Margaret mutters, jittering her leg so hard her Town & Country coupe shakes. "I *know* you do. *I* know *you* do." She has always had a knack for riffing on a theme. Does she want to laugh or cry or join this swarm of dirty people? She squints but cannot read their picket signs—poor penmanship conspiring with bad eyesight. Doubtless they are out of work, or pushing for a union, or hungry, or down on their luck. None of these excuses for blocking the intersection. Margaret leans hard on her horn. One man in a ratty sweater shrugs an apology. Another, in a jacket with no tie, makes a rude gesture. Margaret honks again.

"You are impulsive," Michael said at the beginning, her fingers finding Margaret's bra clasp, her fingers circling Margaret's breast, "and that will get you into trouble." But Margaret hasn't been impulsive with Michael. She's been patient. She has tried to understand. Yet—always—trouble.

Now Margaret searches for the man without the tie. She yanks off a bracelet, a hand-me-down from Michael, and throws it, thwacking him squarely in the back. When he turns and sees her watching him, he moves to thump the bonnet of her car, but she steps on the gas.

"Make way for the rich," Margaret says, and drives through.

■ ■ ■

LUNCH IS AT a quaint Italian restaurant, checkered tablecloths and cotton napkins thick as towels, waiters leaning down with black pepper and Parmesan, refilling red wine. Margaret picks apart a stale piece of focaccia, half listening as her editor, Ursula, and illustrator, Garth, discuss book royalties. Her wrist is still thicker than she'd like to see it, naked now without the bangle. Michael likely won't notice it's gone. She'll be touring for the next few months, and when she returns she'll hardly remember that she passed it on to Margaret. It seems she has forgotten—or wants to forget—about many of the things she's given Margaret. *I won't be your crutch*, Michael will say, but then she'll ask Margaret to lean on her. *You need to be able to form your own opinions*, Michael will say, and then rage when Margaret doesn't parrot back.

"And of course Children's Book Week will be just as overblown as it was last year," says Garth, "and Miss Moore just as determined to exclude us."

Normally this would prompt Margaret to make some clever barb about the children's librarian Anne Carroll Moore, her stodgy sometimes-nemesis. When she squints and says nothing, Ursula and Garth exchange a look.

"They'll be hard-pressed to outdo themselves on theme," says Ursula. "Last year's was so . . . cerebral. 'Books are bridges.' As if the New York Public Library had ended the war themselves with the bravery of its new children's programming."

"This year: 'Books are battlefields.'" Garth laughs.

"Books are battalions."

"Books are bullets."

"Books," says Margaret, "are books."

15

Hosts and ghosts are inextricable. The linguistic root *ghos-ti* is Proto-Indo-European—present in languages across Europe and Western Asia: in Spanish and in Hindi, in Bengali and in Russian, in Marathi and in Portuguese. In English it contributes to *hospital*, *guest*, and *hotel*. It is also found in *hostile*. In *hostage*. Words rooted in *ghos-ti* reference the reciprocal obligations of ancient hospitality. Off you would go to sail the sea, and when your ship sprung a leak, you could stop by and your host would say something like "Oh yes, I knew your father," and invite you in or else be cursed for generations for denying you. I didn't want to be cursed for generations. I didn't want Clara to be cursed. So after asking Michael nicely to get going, I decided the next best thing to do was make my offerings meager, get her to move on to her next host of her own accord. Michael liked beautiful things, so I tried to make us ugly. Michael liked intrinsic mystery, so I tried to make our lives obvious and plain.

"Where did *Madame X* go?" Ben asked of the framed Sargent print that had hung by the bed.

"I'm redecorating," I said. Ben nodded. He didn't care what we put on the walls. The truth was that it smelled of too much luxury, too much sex, too much temptation for Michael. Not that she cared, not that any of it mattered. When Ben left the house for groceries, she snuck into the closet to retrieve *Madame* and broke its glass in a series of quick cracks that spread like the aftershocks of an orgasm. She was telling me she knew what I was doing, that she wouldn't be fooled into submission.

The next morning, we woke up to find volume 1 of my *Oxford English Dictionary* shredded, its vellum-thin pages ripped deliberately from their binding, bunched up and strewn.

"Solly must be acting out," said Ben. "I don't know how she got it down."

I nodded, though of course it was Michael. She was trying to hurt me; she was saying that she knew what I loved and could destroy it. She would go through my beloved objects one by one, the commodities that made up my economy of selfhood slowly ravaged. The dictionary first, because it housed the names, and thus breathed life into the physical objects. A word, broken down into its component parts, was the most powerful magic I had. Michael was a poet. Michael understood. It wasn't garlic, not holy water, but language that would drive Michael out, and we both knew it. Margaret knew, too.

Margaret's poetry was good, which was why she'd lasted. Michael's lacked the lyricism, the urgency, the ineffable spark of longevity. "What will survive of us is love," said the poet Philip Larkin. A pleasant thought, but truly what survives is art—Larkin's Arundel tomb is a statue, a statue is a thing made out of marble and feelings. A painting, oil and feelings; a poem, words and feelings. I'd never been called to make my own art—though of course I wanted to survive—because although I had all the physical materials, I didn't have the right feelings. This was why I struggled to write down my dissertation, though the ideas were all there. Did that make sense? It seemed to make sense, and it seemed to make me an ideal vessel for the next generation: I could give Clara the tools and the parts, and when she was old enough, she'd imbue them with the feelings.

I had the parts.

Michael had the feelings.

Here she was.

This all made an illogical sense to me, but of course I couldn't share it with anyone. Annie was mad, and she'd issued her ultimatum. Ben just thought I was renesting. Kelsey was seventeen. My mother was difficult. I really didn't have any friends.

IF ONLY MARGARET would come back and help me. Every time I went upstairs the door was locked.

ABOUT A YEAR ago, I'd stepped on a tiny shard of broken glass and couldn't pick it out. My skin callused over until it disappeared inside me, and all that remained was a twinge of memory of the pain. Sometimes I thought it had moved through my blood, hardening me. Sometimes I thought Clara was born of the shard of glass meeting an egg, and this explained her transparency, and also her bite. This explained why we were special, why Michael wanted us.

WHILE I NURSED Clara, I thought about what I was going to tell Ben, now that Annie had drawn her line, since it seemed likely Michael wouldn't make things easy and just leave us. I could say that I had postpartum depression, which was probably true. Perhaps that would be enough to placate Annie. Better to say that I *had* had postpartum depression, but I hadn't wanted to worry him and now I was through it. At Clara's checkups I filled out questionnaires about how I was doing: had I blamed myself unnecessarily, been anxious or worried, had I looked forward with enjoyment? Did I have trouble sleeping? Yes, I did, because I was still nursing every four to six hours. Did I feel like things were "getting on top of me"? Yes, an eight-pound baby. It was ludicrously easy to know the right answers, the answers that would have the pediatric nurse nodding and smiling and praising me.

I could admit that I'd lied on the questionnaires. That would be good. That would be vulnerable. Was it still vulnerable if it was so calculated? "Be more vulnerable," said Annie's therapist, but she didn't specify how, didn't specify when, not even for Annie.

But maybe I needed to be less vulnerable. After all, it was the vulnerability of childbirth that had left me, and consequently Clara, open to what I could only call a poltergeist. From the German *poltern*, a disturbance. *Geist*—a ghost. Which begged the question of what ghosts there were among us that didn't cause a disturbance— certainly not Margaret, with her construction projects and her growling dog. Did we breathe these ghosts while sleeping in the way that we supposedly ate spiders? Perhaps this was why Clara, why so many babies, fought sleep. They were close enough to the void that they knew what else was out there, and they didn't want to swallow anything unsavory.

HERE WAS THE problem. Amended: here was part of the problem.

At six weeks old, Clara was turning into more and more of an actual person. When she opened her eyes, it truly felt like she was seeing things, processing and heading toward an understanding. When I put her in the headband from my mother, she looked like an actual baby. She could smile. She was amused by Solly's tail flicking across the waxy floors, Ben's scrunched monster faces, my sneezes. She could push up onto her forearms, and for a brief moment could lift up her head. After she'd eaten, her belly bulged out like an old man's beer gut. Her hair was still downy, but lightening. She was losing her cradle cap, thanks in part to Vaseline and our meticulous combing. In short, she was becoming less of a thing that had happened to me and more of a person who was in the process of happening to herself.

This should have been excellent, as it implied we were, to a certain extent, separating. She was learning how to exist in a body, and while it would be years before we cut the metaphysical umbilical cord, she was well on her way to becoming. We could now go, with any luck, up to six hours at night without nursing. During the day she could be by herself on her mat and not need me for upwards of ten minutes at a time.

This meant I had to reevaluate myself; I could no longer avoid my daily life with the excuse of being necessary. In those ten minutes I had to clean the kitchen, or respond to my emails, or, god forbid, open up my dissertation. The anonymous message-board chorus was still prompting me to write, reminding me I had to keep writing, reminding me I'd pinned all hope of a career, of a self-sustaining life, on this project I'd largely abandoned. Reminding me that writing was most likely the solution to Michael. I didn't appreciate the pressure. The twelve weeks I'd promised myself as maternity leave were not yet up, though the point at which they would be was inching ever closer.

Anon1324: Get back to work. Keep writing.
Anon1325: Clara's asleep, why aren't you writing?

It no longer bothered me that the message board knew me, knew Clara. They could have found us out so many ways: we posted photos of her to our social media accounts, Ben not bothering to make his profiles private. We'd filed her birth certificate and insurance claims and had even put ourselves on the waitlists for day cares, just in case. Of course they knew Clara. What hung me up was that they also knew Michael.

Anon1326: She wants you to write.

It wasn't clear to me how she'd gotten to them, how she'd persuaded them, who *they* even were. But it was clear Michael was using the message-board app as a door I'd unintentionally left open.

One of many doors left open. Now that Clara was closer to emerging from the hazy brume of fourth trimester, she was casting off a part of her protection. She was susceptible to influence, as we all became susceptible as soon as we could use our minds to learn. She was susceptible especially because she didn't yet have language to help anchor herself in a concrete reality. She didn't even know what reality was.

Michael could get Clara by jingling her dangly play gym animals in a particular order, or by playing a particular song. She could turn the crank of the jack-in-the-box and surprise her. She could break the windows and leave the glass in a crystalline pentagram across the living room floor, and while this didn't seem her style, I couldn't know for certain that she wouldn't evolve with Clara's own evolution. A rabbit can outrun the hounds nine times, but on the tenth the dog will learn, the dog will catch it. I found myself checking and double-checking and triple-checking for sharp objects hidden in the short shag of the carpet, for dead animals Solly might have dragged in from outside while I wasn't looking, for the beads of an old necklace scattered across the floor, for tapered table edges, open outlets, dangling cords.

"She isn't crawling yet," said Ben when he came home from work the Monday following Thanksgiving to find me on my hands and knees, one arm fanned under the couch, looking for stray pieces of popcorn. I could hear the ghost of the *even*, the extra syllables of judgment. Ben said, "You can relax."

I'd been meaning to tell him. I was going to tell him. I just didn't know what to tell him. The overhead lights flickered.

"I'll take a look at the breaker later," said Ben. This was the opportune moment, and I slithered up from under the couch, readjusting my sweatpants, breathing deeply. Dust bunnies gathered on my sleeve, made mostly of dog hair: prey formed from predator, ironic. Clara cooed in her bouncer, and I gave her my finger to hold. I thought in doing so she'd lend me some immunity.

"We need to talk," Ben said, before I could begin. "Annie called me."

I had lost the opportunity, the messaging. I hadn't been able to get out in front of it. Ben sighed and came over and sat on the floor next to me, so that we both looked down on Clara, our backs against the bottom of the couch.

"I was going to tell you," I said. I was being honest, yet all the while strategizing how I would discover what Annie had already told him, how much I would have to admit to, how much I'd keep myself from giving away.

"She's worried about you," said Ben.

"Hmm." I scrunched my mouth to the side, and decided to start simply. "Did she tell you I was locked out on the balcony?" Warmth was gathering in the corners of my eyes.

"She didn't."

I turned to look at him, to look right in his eyes so he would know I was telling my version of the truth. "I was locked out on the balcony," I said. "I was getting some air. I'd left Clara inside." I was fully crying now, but not for the reason I knew he would think I was crying. Not because I'd lied to him, or because I'd endangered our daughter. No, I was crying because I was still so calculating, because my brain was still counting the beads on some imaginary abacus, weighing and balancing and planning. Annie's therapist—were we ever to meet—would not be pleased. This was a poor man's vulnerability, a lying man's truth, and I was ashamed of how easily I fell into these clichés, how I took the most undesirable *man's* descriptors and combined them with that age-old archetype, the faithless woman.

From my research, I'd discovered Michael always behaved as if she had no reason to mislead you. The way she felt was not a feeling but an objective fact that you already innately understood, only needed to be guided toward, firmly and gently. I tried to channel her confidence, though I didn't know how much of that confidence was a facade.

Ben was the opposite of Michael in all ways: substantial where she was transubstantiated, tactful where she was blunt, kind where she was funny.

I was still holding my daughter's hand, and I was crying because I knew that this was the closest I would ever be to my husband, and it wasn't close enough.

"It's okay," he was saying, "it happened and it's over and I understand why you didn't want to tell me." His willingness to give felt like a concession. He would hide the hardest parts of me in some dark recess of his mind, pave them over and lock them away. In doing so, he thought he was offering me the opportunity to be unequivocally myself, but he was actually just excusing bad behavior. I felt now that there was nothing I could do that he wouldn't explain away, both to himself and to me.

"I didn't want to make a scene," I said, because I knew he didn't like scenes, and the easiest thing to do now, as I was accepting his truest nature, was to placate him. I would, for now, be who he imagined me to be.

The lights flickered again. Michael did not approve, nor should she. But what could I say to a man who was willing to leave what should have been a larger conversation—why had I left Clara, why had I locked the door, why had I told him nothing—at *it's over*? How could I tell him now that what he thought was just a footprint was a cavern a thousand feet deep? Ben wanted things to be easy, and because of this he had convinced himself that they were, had placed his faith not in God but Occam's razor. I was unspeakably sad for him. For us. For Clara.

"Don't worry," said Ben. "It's okay to let yourself cry." He was prying Clara's fingers off mine, rubbing the small of my back in methodical circles, resting his chin on the top of my head. He was trying to comfort me, and in doing so comforting himself.

I could never, ever tell him.

"Did Annie say anything else?" I asked through a large hiccup.

"Just that you were stressed," Ben whispered into my hair. "That she was worried about you. Should we be worried?"

I knew what he wanted to hear, and because I still loved him in love's simplest form, and still wanted to please him, I said, "No. No you shouldn't be worried. I have it all under control."

"Thank you," said Ben. "Thank you for being so honest."

January 1950

L et's discuss reincarnation," says Michael.

For all their philosophical discussions, spirituality rarely factors into Margaret and Michael's conversation. Neither woman subscribes to traditional religion, and both know that the faith du jour would label what they do together sinful. It has always been easier not to talk about what they do together. Physical love doesn't need language—this, thinks Margaret, is its beauty. All the worlds within a brush of the knee, or a head on a shoulder, a tongue exploring or a palm cupping a breast, spiral out with possibility—a multiverse born of the body. Name it, and the path has been chosen, the reality ordained.

But Michael's tiredness has been named, it has been diagnosed leukemia. At first Michael blamed Margaret's stressful influence and sent her away, hoping the calm she'd leave in her wake would be a cure. When it wasn't, Michael turned back to God, who she'd known as a sometimes acquaintance in her youth. It is now Margaret's fault that God has given Michael cancer; there's only so long one can continue in sin without punishment. Per usual, Michael's contrition is irregular. She's yet to find a doctor who is certain of a cure, and yet to convince herself of an afterlife. She's afraid. She calls often on Margaret.

As a child, Margaret followed her mother into the musty living rooms of Great Neck's dabbling upper-middle-class spiritualists to be lectured in theosophy. Margaret's mother believed in the Oneness of the Universe—that every soul returned to the One upon the passing of its patron, then was sent back to humanity in an occultist appropriation of reincarnation. Margaret's mother is now dead. Margaret wonders if Maude's soul ever returned.

Three years ago, when Margaret posed the question, Michael laughed. Now Michael has work to do—books to write, lectures to give, minds to enrich—and not enough time in which to do it. She's leaving for a clinic in Switzerland in hope of convalescing—Margaret expressly not invited, but summoned to see her off. Michael is gaunt, already pulling on her gloves when Margaret gets to East End Avenue. Luggage sits piled in the hall.

"Ride with me," says Michael. The sixteen miles of traffic between the Upper East Side and Idlewild Airport mean a wasted afternoon, but Margaret nods. She takes Michael's purse while the doorman gets the suitcases. She stands silently next to Michael in the elevator. The doors shutting behind them feel like the ending of a certain kind of life.

Michael smooths her hands over her lap, settling into the cab. "I've been reading about my past lives," she says. Margaret waits. It's like Michael to set this as a trap, and she would rather not be caught in it. "It seems there's no simple way to determine my next body. Whoever I once was got lucky, but that's no guarantee it will happen again. I want to be sure I'm not some bloated politician. Some cad."

"So you've decided not to die," says Margaret.

"I'm going to die. We all will die at some point." Michael speaks as if revealing some prophecy. The car inches over the Queensboro Bridge. Margaret's mouth is dry. "I want to make sure that my soul is in good hands. A metaphysical estate planning, if you will."

Margaret smiles, but mostly because her face isn't sure what else to do. She has always been the fanciful one, Michael grounded in fact. When Margaret thinks about reincarnation, she thinks of the veins across her mother's hands, thick worms under silk gloves. She thinks of airless parlors and stale curtains and frauds in beaded headdresses who promise resurrection. Of Maude too tired for her children, somehow with infinite energy for the occult. Maude so difficult to impress, Margaret still trying.

"I read your poems out loud," says Margaret, shifting in her seat so that her leg touches Michael's.

"And you'll keep doing so." Michael nods. "That is exactly the sort of thing I'm going to need. A compass, for when I return. Something to guide me toward art."

"You'll obliterate life if you keep trying to prove there's no death," says Margaret. They are crossing the East River now, a placid, muddy green.

"If I continue down this path I'll find the secret of life," says Michael.

Margaret says, "The secret of life is being alive."

16

Before Ben had to go to Tampa for work, we would have Hanuk-kah in the suburbs with his parents. It was an annual tradition, which in the past I had survived through heavy drinking. Now, I was nursing, and would have to pass out in the guest double bed without the aid of Linda's off-brand Manischewitz. Still, a night at Ben's parents' could be restorative. Maybe when we got home, Michael would realize she would rather be without us. Maybe when we got home, Michael would be gone.

WE BROUGHT THE pack 'n' play, a sleeve of diapers, several burp cloths, pacifiers, two pairs of pajamas, the swaddles, a pack 'n' play sheet. We brought three changes of outfit, in case of a diaper explosion or spit-up. We brought drool bandanas and bibs. We packed wipes and the play gym and the breast pump and several extra storage containers, because I never knew when I might get engorged. We brought headbands and socks and the baby carrier and a blanket to tuck over Clara once we had her buckled in her car seat. We needed the diaper rash cream and her baby soap and the tub insert that fit into the sink. We needed the monitor and its accompanying acces-sories, the sound machine. We packed the vitamin D drops that I was supposed to put on my nipples before Clara nursed, but almost always forgot. Lotion. Her favorite stuffed duck. Then we had to pack for ourselves.

Once the car was loaded, it looked like we were off to some cave to hibernate for the whole winter, like we would be back in several weeks rather than twenty-four hours.

"We're coming home tomorrow night," I whispered to Michael as I touched up my lipstick.

HOW DO YOU get rid of a ghost? The same way you get rid of anything else that haunts you: run away from it, run far away. Pack your car and your child and hop on the highway and sit in Friday-afternoon traffic while you listen to some podcast about the political resistance, which should concern you right now, but doesn't.

I felt guilty about not being as rapt in the political discourse as Ben was, about not knowing the legalese or politicians' names. Margaret was so apolitical that she'd brag about not reading the newspapers. During World War II she wrote to Gertrude Stein, in Hitler's Europe, about how much she wanted someone to write a fairy tale about invading tanks. Her biographer thought it was tactless, and likely the reason her friendship with Stein never caught on. I didn't think I was as bad as Margaret. I understood the conceptual suffering, and before Clara had followed it closely, vomiting up my dinner on election night, blood pressure rising with each threatened ban. But I couldn't hold all of it at once—my own pain and the country's. I suppose I was more like Ben than I cared to admit in how easy it was for me to pretend and to bury, to stare at Clara and convince myself that pretty soon things would be better, that things were already getting better, that she would grow up in a world that would be cleaner and fairer and kinder to girls. I'd seen on Facebook that someone had drawn a swastika on the walls of my ex-boyfriend's high school, scrolled through the comments, regretted it. Now I changed the input from Ben's Bluetooth to the radio, a secular Christmas song.

"We should play her the dreidel song," said Ben, but he didn't really mean it.

LINDA WAS READY for us, waiting at the window when we pulled into the driveway, ushering us from the frigid gloaming into the house, where a gas fire burned prettily behind glass and a shiny blue banner wished us a happy Hanukkah from the wall above the first-floor landing. I didn't remember such festivity in the past—Linda didn't like her paint marred by Scotch tape, her topiary disturbed, her kitchen spoiled by the persistent funk of latkes. But here were sparkly little stars, here was a vast mixing bowl of grated onion and potato.

"Hello, sweet darling," said Linda in a voice that didn't match her words, serious and low like she was lecturing a group of college students, not cooing at a baby. I appreciated this sincerity; I didn't see what good it did children to be spoken to as such—there'd be no babbling or baby talk for Clara from us. The ushy-gushy cootchie-coos were dangerous, they weren't language and they told an ugly lie about the nature and purpose of language. I imagined Michael leaning over Clara's bassinet, her voice scrunched like an accordion, *Who's a good boogie baby, who's a good ickle boo.* But we were at Linda and Seth's house, ten miles away from Michael, and I wouldn't let her spoil the holiday.

"Can I help in the kitchen?" I asked, and was immediately set to work washing and peeling more potatoes. Linda had bought what seemed like several pounds too many, as if trying to make up for all the past latke-less years.

"Clara just eats milk, Mom," Ben said. "You know that, right?"

"We can freeze the leftovers," said Linda.

Seth brought out the scotch, and we toasted to Clara, the menorah on the counter candle-less and forgotten as evening eased into night. Linda had bought a giant pink teddy bear, three times the size of Clara, and we took photos of her propped in its lap, falling over into its furry paunch, from which she emerged startled but not, we thought, unhappy. This was her general demeanor—surprised but not unhappily so—the excitement of a new place and new people having little effect on her kewpie doll nose, her invisible eyebrows, her cockled, heart-shaped lips. Only when she saw me did she seem truly alert, her eyes casting off that glazed perplexity and sending a beacon directly to my chest.

"She loves her mama," said Linda, giving her approval for what could, for all I knew, be the only time in our shared history. I relaxed into the luck of it all, Ben rubbing my back and smiling, Seth showing us the ice mold that would keep his liquor cold and undiluted, Linda subconsciously conducting the classical music that played as she cooked. I almost didn't want to take Clara downstairs to sleep, I didn't want to lose the balance of this one precarious moment, this small happiness. But I sent Ben out to get more of our gear from the car, because it was nearing nine o'clock, and Clara was lifting her arm above her head in the way that I knew meant she was tired.

I fed her in the basement while Ben set up the pack 'n' play, Clara so hungry that she didn't even turn her head to see what he was doing. We'd brought too much with us, we said. We wouldn't even unpack most of it. I suggested that we skip her nightly bath.

"But will she sleep?" Ben asked, puppy-dog eager. We'd read that it was never too early to establish a routine: a bath, a book, a good night's sleep. Clara would sleep here in the downstairs office—Linda's "craft room"—under the eye of the plug-in baby monitor, while we would be next door, in the narrow guest bedroom. I didn't think she was going to sleep well regardless, in this foreign room with its chilly air and one curtainless window, but I knew that Ben wanted to help with her bath, wanted to comb her tufty hair and powder her and zip her into the sleep sack with the cows leaping the moons. This was the house he had grown up in, and he wanted a similar childhood for Clara.

Afterward, the three of us sat together on the floor by the pack 'n' play and read stories, Ben holding Clara so that she could see me turn the pages, though her eyes never settled on the book. She was looking at the window, high in the wall, looking out onto a composite night. Something brushed against the glass—whatever still grew in the gelid ground of Linda's garden, a barren bush, a bramble. *Tap tap tap.*

As I turned the final page, we saw Clara's face melt into the satisfied smirk of having just released her bowels. Ben winced at the smell.

"I'll change her and put her down," I said. "You go visit with your parents."

Tap.

It's difficult to change a dirty diaper on a carpet.

Tap tap.

I sang to Clara, put her in dry pajamas, zipped her and folded her into her swaddle. The sound machine sighed pleasantly, and she had her eyes open when I placed her in the pack 'n' play, on her back, just under the monitor's camera. While I climbed the stairs I stared at her image in the display screen, two shining orbs her open eyes. She squirmed a bit, but didn't cry.

Tap tap tap.

THEY'D MOVED INTO the living room—Linda, Ben, and Seth—and moved on to a third round of whiskies. I sat on the bench of Ben's childhood piano and watched his mother swilling her tumbler, watched the tremors lacing through his father's hands.

"We forgot to light the candles," said Linda. Then the debate over whether we had missed the crucial moment—sundown—and would be better served waiting until tomorrow. I thought that if God cared about when we lit the candles, then God was no better than Michael, just another petty ghost. We should light them; we should put the menorah in the window and announce ourselves. But Linda didn't want to, and it was Linda's house, so we didn't.

Seth started talking about candles. He was drunk. He talked about how in Judaism candles represented the soul, flickering, weak, eventually snuffed out. All the while Linda did that thing where she looked at me, squinting, trying to figure out if I understood the basic tenets of the faith in which I had been raised. I ignored the stare in favor of the memory of her praise.

It made sense that Jewish candles were lives, that flames were souls. With the exception of the Ner Tamid, the flame that burned forever in the synagogue, the candles that we lit were designed to burn out. They were long and thin and crammed into their holders, threatening to fall. Nothing like the candles I lit throughout the year at home, which came in squat jars with lids, which were meant to be snuffed and relit, which emitted cloying vanilla and mulberry and barely even flickered.

Seth was tossing around Yiddish like a name-dropping socialite trying to score an invitation to a party, Linda bobble-headed, well aware that she'd be his plus-one. Ben's glass was empty. He was rising from the couch to refill it when we heard Clara scream.

The sound came, tinny, from the monitor, but she was loud enough that we also heard her cries from downstairs. I took a breath, trying not to be hasty. Sometimes she'd cry out in her sleep and then settle, and letting her handle herself could save me hours of grief.

"Time to sleep," I whispered, as if she could hear me. I pressed the button that should show Clara's image, but didn't see her little body on the screen. The monitor had arrows that controlled the camera's pivot, and I searched with the track pad, scanning up and then down. The crying had stopped. She was probably fine, but I still couldn't see her.

"Ben," I said, "come here." I showed him the swerve of the camera. "Where is she?"

"Hmm," he said, repeating exactly what I'd just done as if he could do it better. "Short-circuited, maybe? I bet it's the picture from before you put her down. She isn't crying anymore. We shouldn't bug her." As if seeing her mother would be an inconvenience. As if Clara had better things to do.

"If you need to go see her, you go down and see her. You do what makes you feel safe," said Linda, again in my corner. But I had no time to thank her, no time to register my surprise. Clara was crying again, the red light on the monitor flashing. I stared at the lack of her as I took the stairs two at a time, already knowing. The greasy, undigested remnants of my dinner roiling in my stomach, a heaviness settling across my chest. The crying triggered something primal, a mix of guilt and self-importance, a centuries-old fear.

I paused outside the door, willing Clara to be there, willing an electrical fault or a dead battery, a simple explanation. As I walked into the room I prayed silently, *Leave us alone.*

Until I saw Clara lying in the pack 'n' play I didn't know how tightly I'd been holding my shoulders, my breath. She was whimpering, come undone from her swaddle, one hand pressed against the mesh sides of the crib, the other clutching a pacifier, which I supposed she was unable to return to her mouth on her own. But this wasn't why she was crying, at least not solely why.

The overhead fan hadn't been on when I left the room—I knew because I'd worried about the cold, dressed Clara in her fleecy pajamas, debated adding a blanket before deciding that I wouldn't because the risk of SIDS was greater than the risk of being chilly. Now the fan was spinning so violently, I thought it would detach from the ceiling. Linda's knitting had been thrown from the desk, a luminescent snarl of yarn. Her scrapbook materials were scattered, a pair of scissors open on the floor. The desk chair was overturned, the computer monitor flashing. I was afraid to touch any of it, afraid that it all contained Michael. She'd touched these things and might be waiting. I'd be stupid to open myself up to her, to try to move the things she'd already infused. Instead I scooped Clara from the flat mattress of the pack 'n' play and held her very close to me, shushing her, nuzzling her, telling her not to cry.

The door slammed shut behind me. The monitor's camera scanned the room, circling and wheezing. The console sat on the floor next to us, untouched. This was not Ben, or Linda. This was not Seth, or Solly, or my sister. Not Arthur upstairs, not Garbage Greg. This was not lack of sleep or grogginess from painkillers or hormonal shifts. The camera settled right on us. It crackled.

Then the computer monitor flashed again, the little LED light in the corner blinking on and off. The fan aggressive, threatening. A howling wind outside. If I had been hidden within the eye of the storm when I entered the room, it had now found me.

If I took Clara upstairs, Ben would comment. He'd say something like "I thought we agreed to let her cry it out," which we had not agreed to, but which he liked to bring up as if we had, couldn't not mention. Linda might be on my side. Linda, who knew what it was to be a mother, who still called her sons every few days, who still reached out for them with clear-polished fingers. Linda would say "If this is what she needs, you do it," and I would feel profoundly grateful. I wouldn't have to explain, but could tuck Clara between us on the guest bed, keep away from this office until morning.

I balanced Clara on my shoulder, headed toward the door. As I reached for the doorknob I felt the craft supplies following me. Drifting at first, then gaining speed. Expensive scrapbook stickers—WELCOME BABY, a miniature bottle, little mixed-media choking hazards—swirled up around me, and I ducked to avoid a sharp-pointed cardboard star. We were steps away from safety. My hand was on the doorknob. And then suddenly the doorknob was hot, gleaming turquoise, liquescent. Gasping, I shot backward, my fingers pulsing from the burn. I felt dizzy, as if I myself were melting. We were trapped in this room and the doorknob was melting. My eyes peeled wide, I watched it melt away until there was only the solid wood door. We were stuck here, the crafting scissors sharp and gleaming.

Clara sensed my fear, and again began to cry.

"Please," I said to Michael, but I didn't know what to ask her that I hadn't asked already. Ribbons floated up like seaweed, weightless at first and then creeping into my hair, binding my wrists. All I could do was make a fortress of my body, sit with Clara in the armchair and bare the brunt to protect her.

"You are ribbons," I said, because to acknowledge them as ribbons, to name them, *ribbons*, broke the spell. And as I spoke they—one by one—became inanimate, dropping suddenly, in the way of the dead. "The ribbons, the ribbons, the ribbons." Down and down and down. Naming gave power to the namer. Power, like a state of matter—it couldn't multiply; it must be redistributed. I would name the objects, and thus take power from Michael, who couldn't speak.

"The stickers. The scissors. The books." I spoke rhythmically, with the accentuated iambs that would help to calm Clara. "The knitting needles." Sharp, too near our eyes. "The yarn." Unraveling: a pair of mittens too small for a child, too large for my girl. "The doorknob?" But it couldn't be a question. "The doorknob," I asserted, and it reappeared. "The door. The window. The light."

Clara was falling back asleep, her body slack, and I tightened my grip. I was afraid that in her sleep she'd go to Michael, and was tempted to pinch her awake. But the room was settling. The fan was slowing down. The computer had ceased its relentless flashes of light and had faded to black.

"The needles. The thread. The carpet. The dried flowers."

A mantra of the physical. A prayer. I was praying mundanity back into existence. Time passed. "The spinning fan. The desktop computer."

I put Clara back in the pack 'n' play, where she lay still but for her breathing, yet I kept rocking. I kept whispering. "The keyboard. The stuffed giraffe. The armchair. The lamp." Upstairs, Ben was walking across the kitchen floor, opening a cupboard, shutting it. Linda mumbled something, and Seth laughed.

"The throw pillows. The white noise." But no, now I was incorrect. I'd named it incorrectly. The noise was not a tangible thing, thus could not ground me. I braced for impact.

My phone sat in the corner, turned facedown so that the light wouldn't disturb Clara. It was vibrating, a harsh buzz against the plastic rug protector. There was no internet or cell service down here in the basement. Linda always missed our calls when she was crafting. We'd emerge from a night at Ben's parents' with a wealth of social media notifications. But there it was, ringing.

Would I answer? Was I capable of answering? I didn't even like to answer the phone when I knew who was calling, when I liked who was calling. I really only talked to Annie, or to Ben. I wouldn't answer.

I waited, clutching my elbows. The vibrating stopped. The room was still. And then, as I had known it would, the cell phone shuddered as a voice mail chimed through. *Delete it*, I told myself. I didn't.

I pressed play and held the phone to my ear. I heard piano music, very soft at first, almost imperceptible. Little runs of notes, familiar but not enough to place until the bass line came in, the pounding chords I knew were Chopin's "Raindrop" prelude, because I remembered my childhood piano teacher tapping my shoulder, stressing the importance of the rhythm. I remembered my hands struggling to keep pace, her stern call for forte. I'd quit lessons not long after, complaining that she made me take the polish off my nails. My mother had said, "Fine then, save me the money."

There was a voice now, too, although it did not call for forte.

Then methought the air grew denser
Perfumed by an unseen censer
Swung by seraphim whose footfall
Tinkled on the tufted floor—

It was a woman's voice, her recitation crackling as if filtered through an old radio or gramophone. I could place the poem from its obvious rhythm, although at first I didn't recognize the words: a later verse of Poe's "The Raven." The voice mail was forty-five seconds long, cutting out mid-*nevermore*.

I wasn't sure what to make of it. But then a notification popped up from my What-to-Expect message board.

MichaelStrange: After this program I received a call from a neighbor of Poe's who lived just opposite his cottage at Fordham, saying, "If only Edgar could have heard you, you've practically spoken for him."

"Why," I whispered, "are you telling me this?" No answer, no movement, no whir of the fan, no glossy stickers sashaying to the floor. I turned the phone facedown on the carpet. I walked to the door and sat against it.

Michael wasn't haunting our condo—a 2012 remodel without creaking floorboards or mysterious paneling, just a building in a line of buildings, its only noteworthy quality a locked turquoise door. She wasn't haunting me—I had spent weeks alone in the condo, I had spent months alone in our apartment in New York, I had spent years alone, decades. I sat with my back to the inside door of Linda's craft room, watching my daughter sleep. Thinking. Calculating.

I knew little about séances, or exorcisms. I hadn't even seen *The Exorcist*, the film, just knew the scene where the little girl's head started spinning, where she talked in a comically low voice and spat bile. Clara's wouldn't be that sort of exorcism. Clara wasn't *possessed*. She wasn't anybody's puppet. It was more like she'd been overrun. It was like when I'd gotten bedbugs—I hadn't realized they were there, but once I did realize, I could leave. I could take action. Call the pest management company to fumigate. Seal all my good clothes into plastic bags and wait until everything was dead.

Demand back my down payment and first month's rent. Find a different place to live.

I WENT BACK upstairs to say goodnight to Linda and Seth, to tell Ben I was going to bed. They were already cleaning, tying trash bags, lining wineglasses up next to the sink. I thanked Linda for dinner, faked a yawn, and then went down and got in bed with my clothes on. I knew Ben wouldn't notice. When he came to lie down next to me, I pretended to be sleeping, breathing heavily until I heard him breathing heavily.

Once the house was quiet, I went back into the craft room. Clara was lying there with her eyes open, gumming a finger. I put her on the floor while I folded up the pack 'n' play and tossed her diapers and creams and the rest into my own overnight bag, grateful we'd left most of her things in the trunk. I didn't want to leave her alone in the craft room, so I brought her up and lay her on the living room carpet while I wrestled her stuff up the stairs and out to the car. The front door beeped each time I opened it, but in their whiskey stupors, no one noticed.

Part III

If only somewhere there was a way to sustain this dream—the only reality I have ever known.

—Margaret Wise Brown, in a letter to
Michael Strange, October 1947

stopped at home to get my laptop, which was charging on the kitchen table. Solly whined while I fed Clara, but I didn't let her out of her crate—the dog walker had come that night and would come again in the morning. I took a few extra pairs of socks and underwear, a few half-filled notebooks. Some tinfoil-wrapped brownies to snack on while driving so I wouldn't fall asleep.

Before I left with Clara—and therefore with Michael—I went to recruit Margaret. I thought I'd try one last knock at the turquoise door, which, as I climbed the uncarpeted back stairs, I thought might no longer exist. It might have disappeared entirely, or else she might have bricked it up and painted it over. I braced myself for how I would feel if it was there but still locked, how I would feel if I could hear Margaret's dinner party, Margaret's construction work, Margaret singing to herself in the bath, and couldn't find my way in. The stairway smelled like rotting pumpkins. The door to the roof was cracked open, an empty airplane liquor bottle wedged in the jam, putrescence funneling down in currents of cold air.

The turquoise door was also open. Margaret stood in the frame, wearing a fur coat and gloves, her traveling case in hand.

"Are you ready?" she asked me. "Crispian, come." Apparently she had been waiting for me. Apparently she and the dog were a package deal. I was glad to have the corporeal company. I needed somebody to help me manage Michael. I needed somebody to read the map I was planning to buy at the gas station once we'd hit the highway. I couldn't use GPS—I'd left my phone in Linda's craft room.

BY THE TIME we got on the road, it was nearing two o'clock in the morning—Clara had to eat again, Margaret had to find her lighter. When we finally pulled out of the garage and down the empty alley, I had one eye on Margaret, wondering if she'd fade or crackle, disappear with the condo or the last view of our street. But she remained solid beside me, fingers yellow with nicotine, her fug of smoke and fur and perfume so pungent that I cracked the driver's-side window despite the frigid cold. The streets had other cars, had people huddled in their winter jackets, trudging toward the el or toward home. We even hit traffic passing through downtown. Just before I-90 split from 94 I pulled off to get gas, and ran inside for a map of the tristate area and a warm can of soda. I took Clara with me. The car seat bumped against my hip, the handle digging into my arm when I rummaged in my purse for my wallet.

And then finally we were sailing, Clara lulled to sleep, Margaret fiddling, trying to refold the map. I wanted to instruct her—if she just flipped it over, it would pleat back into place—but I was awkward, worried she would change her mind and be finished with me, that when the time came, she'd refuse to help me separate Michael and Clara. I didn't know why she'd locked me out of her life, or why she'd now let me back in; I didn't want to risk upsetting her. So I let her crumple the map into the glove compartment, let her prop her feet on the dashboard while she stared out the window. Illinois flat as ever, warehouses and outlet malls and low clouds that dirtied the darkness. A burned smell was coming from the heating vents. Crispian was asleep. He was snoring.

We were headed to central Wisconsin, where Jeanie's brother owned a cabin. When we were kids, Annie and I had tagged along with Sam and Kelsey on occasional summer weekends, and I re-membered where the spare key was kept, how to get in, that they closed it up in winter because the lake didn't freeze over enough for skating and there was nothing to do in the nearest town.

The cabin was the closest thing I knew to solitude. It was the closest thing I knew to The Only House, Margaret's summer home in Vinalhaven, Maine. Unlike The Only House, Jeanie's brother's Wisconsin cabin had plumbing and electricity. I didn't think that Margaret wouldn't know the difference—I wasn't trying to trick her—but I hoped that she'd appreciate my effort to find somewhere she could be comfortable.

I suppose I was operating on a number of assumptions: that the roads wouldn't be iced over, that my half brother and his friends wouldn't have snuck up with a keg, that the pipes would work. But I figured Margaret could handle any problems that arose: she was used to harsh climates, she liked roughing it. For a wealthy New Yorker, she was surprisingly outdoorsy.

At least she seemed outdoorsy in her letters. At least she was in her biographies.

It occurred to me the woman sitting here was something other than what I had read in her books and her letters, somebody outside the frame. No matter how well a biographer studied her, they didn't know her fully, which meant I didn't know her fully, even with years of research. I looked at her—smoking again, despite the fact that I had told her I'd prefer that she didn't, her cigarette poking through the slit window—and felt a great divide between the person I had been during graduate school, holed up in the library, and the person I was now. I'd been so sure of myself. I'd thought that history could be reconstructed. I'd thought that the world could be known.

ROAD TRIP FILMS imply that it's easier to speak on the road, to bare the soul while staring at some stranger's taillights. I kept glancing over at Margaret, the slight flush of her cheeks, her pinned-back hair, which was hay-yellow with just the slightest frizz. I was placing her at about thirty-four, about my age. I wondered if she knew that in less than ten years, she'd be dead. I wondered if she knew she was already.

How surreal to know the moment of another person's death. Honestly, I had a lot of power. I could tell her not to go to France, where her appendix would swell, where the surgery would go well but the subsequent bed rest would go about as poorly as one could imagine. I could tell her to trust herself, not the doctors. Margaret would want to get up and walk around, the way she knew you were supposed to after surgery, but her French doctors would tell her that she shouldn't. That was not how things were done then, in France, where the medical care was so recognizably inferior that travelers were advised to carry cards instructing that they be taken to the American Hospital in Paris if they became ill. But Margaret would be in Nice in 1952, and she'd require an immediate operation. The French doctors would remove her appendix and a benign ovarian cyst, and then tell her to lie in bed, and all the while a blood clot would be gathering. After a few weeks a nurse would come and ask Margaret how she was doing, and she'd kick up her leg and grin, because she was feeling just fine and at last was engaged to be married to a man that she loved. His name was Pebble Rockefeller, and he built boats and he sailed, and she was going to sail off with him, just as soon as she was finished with this lie-in. After years of unrequited love, years of love that felt like prison, of love that felt like a freedom she couldn't keep, love that wanted her to abandon her career, love that wanted her to change her career, love that wasted away with cancer, love that wouldn't leave his wife, love that left her husband but wouldn't commit, love she couldn't find for her own self, she would be happy. She would be forty-two years old and would can-can her leg for the doctor, and when she did so, that blood clot would take off toward her heart. She would be dead in under a minute.

I didn't tell Margaret anything. I just stared into the taillights of the semitruck in front of us, thinking about different kinds of pain.

WE STOPPED AT a rest area around six in the morning, so I could feed Clara and Margaret could take Crispian for a walk. The restrooms were locked, so I crouched down and peed next to a bush, Clara watching me with cold, impassive eyes. I brought her back into the car to feed her, the heat still on, the windows fogging. When we got moving again, Crispian was restless. I heard him whining in the back seat, scuffing at the floor mats. Margaret had owned two Kerry blue terriers over the course of her adult life, and I suddenly remembered reading all sorts of accounts of one of them causing trouble—ruining photo shoots and dinner parties, Margaret having to bribe her friends to watch him while she traveled. I wasn't sure which one this was, and I didn't know how to ask. She'd had the bad dog when she first moved in with Michael; there had been some sort of argument about it. Or had she gotten the bad dog once she was already living with Michael?

Not living with. They never lived together. This was 1943 or so, and Michael didn't want to stir up trouble. They'd had apartments across the hall from each other, the doors left open and unlocked.

In the back seat, Crispian nudged Clara's blanket. He howled.

"The dogs didn't always get along," said Margaret.

"What?"

"Smoke and Cricket. And then Crispian and Cricket, once Smoke died."

"What?"

"When we all lived together. At East End Avenue. It was wonderful, for a time. Michael can host a rip-snorting party, and always so many celebrities. It was a shame, about the dogs."

"Oh," I said. Was she implying that Clara was a dog? That Michael's dog was part and parcel to this haunting? I wanted to pull over, get Margaret's dog out of the car before he decided not to get along with Clara. Instead I drove faster, passing the semi we'd been comfortably tailing, letting the power of my foot on the gas relieve all other want of power.

As we neared our destination, I began to get the distinct feeling that somebody else was in the car with us. Not Clara, whose every stirring had me bracing for a meltdown. Not Margaret, who continued to chain-smoke with the focus and precision of a surgeon. Not Crispian, who had shimmied his way up to the console between the two front seats and put his head down on my open Diet Coke, a small string of drool collecting on the pull tab. I kept catching whiffs of lemon verbena, of tiger lily. Something was pushing on the back of my seat. I drove faster.

WHEN WE PULLED off the highway and passed through the small Wisconsin town closest the cabin it was six thirty a.m., the utter blackness of night dissolving slowly to morning. This was lucky, because once we passed the town, we had ten miles of highway with only my headlights to guide us. I found the turn onto the rambling drive from memory, the only marker a weatherworn boulder at the edge of the main road. It had snowed here, long enough ago that the melt had muddied the road to the house, and I drove slowly, afraid of spinning out. The car creeping, Margaret tapping a finger on the inside of the passenger-side door, something or someone that was not Crispian or Clara displaying a similar impatience in back.

The cabin rose from the mist, its pointed roof and widow's walk, the rock garden and empty fire pit, the dock leading nowhere, the lake a film of ice. It was smaller than I remembered, but I was used to the stuff of my childhood being smaller than I remembered.

I made it to the covered car park, asking everyone to stay put while I dug around for the fake rock that housed the key, which was so easy to find that a part of me wanted to call Jeanie and tell her that her brother was an idiot. Or maybe I was the idiot, up here in early December, the landscape barren, and the morning so cold that my nipples felt like shards of cut glass. I pictured them as icicles, I pictured myself leaning down to Clara, her mouth open, my icicles piercing the back of her throat. I unlocked the door.

This cabin was truly a cabin—not the mini-mansion variety so many of the kids Ben knew in high school moved up to in the summers. It had a galley kitchen and a sparely furnished great room; a downstairs master bedroom, and two upstairs rooms filled with rickety bunk beds. The appeal of the cabin was the property it sat on: the acres of untouched forest, the lake. There was only one bathroom, without toilet paper.

Inside, I cranked the heat as high as it would go, and ran the water in the sinks until it came out hot and clear. Then I went back to turn off the car and get Margaret and Clara. Crispian was running in circles outside, Margaret was writing something down on the back of a Starbucks napkin she'd found in the glove compartment. Clara was sleeping.

Margaret helped me carry Clara's things into the house, tottering under the weight of the pack 'n' play. When we got inside, she seemed to approve of the cabin, dropping the baby paraphernalia in a clatter and wiping frost from the windows with a gloved hand, sticking her nose right up to the glass. We started a fire with the wood that was already piled up inside, and brought another few logs in from the shed. I nursed Clara sitting on a wide red leather couch, staring into the flames.

There were a few non-perishables in the pantry—a tin of sloppy joe sauce, a can of green beans, a stale sleeve of crackers—and we made breakfast of these and the brownies I'd taken from home. Once we'd finished, Margaret helped me rinse the dishes and pile them in the sink. She ran the tap to fill the rusty stovetop kettle. I was settling back down on the couch—Clara doing her tummy time on a blanket by the dining table—feeling for all intents and purposes that this was just another awkward family trip, when I heard a sharp knock at the front door.

I thought at first it might be Ben, but Ben would just be waking up. Ben would be turning to find my side of the bed cold, would be thinking I'd gotten up with Clara. Soon he'd pull on a sweatshirt and stumble upstairs to find Linda making coffee, Seth unloading the dishwasher. They'd look for me. They'd notice the car was gone. They'd find my phone.

But I couldn't think about any of that—Ben's panic, how he'd feel and who he'd call. To think about any of that would make everything else pointless: the four-hour drive, the cabin, the slimy tinned breakfast. And besides, someone was knocking.

The front door was unlocked, which didn't matter. I had invited Margaret in and I had carried in Clara, and because she was already in both of them, Michael didn't need me to turn the knob, to tell her where to put her shoes or hang her coat. She was knocking out of politeness, knocking to let us know that it was time to pay attention.

The knocking stopped, and Clara coughed, and what happened next was difficult to describe, although I'm going to try to describe it, because otherwise what use is language, otherwise what use are words. Clara coughed up a bit of half-digested milk, creamy fat collecting like algae on the edge of the small pond of spit-up that formed before her on the play mat. Something was caught in her throat, and I moved to lift her upright, but before I'd even reached her, she'd cleared it—cleared it such that it was swirling up out of her in a steady exhalation, her forehead wrinkled with distaste, her eyes making the same cynical sweep that they had of Linda's teddy bear, of the back seat of the car. There wasn't any sound to it, other than her breathing, but if there was a sound it would've been the ringing of a gong, reverberating low and warm, a deep, extended gasp.

The word *ghost* comes from the Old English *gast*—a breath.

And then Clara sneezed and stuck her hand right in the little pool of spit-up, flinging it off the play mat and onto the thick, cork-soled high heel that suddenly stood solidly in front of her. Velvet, and gluey with Clara's secretions. A shoe strapped onto a foot, connected to an ankle. A pair of cropped pants. A long camel-colored coat, a man's coat, buttoned on the left, with a dark collar and gold epaulets attached to the shoulders. A scarf, striped blue and black, tucked under the coat. And then the face.

Michael was younger than I had imagined her—I guessed in her mid-forties, a good five or six years younger than she would have been when she first met Margaret. If she was able to choose, it made sense she'd want a body in its prime. She had sharp cheekbones and small, dark eyes, and a beaked nose that had thinned at the nostrils with age. She wore her hair parted severely to the side, a fluffy swoop of dark curls falling over her right eyebrow. She moved with authority. She smelled of lemon verbena.

Outside it began to hail, an inconsistent pattering. *Tap. Tap-tap. Tap. Tap-tap-tap.*

Michael glanced down at her shoes, then tightened her lips, closed her eyes, straightened her shoulders. A practiced gesture, a deliberate dismissal of a minor inconvenience. When she opened her eyes again, she'd recovered her charm. She knelt and unbuckled her shoes, placing them gingerly next to the sofa.

"Well," she said. She smiled at me. "That's better."

18

Michael sat down on the couch as if she owned it, legs spread wide, leaning back like a caricature of masculinity in some bad period drama.

"Well," she said again, obviously waiting. Was she waiting for me? For Clara? I spun around to look for Margaret, who had been standing in the galley kitchen, boiling water for tea. I didn't see her. "I'd asked Margaret not to come near me," said Michael, following my gaze. "I'd hoped she could respect my wishes."

"What?" I was a caught fish, my mouth gaping. A little rabbit, cornered at the end of the hunt.

"Margaret heightens my anxiety. The doctors agree."

I looked from Michael to the door—ten paces or so, fifteen if I got Clara. But the car seat was in the far corner, the car keys were in the pocket of my coat. I could realistically grab one and not the other, yet each without the other would do me no good. So far the morning had played out much as I'd imagined, but I hadn't really planned for Michael's rebirth. I suppose I'd thought that once we got here, I would give Clara a hot bath, or do some sort of cleanse to release toxins, and Michael would float away on the breeze. I'd thought Margaret might help me confront Michael. I'd thought Margaret might stand up for herself, that she and Michael would either reconcile or finally part ways, and they would stay here in

Wisconsin so that Clara could open her eyes, easier. Changed. We'd hop in the car and magically be back at my in-laws' right as Ben was waking up; I'd tell him that we'd just been out for coffee. I hadn't counted on time passing, on this distance between me and the door. I hadn't counted on this conversation.

"I need you to be my legacy," said Michael.

"What?" My eyes still darting, my boots on the doormat. All I truly needed were my keys. We could hunker down in the front seat, blast the heat, wait for Margaret to find her way back and handle Michael. Clara wouldn't know the difference. Clara would remember none of this. She'd be happy in my arms, blinking out at the crystalline sun. Watching the shadows of the birds migrating south over the lake.

"My legacy," Michael said again, rolling her tongue on the *l*, the guttural *g*, a final hiss and then a deliberate, elucidated closure. Often when I spoke I found myself dropping the ends of words, a consequence of vocal fry, a consequence of being a woman. Michael spat, rather than swallowed. Her diction was perfectly clear. And here I was, a blurry version of who I wanted to be, leaning down to mop spit-up off my kid with the sleeve of my sweater.

"What?" I dabbed Clara's cheek, fumbling.

"My poetry," said Michael, very weary, very tired, luxuriously basking in how much she had been put upon. In this she reminded me of a wealthier, mid-century version of my mother. "My poetry," she said again, "the best and most true thing that has come out of me."

"I'm sorry," I said. "I don't think I understand. You want us to read it out loud?" Clara in my arms now. If I scooted us both to the side of the sofa, maybe we had a chance. I inched along, my leggings snagging on a nail that jutted out in the wood floor. I heard the rent, felt the pressure of the nail head against my thigh. From this angle I could see that the dead bolt was unlocked, that all it would take was a turn of the knob, and then freedom.

"Of course that isn't what I mean. How silly," said Michael. "How very childish."

One.

"Oh."

Two.

"Excuse me."

Three.

"I'm sorry." And then I was off, grabbing my coat, tucking Clara under my arm, her neck supported by the crook of my elbow. I pushed through the door, dodged a puddle—gravel piercing sharp and cold through my wool socks. A huff of breath delivered to the top of Clara's head to try to warm her, an awful rawness in my throat, my fingers sticking to the door handle, the two of us inside. I cradled Clara in my oversize sweater. I turned on the car, willing the air to heat quickly. I looked at the cabin.

In my rush, I hadn't bothered to close the door behind me. I could see Michael sitting on the couch, facing the fire. A gust of wind scattered a mound of dead leaves. A static-ridden radio program whinnied through the car speakers, although I hadn't pressed any buttons. Clara wasn't thrilled to be up next to the air vents, but I held her close enough that her lips lost their tinge of blue, the tops of her ears reddened. Lifting the bar to push the front seat as far back as it could go, I sat on the floor in front of it, picking caked dirt out of the plastic mats, my heart pounding.

"You might as well go back inside," said Margaret, and I jumped, banging Clara's head against the dashboard, making her cry. The car had been empty when we climbed in; now Margaret was peering down from the passenger seat. "You'll be more comfortable there."

I didn't say anything. There was a chance that my silence would vanquish both women, that I could exorcise them both with compression, like when I had to pee, but held it in so tightly that all of a sudden I didn't. Margaret blinked and reached for the volume dial, the voice on the radio crackling to life.

And the Raven, never flitting, still is sitting, still is sitting
On the pallid bust of Pallas just above my chamber door.

"She did a whole series of great poetry set to music," said Margaret. "She even did the Bible. But it wasn't commercial enough. Michael didn't want to sell soap after losing herself in Poe, so they canceled her program."

Clara was still crying, a whimper not appeased by me rubbing her back.

"Me, I'd sell whatever they asked me to," said Margaret. "After all, it is business."

"You broke your contracts," I whispered. "You constantly forgot to pay your electric bill."

"Well," said Margaret. "Michael says I never really outgrew my childhood."

Clara was moaning now, a sound that cut through the radio static, through the toasty itch of my sweater, through Margaret's musings.

"You should take the baby back inside now," said Margaret. "Before Michael gets frustrated."

Clara's lips were turning blue again. The sound she was making was not fear but pain—the sound of sinews overstretched, a rope pulled to fraying. A keening. Cover the mirrors, rend your clothing, mourn. I no longer wanted to squeeze her until she burst, or shake her until she went quiet, and I understood that this was love, this hurt my heart was holding on to for my daughter, this hurt I wanted not to stifle but absorb. And now I had absolute proof: Clara would hold Michael within her, no matter where we'd gone. I was a crocus in a hidden garden, and here was Michael: *I will find you.*

I took Clara back inside, and Margaret stood next to the car, huddled in her furs, waiting. Margaret was used to traveling great distances to reach Michael, only to be turned away. Margaret was used to waiting.

HAUNT: FROM THE Old French *hanter*, which means to practice. To indulge in. To cultivate. Possibly taken from the Old Norse *heimta*, to bring home.

BACK IN THE cabin, Michael was unfazed, still watching the fire. "It seems to me," she said when she heard me shut the door, "that my remembrance is corrupted. I've had the unfortunate luck of being incorrectly recorded."

Clara was settling now, nuzzling into my shoulder. No longer blue, no longer hurting. I brought her closer to the fire.

"These *biographers*, you know." Michael's face puckered.

Michael had no biography of her own; she'd only played the villain in Margaret's. Her out-of-print autobiography was a rambling, self-important opus disguised as a letter to her mother. Parts were lovely. I enjoyed elaborate language, and reading Michael felt at first like eating French pastry after academia's brown bread. But like French pastry, she was easily overwrought, there was too much puff and not enough substance. Overly rich, and difficult to digest. Michael's book was buoyant, always another aspiration, always a new career or husband around the bend. Unfortunate things happened—a failed marriage, a scathing review—and she still called her life delicious. But autobiography as genre is a trick of smoke and mirrors. Selfhood is reflexive, autobiography performs. After reading Michael's book, I didn't *know* her.

What other people had written of her—what she claimed they'd gotten wrong—seemed closer to the truth. The person that she was, as opposed to the person she wanted to be. We say the ego swells because it bloats the idea of the self to something unrecognizable. Michael was resting on her ego, had survived on her ego. It had buoyed her across the river Styx and into my Chicago condo, and I'd driven it up I-90 to this cabin, where it was sitting on my stepmother's brother's couch.

When you fashion yourself a new name, when you marry an actor. When you have your suits tailor-made in a style no one else in New York is wearing. When for several shining years you feel the heat of the world's spotlight, and then spend the rest of your life trying to get that glow back.

Of course she wanted a new legacy. Of course she wanted me to write it.

"You're not really my focus," I said. "I've tried to incorporate you as much as I can, but I'm writing more about children's books. More about Margaret."

"Margaret, Margaret." Michael sighed dramatically, leaning farther back into the couch. "Always Margaret, my god. She's going to give me a heart attack. You know that she gave me leukemia?"

"What?"

"Leukemia. A cancer of the blood."

"No, I know what leukemia is, it's just, you can't catch it. You can't *give* it to someone. It's mutations of the—" Michael gave me a withering look that stopped me further plumbing the shallows of my medical knowledge. I changed tactics. "You had children. Didn't your son have children?"

Michael sniffed. I tried to imagine my parents discussing the "best and most true thing that had come out of them" and wondered if that thing would be me. Wondered if, for me, the best true thing would be Clara. I was banking on it being Clara, resting on the laurels of her birth. Before, I had been resting on my dissertation, investing in the work with the thought that someone would one day read it and attribute it to me and say "Well done." God, I was typical. Mommy and Daddy didn't love you the way you wanted to be loved, so you go begging for love elsewhere.

Margaret's parents had an awful marriage. They would argue, and her father would go live on his boat for weeks at a time. Divorce wasn't done, then. Too embarrassing. Margaret's mother became involved in spiritualism, desperately trying to shore up the cracks. Her father would bring his children into his study and start off reading out loud to them, but get so immersed in the story he'd forget them and forge silently ahead. Neither parent spent much time on Margaret. They weren't especially proud of her success.

Michael, on the other hand, had two doting parents.

What sort of parents would Clara have? In one sense, I supposed it would be up to me, but in another sense it wouldn't. I couldn't choose how I felt—I could choose only how I acted—and at some point she'd be old enough to see behind the mask I wore and know. How old would she be before she sniffed out my resentment? Or at some point would I no longer resent her? Would the love—which now felt about equal to the resentment, about the same weight on the scale—fatten up and decisively surmount it? Maybe I would gladly give up hopes of a stratospheric career, and go teach high school. Maybe motherhood would soothe my frustrations, and I would be so grateful that Ben was a good father that I'd start to really love him. Maybe I'd become the person he thought I was already, gradually softening, accepting the mold.

If I had to teach, god forbid it be high school.

All the while I was thinking this over, Michael was waiting for me to speak. She sat with her back very straight, tapping a finger against her knee to the beat of phantom music. Clara passed gas in her sleep.

"No," I said, finally. "No. I think you'll have to rely on your children. Or great-great whatever children. I really only have revisions left. I've added as much of you in as I can, and it's crazy to think I'd rewrite everything. My advisor would never agree to it."

Michael hissed in a breath. I thought she might swell up like a Halloween ghost set up in someone's front yard, all shimmery at the bottom, full of hot air. Instead she flared her nose and stood, patting the creases out of her pants. She went to the window and nodded. Margaret was out there, her ankles bare, thumbing the cuffs of her coat. Michael opened the door and stuck her head out into the cold.

"Bunny," she called sharply, "come here."

19

Margaret came when called. I knew women like this, spaniels heeling their lovers. Women who would cancel plans, travel halfway across the city to deliver a forgotten brown-bag lunch, dye their hair and get waxes and try to lose those last ten pounds. It was an epidemic, and it spread because you'd think to yourself, If she does all that and *still* nobody wants her, what will love look like for me?

Michael watched Margaret through the window, her eyes dark and narrow. Calculating.

"Maybe," I said before I could stop myself, "if you wanted a better legacy, you could have been nicer to people when you were alive." This was the bitterness that had rooted in me upon Clara's birth, the trauma that was only soothed by the expression of the anger. A bruise I had to keep pressing on, no matter the pain, because otherwise it would be gone, it would be swallowed, and without it, who would I be?

Michael ignored me, watching Margaret come inside with that kicked-dog slump of her shoulders, that loyal-dog shine to her eyes. Michael rose and laced their hands together, and I could see how the squeeze lit up something inside Margaret. I could see where the love had been, where Margaret thought it still could be.

"Come," said Michael, and of course Margaret came. Michael

took Margaret upstairs, her stocking feet silent next to Margaret's clacking pumps, her dark head bobbing next to Margaret's gold one. The cabin had a winding metal staircase, which was terrible for children and made you feel that you were climbing up to something far more interesting than what you actually found at the top: a widow's walk that circled the top of the great room, leading to bedrooms tucked away over the kitchen. I watched Michael and Margaret, who didn't seem to know I was watching them, step into the larger bedroom.

I COULD HAVE left then, but I didn't. Instead I opened up a can of baked beans, and heated them on the stove. Nursing made me hungry.

Falling in Love

Margaret Wise Brown and Michael Strange first met in Maine. Michael was fifty, Margaret twenty-nine. They were both romantically involved with "Big" Bill Gaston, a well-to-do lawyer and philanderer, through whom they were introduced.

Over the years Michael saw Bill sporadically; she had many lovers. Margaret's only consistent lover was Bill, who was older than she was and owned a house across the water from her cottage in Maine.[1] He kept telling her one day he'd settle down, or else she kept telling herself that he meant to tell her, that that was what he meant when he told her what he actually did tell her. He would visit her in New York, and she would write to him, imagining the family they'd have. But then Bill got another woman[2] pregnant, and he married her instead. Margaret stayed away until she didn't, because Bill was a flirt, and she loved him. His wife Lucille found the two in bed together and mentioned divorce, and so Margaret—clever, Margaret, not always kind—talked to the tabloid reporters about his failing marriage. She

---

1 The Only House, half hidden in the trees, the boudoir out on the lawn, the rock face angling down to the water. In a nearby stream, Margaret is cooling a large bottle of white wine. A jar of milk sits at the bottom of the well, tied to a rope for its retrieval. There is no refrigerator.

2 Lucille Hutchings.

thought she could change Bill, she thought she could play God. And in a way she did play God, because that summer Michael read the article about Bill's imminent separation and came to Maine to comfort him.

Michael and Margaret struck up a vibrant friendship. Back in New York, they went to lunch at one of Margaret's favorite haunts in Greenwich Village. Are you dating anybody? asked Michael. How's the sex?

Margaret drank a vermouth cassis.[3] At this point she had published with Doubleday, Harper, Golden Books, and W. R. Scott.

"You should stop writing those silly furry stories," said Michael.

---

3 One and a half parts dry vermouth, four parts soda, one half part liqueur. Crimson, with a slice of lemon floating at the top. Margaret stirs it slowly.

20

They came back downstairs as I was opening my laptop, debating whether or not to turn on the Wi-Fi. The cabin hosted the only available network, which was locked, but I was pretty sure I could guess the password: something stupid like GOPACK or 12345. The trouble was, once I got into the Wi-Fi, Ben could find me. Everything was interconnected: the tablets and the cell phones and the computers and the cars. I didn't know if I was ready for Ben to find me. I didn't know what it would mean to be found.

"Margaret," said Michael, "it's time."

They stood blocking the staircase, arm in arm, neither of them smiling, although Margaret had a slight twist to her upper lip that signified pleasure. She loved a good game, a good surprise. I picked up Clara, who usually melted into being held, but now was wiggling with a strength I didn't know she had. She'd only discovered her hands a week ago, and she was already reaching with them, using them to grab at something past me.

Crispian whined and circled the dining table, a conduit for the awful energy coursing through the cabin. Michael clucked her tongue at him, and he appeared somewhat chastened—instead of trotting, he slowed to an amble. When he reached her, she put a hand on his back. Clara wanted the dog. She wrenched out of my arms, trying to reach him. I couldn't contain her, couldn't save her, and I panicked as she dove away from me. Now I had only her legs, which were kicking to be free. Soon I would drop her altogether. But before Clara could plummet to the floor, Margaret walked over with a *tap tap tap*, crouching to meet her wherever she was going. I tried to grab on to Clara's ankles, I tried to reposition myself to protect her. I was left holding a tiny purple sock.

Sleet fell in sheets outside, pattering against the roof, splurging against the window.

Margaret disappeared. Margaret was gone. And with Margaret, Clara.

21

They were only invisible, only away, for a minute. Clara and I were inextricable. My breasts were heavy and my bra wet where my nipple chafed the cup, and so I knew Clara was hungry. Michael sighed when Margaret reappeared. She rolled her eyes when Margaret handed Clara back to me.

"She eats every three hours," I said. "During the day."

"Go," said Michael, and I didn't know what she meant, but then I did, because Margaret was going. She was going into Clara the way Michael had come out of Clara: Aladdin's genie into the lamp, Red Riding Hood into the mouth of the wolf, a little fur child into a warm wooden tree. Clara's pupils dilating very quickly, until I could barely see the darkening blue of her irises. Clara's body very hot, very frightening. She opened her mouth, and I could see the nubs of teeth sprouting from gums where there had not been teeth before. Her nostrils flared, and her mouth turned up at the sides. Amused.

Amused and hungry. She was wrinkling her chin, butting her head against my breasts. I dropped her on the play mat because I didn't know what she was anymore, who I was to her. Clara couldn't speak, couldn't say *Mama*, and I wasn't sure any longer if I was her mama. The word *mama*, the sound of it, is universal in almost every Indo-European language. *Mamma, mama, muhme, maman, mam.*

Linguists think it's an echo of the sound made while sucking. The lips together, the wetness. The feeling of being so disgustingly fecund, then empty.

On the mat Clara bellowed, demanding to suckle. Michael looked at me impatiently, doing everything but tapping her imaginary watch to tell me to get a move on, to feed Clara so that they could do with her whatever they would. It hurt me to withhold from Clara—the pressure of my full breasts, the anguish of watching her cry. The knowledge I could sate her appetite so easily.

But I was afraid of her. I'd been afraid of her since she first slid out of me, since the nurse dried her off and put her on my belly and told me she was mine. Now that Clara had teeth, now that Clara had Margaret inside her, it was easy to look back and see how much of my resentment had always been fear.

Her crying stirred something native, summoned all my deep maternal instinct. She was so much louder to my ears than to anyone else's. She would have to eat, regardless. If I wanted my daughter back in her body, that body would have to be fed. It would have been much easier if I'd brought the pump, much easier if I had used formula.

Clara's new teeth were tiny and sharp. I brought her to my breast, and they drew blood. She ate, and when she pulled off the breast she had a ring of red around her mouth, a popsicle mustache of milk-watered cruor. She repeated her work on the other side, deliberate and symmetrical, and then Michael came and took her from my arms and then she was gone.

I sat with my nursing bra unclipped, my breasts goose-pimpled and limp from being recently unburdened. I was alone in the cabin with Margaret's dog. I started to cry.

Being in Love

When she first met Margaret, Michael Strange was a prominent member of dizzying social circles: old money that tolerated her artistic flirtations but would never stand for explicit lesbianism.[1] She was sophisticated and confident, a mentor to Margaret. She'd had secret romantic dalliances with women before.

Margaret and Michael took walks through the Central Park Zoo, where Michael played games: showing up incognito and trailing an increasingly panicked Margaret, hiding just out of sight, laughing, before revealing herself to have been there the whole time.[2] They took walks through the Village, where Michael suggested they wander down the less savory alleys, engage with the less savory men. Margaret went to cocktail parties at Michael's grand Upper East Side apartment. They spoke on the phone at all hours. Margaret befriended Michael's daughter, Diana, who was off to Hollywood to be a star.

On the night of Diana's farewell party, Margaret stayed at Michael's after all the other guests had left. Taking Margaret to her bedroom,

---

1 "It is one thing to be avant-garde," says Michael gaily. "Quite another to be avant-honte." The sycophants twitter. The party goes on.

2 "She'll never recognize you in that get-up." Harry frowns. Michael giggles and adjusts her large blue hat. With the veil over her face, she might be homely. She might be disfigured. She might be Broadway elite.

Michael put on a lace negligee; she read poetry out loud. She complained about her husband, voiced concern that he was seeing another woman, that he mistreated her in front of the servants, that he would never understand her the way Margaret understood her, that she could never love him the way she loved Margaret. They were drunk. This was the night they became lovers. Michael told Margaret they must write a book together. She told Margaret to stop writing the children's stories and do some meaningful work. *You're a son of a bitch*, she said to Margaret. *I will love you until the day you die.*

clipped my bra back together. I stood up. I put the remains of the baked beans in Tupperware and washed out the pot. I wiped the slushy footprints from the front hall.

I DON'T KNOW if it's better to be the one who loves too much, or the one who loves too little. I don't know if it's better to be left or to be leaving. The scale of love measures the fatty red weight of the heart, which, when beating, looks nauseous and seizing, overeager and aggressive. Embarrassing.

I WIPED MY eyes. I booted up my computer.

The message-board mothers had wanted me to write. Michael had wanted me to write. And so I started furiously typing. I opened myself to the muse—to Margaret, to Michael—hoping that documenting their relationship would somehow bring them back to me. Hoping documenting their relationship would bring Clara back to me.

It didn't.

WAS I WRITING them down wrong? Did they dislike it? I was trying very hard to only state objective truths.

Mixed Signals

In 1942, Margaret summered on her own in Maine so that Michael
could give her marriage one more effort. But when she got back
to New York, Michael called up in a frenzy: her husband had discovered proof of their affair, had called a doctor to treat her for what
he claimed was mental illness. *Homosexuality. Lesbianism.* Margaret
helped Michael get a room at the Colony Club, an expensive women's
social club for Manhattan's elite. She helped her organize a formal
separation. People talked.[1]

Michael bought a new summer home in Connecticut, where she
brought Margaret. The women would write together, Michael rag-
ing, Michael correcting Margaret's grammar, Michael telling Margaret to pack her things and go, Michael bringing Margaret into
the bedroom, Michael promising to love Margaret forever. Then the
New York Journal-American published a scathing exposé about Michael's divorce, "The Sappho of Long Island."[2] Michael told Margaret not to call her, walked the city in disguise to avoid gossip. But

---

1 "Michael has had her fill of men," says Bill Gaston, calling long distance. "Maybe
from there she'll move on to a goat." Margaret grimaces, twists the telephone cord
around a finger.

2 *Maybe from there she'll move on to a goat.*

after several months—as always—Michael changed her mind. She rented two apartments on East End Avenue, across the hall from each other, doors always unlocked, often open. Margaret gave up her own apartment, and moved in.[3]

---

3 The light is better in the front room. Margaret pushes her bed toward the window. Michael tells her she's a child, but with laughter. With a kiss.

23

If it didn't hurt so much, I thought it might even be funny, Margaret's timing. Michael's timing. My own. The second I'd realized that I loved Clara—the night that Ben came home from his first business trip—Michael had swept in to claim her. Michael had held on ever since. The joke was that as soon as I recognized love, as soon as I named it, its object was no longer mine.

I paced the cabin and thought about how else I might lure them all back. I went upstairs and opened the windows—cracked them each a perfect inch. I stoked the downstairs fire, feeding it crumpled newspaper. The play mat, with its pervasive sour spit smell, sat empty in the corner of the living room, next to the leather couch. It had a quilted pattern, purple and green paisley next to pink and white polka dots. It looked like the patchwork of the ground seen from an airplane. It looked like a world I could fall into, if I lay down and inhaled the place where Clara had been. It looked like somewhere I might find her. I lay down, my head on the stain she'd left. I closed my eyes and let the dry heat of the fire hold me.

24

When I opened my eyes, it was spring and it was muddy and I was alone in an untamed field, shoeless and itchy in wool. Where was Clara? I heard instrumental horns in the distance, loud and large and inappropriate, given the pastoral scene. A tension in the air, the recognition that for now the world was still but soon something was coming. Where was Clara? The yipping of the dogs, the subtle rumble of the ground as they cantered and yelped. The fear and desperation of the rabbit almost palpable, although I couldn't see it. Where was Clara? Every rustle in the trees, every rumble, I thought, signaled the rabbit's arrival.

SOMETIMES, WHEN CLARA was asleep, I missed her. I'd say to Ben, "Ben, should I go wake her up?" When she was awake, I would count down the hours until she was asleep again, and then, when she slept, I would say "Ben, should I go wake her up?"

REALLY IT WAS a gorgeous landscape, unlike anything you'd see on Long Island today. And this had to be Long Island—somewhere ritzy like Old Westbury or Glen Cove, where Margaret and her beagling club would meet weekly to hunt. Mansions and gardens and stables, the Long Island Sound glittering in the distance. I was lucky I hadn't had to brave the traffic to get out here, lucky I could pretend myself carefree and rich, Daisy Buchanan or at least Jordan Baker, picnicking in style, the wind in my hair. But I couldn't enjoy the fresh air, or the sound of the water. I couldn't relax, couldn't explore, because of Clara.

It felt very unfair that because I loved her, I would always have to wonder where she was, what she was doing. Very unfair that there was now a part of my brain forever focused on Clara—I couldn't escape into my research or writing, I couldn't zonk out in front of the TV or get gluttonously high and play video games or take an impromptu vacation or even lounge about, enjoying my own heightening delusions. This was so obvious, this had been creeping up behind me all along, but it was only here, as I was beagling without her on Long Island, that the unfairness of it hit me.

I do think that sometimes it takes a recalibration to confront the obvious. It takes an escape, then a return. And this was the obvious that I'd been skirting, the ugliness that I'd been avoiding, the shard of glass in the corner of my eye: I wasn't sure that I enjoyed being a mother.

But maybe I did.

The grass was wet and smelled so sweet and young that I couldn't help but think about Clara. The darkening blue of the sky was her eyes, and the little roots that crawled the dirt, her hands. I didn't *not* enjoy being a mother. I didn't want somebody else to mother Clara, I certainly didn't want her possessed.

It was about control, this whole thing: Clara's abduction, the hunt. Michael liked to be in charge, and Margaret liked to play games—she liked a sense of fun, a challenge. I wasn't sure what I liked. Not this. Not twisting a blade of grass around my finger, pressing my palm to the bark of a tree. Listening. Hoping. Chewing my tongue bloody with the anticipation. Where was Clara? *Ben, should I go wake her up?*

You're never in control when you are the one waiting, when you depend on the actions of others. *Depend*: from the Latin *pendere*, to hang. Hang your hopes, hang your hat, hang yourself in a noose if you've hung a yellow ribbon on the old oak tree and heard nothing in answer. Margaret had some plan but I didn't know if she was the dog or the rabbit, or thought she was the dog but was actually the rabbit, or didn't cleave to any stupid hunting metaphor because she was a woman, and a woman was of her own breed.

And now here came the dogs, drooling, snapping, lusting after the rabbit I'd yet to see. And here was Margaret in her knee-high boots, grinning and running with them. She was far enough away that I couldn't tell if Clara was still part of her. I couldn't tell what she'd done with my baby. In the sixteenth century the word *baby* meant the tiny image of oneself seen in the pupil of another person's eye.

In my wool socks I slogged through the muck to get to Margaret, who was surprisingly spry.

"Where is Clara?" My voice brought to mind the old expression: I've a frog in my throat. *Get it out, please. I'm so desperate I can no longer speak.*

"What, the baby?" Margaret called to me, laughing. I wanted to slap her. She gestured to the dogs.

I'd been worried that Solly wouldn't take to Clara. Supermarket checkout lines displayed tabloid cover stories about infants mauled by previously docile family pets, babies with reconstructed faces and glass eyes. Tabloids were called "rags" because they were unserious, because these stories were not to be believed. Was I unserious if I paged through them while waiting for my groceries, if I bought them at the airport before boarding the plane? There was a certain unseriousness ascribed to me, regardless. Me, the only woman at an academic conference in a city I didn't know, sipping the house white wine alone at a back table. Me, my bathroom trash can full of disposable ice packs and the heavy, bloodied gauze I'd packed into my large postpartum underwear.

"The baby?" Margaret asked again, arresting me mid-flight.

"Is she—" I couldn't finish. Margaret grinned and adjusted a hairpin. Sweat beaded at her hairline, trickling down her ear. The pack's excitement heightened, and we watched the dogs circle a tree stump, and we heard the dogs yelp, heard the dogs cheer.

"What is that?" I asked Margaret, slowly. And then I was running, pushing past the eager animals, kneeing them, braving their teeth to reach their prey. I was wading through dogs, fighting my way against their tide. They were endless, writhing, licking me, panting. Some snarling as they blocked their kill, others jumping with excitement. Their tails were stronger than I'd have expected, solid bone, and they smiled up at me, waiting to be told they were good boys. Muzzles red, viscera dripping from their teeth. A united front that I couldn't break through. "What have they caught?"

The thing was dead; it had to be, to provide the dogs' noses such color. There was a heat. There was a smell. I thought of savory pies, steaming, thought of prodding my spoon into the tender center of a chicken potpie and casting off the shell of crust. With an internal temperature of 98.6, or thereabouts, it did make sense there would be steam, when the inside moved outside.

I couldn't look; I couldn't look away.

On the one level, I'd thought before, if something out of the blue happened to Ben—a plane crash or some quick terminal illness—I wouldn't have to make any rash decisions, and the monotony of my marriage would be solved. Could I say the same now, about Clara? Was it simpler to let circumstance take over?

But then I vomited all over one of the nearer dogs, which startled him. I couldn't catch a breath of this good, unpolluted air, and I couldn't stand upright, had to crouch with my hands scraping through my hair, had to start keening.

"I didn't take you for such an animal rights sort," said Margaret, coming over to examine the results of the hunt. In response I spat leftover bile. "It's only a rabbit."

I looked through the lattice of my hands, my face still covered.

The dogs parted for Margaret, to reveal matted fur. A torn stomach displaying small round pellets. It was only a rabbit.

"You thought it was the child?" said Margaret. "Of course not." She was droll about it, but I could tell she was offended. "What do you think we are?"

"Where is Clara?" I asked.

"You've read the book," said Margaret. "Given your own work, I assume you've read mine."

"What do you mean?"

"Once," said Margaret, "I wrote a book about a bunny who wanted to run away."

"What?"

"He told his mother, 'I am running away.'"

"Clara's a she," I said. "And she doesn't want to leave me. She hasn't run away, you've taken her."

"But do you?" asked Margaret.

"Do I what?"

"Do you want to run away?"

MEMORY, MARGARET WROTE once, is a wild and private place to which we only return by accident, as in a dream or a song.

When I was eight and my mother was sick, I brought her pre-packaged Jell-O cups because that was the only food she'd eat. Her room smelled like rotting fruit and cat piss, like unwashed bodies and my father's cologne. I peeled back the lid for her, and used a plastic spoon to mix the set slime into something more appealing. A TV tray was set up by the side of the bed. The curtains were shut.

"I didn't want it from you," my mother said when I put the cup down on the TV tray. At the time I heard: *My mother doesn't want me.* I'd left the room to go cry by myself in the downstairs bathroom, but now I understood what she meant. She couldn't have me there. She couldn't be the wronged princess, pining in her tower room, and also my mother. She couldn't be desirable to my father and have birthed me from her once-taut stomach, couldn't be a sweet young wife and at the same time have these two fast-growing girls.

Margaret, however, always embraced incongruity. This didn't mean she was happy, didn't mean she did not want. But here she was, incongruous, a hunter and an author of cute books about bunnies, a children's icon who didn't especially like children, an extrovert who loved being alone. Here I was, pondering the incongruity of being a mother and an academic, of devoting oneself to two projects, which is to say living a life, which is, I guess, no incongruity at all. Merely living, merely choosing, in each moment, who and what to which you will attend. The Latin, *atendere*, means to stretch.

"NO," I SAID. "I don't want to run away."

"Then go and find her."

On Whimsy

M argaret worked with a variety of illustrators over the course of her career, but none more closely than with Clement Hurd and Leonard Weisgard. Clem found Michael abrasive; he didn't care that Margaret was with a woman—he just didn't like this particular woman. He mostly kept his distance once Michael came on the scene.[1] Leonard, for the most part, weathered Michael.

"Leonard," Margaret would say, "I'm feeling rich," and they would go to eat foie gras with port wine or thick, decadent alfredo at La Crémailère or Aux Gais Penguins or Pappa Monetta's. Margaret's rich feelings had little to do with money—she generally didn't keep money in mind. She'd grown up with money: a Swiss boarding school, a Long Island property, visits to relatives in stately southern homes. She spent the entirety of her first manuscript advance on flowers, cashing her check and buying up the total wares of a horse-drawn flower cart on her walk home from the bank.[2] Whimsical. Annoying.

---

1 Clem and Posey return from a dinner at Michael's apartment. "She's so cruel," says Posey, unbuttoning her coat. "It's devastating to watch her demean Margaret."

2 The apartment is a floral fantasy, though Margaret coughs each time she waltzes through the kitchen. Gladiolas in the teakettle, peonies lining the windowsills, Margaret's underwear drawer bursting with gardenias. The injured flying squirrel that has been living in the bathroom while Margaret nurses it to health seems confused. The cats keep throwing up daisies.

When she said she felt poor, she meant that she was suffering a dearth of creativity.

It was Leonard who talked Margaret down off the ledge when Michael was cruel, and Leonard who collaborated on her only Caldecott Award–winning book, *The Little Island*. Leonard who said colors and shapes could be translated into sounds, and thus Leonard who illustrated Margaret's Noisy Books.

In the first *Noisy Book*, Muffin, the little dog, is having eye trouble. As he leaves the dog doctor with a bandage over his eyes, he hears a variety of city sounds: feet walking, cars honking. He hears a *squeak squeak squeak*, and he wonders what it could be. Not a lion, not a policeman, not an empty house. It turns out to be a life-size baby doll with bright blue eyes and yellow hair. The unspoken assumption that all blind dogs must be in want of a little blond baby was a strange one, but it fit Margaret's aesthetic.[3]

She enlisted an actual dog—progeny of her own Kerry blue and Bill Gaston's prizewinning standard poodle—as an artist's model. It peed on Leonard's paintings.

---

3 Margaret and Leonard take the book to Bank Street School for a test run. An adenoidal boy stands up, uses his arm to wipe his nose. "Cars don't go *honk honk*," he says. A child next to him agrees: "They go *awuurra awuurra*." Leonard laughs. "Well then, the cars will go *awuurra*," says Margaret.

25

The cars I passed were loud, but I wasn't sure how to describe the noise they made. There is no Old French or Latin to ground onomatopoeia, no history to explain it. There was no explanation for how fast the scenery shifted, how one moment I was standing in an open field with Margaret, and the next I was here, alone at the center of a city stylized in primary colors, the sky cerulean, the clouds strangely thin. It was New York, I thought, or was it Chicago? There were no other real people—not Margaret, not Clara— just abstract empty-faced ciphers completing their urban activities: waving a child across the street, walking a dog, hammering at the side of a white building one hundred feet up in the air. It felt like the natural evolution of any city, the culmination of the claustrophobic crowds that only amplified your loneliness, the people who walked past you like you weren't even there.

If I closed my eyes, I sensed the outline of a dying fire, a towel spread next to a sink where a saucepan sat upside down, drying. With my eyes closed, I could hear a baby whimpering, the onslaught of sleet, the sighs of radiant heat: a cabin in the middle of nowhere, dusty and itchy winter dry and inaccessible. But with my eyes open, I could make out the old Chicago skyline drawn in black and red, beside the ink-blotted lake.

I started walking, looking for Michael. Hoping Michael wanted to be found.

IN LATE WINTER of 1929, years before she met Margaret, Michael visited Chicago as a stop on her midwestern lecture tour. She didn't have good things to say about the Midwest, but this wasn't a surprise, as not many New Englanders I knew had good things to say about the Midwest. When I lived in New York, everyone complained about Chicago winters, about what they sneeringly called midwestern niceness, as if niceness was something to be pitied. The city I'd grown up in had never been nice, had been, I supposed, only nominally midwestern. "Be nice," said my mother when my father came to pick us up and take us to the suburbs, when her boyfriends came over to pick her up for a date and Annie and I sat eating potato chips in bare feet on the couch, narrow-eyed and judging them. "Be nice" to all the little girls, the babies baring teeth.

Michael was certainly not nice. During her visit to Chicago, she'd gone to look at the bullet-pocked doors where just months earlier two gangs had played their parts in the Saint Valentine's Day Massacre. She was proud of the risk she imagined she was taking, even bragged about how one of the guests at her hotel had a string of pearls robbed right off her neck while returning late at night on Lake Shore Drive.

I thought I might find Michael at that hotel—the Lake Shore Drive Hotel. She would have a suite, of course. This was Michael's natural habitat: a luxurious hotel suite from which she could opine, a polished antique desk with curled legs and handles made of actual gold, heavy paper, and expensive ebon ink. If Margaret's archival display was the beagling, then Michael's would be the trappings of the artistic elite.

The cars here in this picture-book Chicago sported very round red wheels with blue axles. Brickwork was carefully outlined in black, and eaves were patterned in bold shadow. Every door was the same: red, with four mismatched decorative panels. No leaves on the trees. The sun a perfect ball of light.

The desperation I'd felt for Clara was gone now. Margaret's genuine pain when I thought the rabbit was Clara reassured me. She was happy while hunting. She wouldn't hurt my daughter. She didn't like children, but she did understand them. Or did she?

Was Clara only safe if Margaret was happy? I wondered as I walked. It seemed impossible for Margaret, who needed so much from her lover, to be the Margaret she presented—elusive and laissez-faire and droll—and at the same time be happy. And it was obviously impossible for Michael to be happy, because she'd never actually become the Michael Strange that she wanted to be—powerful, universally praised. The solution of course, was to throw the two unhappinesses together so they could cancel each other out, which it seemed they sometimes did, though mostly didn't. But maybe Margaret's unhappiness was deeper than Michael's, or maybe Michael's need was shallower than Margaret's, or maybe two negatives would not make a positive, no matter what high school chemistry teachers claimed.

I walked past an empty-faced policeman in an ill-fitting uniform, his hand raised against traffic. I nodded to thank him. I walked past a fat red horse.

The issue was that their love story had no true conclusion. Throughout their entire relationship, Michael pushed and pulled, and Margaret let her. This wasn't sustainable. This wasn't a way to live a life. Both knew, by the end, that they should separate completely, but neither seemed able to do it. And then Michael was sick. Michael was dying.

If they'd officially parted ways before Michael died, it could have been a classic tragedy, a satisfying resolution. Or if Michael had died, adored, in Margaret's arms, their love could be preserved as something purer than this odd amalgamation of possessiveness and fear. But Michael's illness had forced these women's hands, and now their history was contorted, and I couldn't get closure until I knew how to fix them, and until I fixed them, I couldn't fix Clara.

Margaret had sworn she'd uphold Michael's memory, but I thought she'd been bullied into the promise. If Michael hadn't gotten sick, I thought Margaret would have wised up to the fact that she was being used. Based on conversations with her friends around that time, it seemed that maybe Margaret had wised up, but what could you do when your lover was dying of cancer? After Michael's death, those friends said sotto voce that she'd seemed almost relieved.

IT WAS MUCH easier to think about this than the snow that was now falling outside the cabin in thick sheets. I kept my eyes open. I kept walking.

MARGARET HAD NEVER, to my knowledge, visited Chicago with Michael. She'd been up and down the eastern seaboard, been to Europe, been out west, but never here in this middle ground that I knew was Chicago, although it looked an awful lot like Margaret's *Noisy Book*. In fact, the Lake Shore Drive Hotel when I arrived looked an awful lot like the empty house that Muffin the dog knew did not go *squeak squeak squeak*. The actual Lake Shore Drive Hotel did not have a yellow exterior, a large red door with a blue pediment, three blue windows, a blue-speckled roof. But the sign outside said Lake Shore Drive Hotel, so I walked in.

It smelled suspiciously like dog urine.

Inside Michael's autobiography it was 1929, so all the ashtrays were white with curled burgundy script. Palatial, Michael had described this hotel, and palaces were often very cold. The high-ceilinged lobby was empty of guests, the elevator new and old at once—newly built but not what I was used to—and I scraped my palm while pulling the cage shut. It rose without my say-so and deposited me at one end of a long hallway lined with carved white doors. Outside each door, a gold-plated number, a side table with fresh flowers, a plush rug.

At the far end of the hall, one of these ornate doors was open. I walked in, and there was Michael. She stood next to the drawn floor-length curtains, looking out, one hand resting on a varnished wooden desk, the other pressed against the glass of the arched window beside it. I waited.

"Once," Michael said to the view, "when I was very ill and depressed after leaving Jack, I was recovering at a sordid little French hotel and saw Walt Whitman sitting in the chair beside my bed." This I already knew from her writing. Michael tended to repeat herself.

"What does that have to do with me?" I asked.

"I say this so you know that we look out for one another, we true artists. Our words remain and act as balms, piercing the wretched little lives we find ourselves living, promising us more."

She'd mixed her metaphors, but who was I to point that out?

"I'm not an artist," I said. "And I don't think my life is wretched."

"To each his own," said Michael and adjusted her scarf. She sat down at the writing desk, started scratching something out with her expensive gold pen. I supposed despite the promise of being my balm, she didn't actually care much about me. She'd said what she needed to say, and I hadn't been receptive.

"Are you just going to hold me here, then? Just going to hold on to Clara?"

"Why, whatever do you mean?"

I was getting pretty tired of these mid-century women and their typical mid-century language. I was getting pretty tired of being their playing field, of housing them inside my body. I knew I was a pawn in their game—and it made me feel like myself as a child, when it wasn't really me that mattered. It wasn't *me* my parents wanted, but the satisfaction of getting full custody. When he proposed, it wasn't *me* that Ben wanted, just the illusion of marriage. Even Clara just wanted my milk, wanted my warmth.

"Is Clara here?" I asked. "Is Margaret?"

"Through that door," Michael said, nodding. "To the left."

26

In the great green room there was my daughter, lying on a massive bed, with Margaret knitting in a rocking chair a few feet away.

"Can it be over now?" I asked. The fire was lit in the hearth, but it was cold, getting colder. I stood in the door, on the precipice, unable to come in. Each time I tried to take a step across the threshold I was halted by a wave of cold, a soul-deep freeze, an ice wall.

"Close your eyes," said Margaret.

But I couldn't.

The Makings of a Classic

Goodnight Moon was illustrated by Clement Hurd, who also drew *The Runaway Bunny*. In 1946 Clem was coming home from the war. On his return, Margaret knew Clem would feel lost after the trauma of the front, and so she housed him in her studio, a strange little two-story cottage called Cobble Court tucked away in Lenox Hill, a few blocks south of the Upper East Side apartments. A small white clapboard house with ivy around the door and a sunroom full of square-paned windows, the ghost of a long-dead New York hidden behind a block of commonplace apartments. Margaret told Clem and his wife Posey to stay as long as it took to get back on their feet.

Margaret had her editor at Harper send Clem a copy of her newly finished manuscript. She requested that he draw her a "fabulous room" with a "Little Boy Bunny in bed." The room would be big and bright, but would grow darker.

27

Michael couldn't enter the room, and because of this I couldn't enter the room. We were somehow intertwined, somehow connected. Maybe the room was afraid of Michael's heat. Or was it because Clement Hurd, its artist, didn't like her? Had he cast some sort of spell to keep her out? I'd had friends who didn't approve of my choice of past romantic partners. They mostly said *I never liked him*, and sometimes they said *Well, now I guess we'll have to pick up the pieces again*. All of my friends who met Ben had agreed he was solid.

Clara was lying on the bed, awake, but not crying. I didn't want to run away from her, but I also didn't want to run toward her. This understanding didn't temper my relief. She was whole. She was there. My little baby, being such a good girl. Being so quiet.

The books said to put her down in her crib when she was drowsy but awake, so that she'd learn to fall asleep on her own. So that she wouldn't need me. Well, that wasn't really it, it was really so that I wouldn't have to nurse her to sleep, or always rock her, or maybe so that when she half woke in the night she could soothe herself back into restfulness or REM, so she could wake up refreshed in the morning. I couldn't remember, now, why I was supposed to try to put her down drowsy. I couldn't remember why it was better for her not to need me, why it was better for us to be two separate people, not one.

"I understand," I said to Margaret, "how you can feel both more and less yourself with someone else."

She didn't look at me. Neither did Clara. The room was so cold.

And now Michael had come to stand next to me, looking in on the encapsulated night.

"What do you want from me?" I asked her. My teeth were chattering. I'd left all the windows in the cabin slightly open. The snow was coming in and puddling on the sills, prickling my neck, wetting my fingers when I braced against the doorframe. The wind was fierce.

IN GHOST STORIES, we generally discover what the haunting signifies. By the end of the story or the novel or the film we know who died and why they're restless, we know that somebody disturbed some ancient orb or moved into a toxic house. But in the story of my life I couldn't say why I was haunted, why I needed these women, in this moment, and why they needed me. There is a room, and in it are objects, and I suppose that is enough.

A PHONE WAS ringing in the kitchen, at the cabin, and I lifted it from the wall, closing my eyes so I could answer.

"Thank god," said Ben from far away. "Are you okay? Is Clara?"

I coughed, and said, "We're fine." Then I started to cry.

"Can you drive?" asked Ben. "Never mind. I don't think you should drive. I talked to Annie about your—you know, your—Anyway, the roads are bad. We'll come to you."

"Okay," I said through hiccups, "but I think maybe you shouldn't."

"It'll be okay," said Ben. I didn't like his forced amiability. I didn't want him to come. I was in the middle of something, and he had interrupted.

"I have a lot going on," I said. I waited for Ben to respond, but all that came back now was static. "Did you hear me?" I said. "We have a lot going on." A few more seconds of that strange, whispering buzz, and then silence. A lightness told me that the cord was no longer connected to the wall. Someone had cut the line.

"Focus," said Michael, "on what truly matters."

I opened my eyes.

AS THERE HAD been in the upstairs house Margaret built in our condo, as there had been in Margaret's Only House in Maine, there was, in this great green room, a door that led nowhere. A frame, and then a fifty-foot drop, whatever stairs that had once led down to the earth long since demolished. Outside there was the lake, the wind, the snow.

"You're always telling me I've killed you, and that's what's wrong," Margaret was saying from her place in the rocking chair.

Clara was propped up on a pillow, looking from one woman to the other, as aware of her surroundings as I'd ever seen her.

"You're being dramatic," said Michael. "You're hysterical."

I didn't think I'd ever heard a woman tell another woman she was being hysterical. Hysteria was a term reserved for men's use, a male explanation for the wrongs of the world that men couldn't be bothered to remedy. *Hysteria*: an early-nineteenth-century medical term coined from the Greek *hystera*, meaning womb.

"Technically—" I began from my place in the doorframe, my place next to Michael, and all three of them—Margaret, Michael, even Clara—shot me daggers.

"This isn't about you," said Margaret, even though I was on her side. I'd been trying to stand up for her. And it *was* about me. They'd called me here, they'd stolen my child. Didn't they want me to take sides? Why else would they have brought me?

I didn't think I'd taken the wrong side, though I supposed it was possible. I supposed I had to know which one I was, Margaret or

Michael, had to know which one was Clara. Once I knew for certain, I could understand why I still didn't know what I wanted—despite knowing I loved Clara, despite knowing what I should want, what I didn't.

I'd filled out all the online tests: Myers-Briggs, Enneagram, Which Sex and the City Star Are You—I knew I must be one of these women or the other. Since adolescence I'd done everything I could to find the category that would explain me to myself, the category to do the work of self-examination for me.

A category is a name, and thus an incantation.

"Margaret," I whispered, wishing myself the overborne, not overbearing.

"What?" she snapped. I had romanticized her, somewhat. In wanting to be Margaret, I had made her in my image. In casting Michael as the villain, I'd forgotten that Margaret could be cruel as well. She'd fallen out with her first publisher, Bill Scott, over payments. She would write letters in anger and then send them, and then later send short notes of self-reproach. Margaret was ashamed of her short temper, but there it was, she said, and there was nothing to be done about it.

There was Margaret: seeing herself, disliking herself, telling herself there was nothing to be done. And then there was Michael, seeing herself a magnanimous, merciful queen.

I didn't say anything else, and they kept going.

"What's really wrong is that you've lost yourself in this psychoanalysis," said Michael. "All this luxuriating in the past is your excuse not to grow up, your excuse not to make the necessary changes in your art. You are denying your own evolution, and it's very unattractive. The whole thing is obscene."

"You know the psychoanalysis is only a temporary treatment," said Margaret. "By nature, it's a temporary practice. Once you've faced the desolation, you're free of it. You meet the pain, and face it as you once were unable to face it. You feel it again, and this time you stand it."

"I don't like what you're implying," said Michael.

"I'm not implying anything," Margaret said. "I'm only trying to explain why our views differ, you and me." She was still sitting in the rocking chair, but rocking more quickly, her irritation obvious in the scuff of her foot on the floor. The chair made an ominous creak under the pressure.

"You and I," said Michael. "Not *you and me*."

Lovers Quarrels

1. Margaret was still undergoing psychoanalysis, Michael still didn't like it.[1]

2. Margaret was still writing for children, Michael still didn't like it.[2]

3. Margaret thought that Michael liked to feel abandoned, which was why Michael kept pushing her away.[3]

---

1 The guests have retired to the screened porch. Margaret stands in the doorway, watching Michael opine. "This Freudian obscenity," she is saying, and someone is laughing and Margaret is feeling small. She walks out to the dock. The rain is coming—she can smell it on the wind. The world feels vast and deep.

2 "I heard you took tea on the library steps." Michael laughs. Margaret says, "Yes, I'd forgot my invitation. They wouldn't let me in, so Ursula and I had a Children's Book Week luncheon of our own." "She's a terrible influence." Michael doesn't say more, because it's already been said. Michael has made herself painfully known. "It was my idea," says Margaret, setting her coat across a chair. "Exactly," says Michael.

3 Each time they speak, Michael tells Margaret that they have been living in sin, that Margaret is sinful. She has cast Margaret out of the East End Avenue apartments, cut off all contact. She is sickening. She is dying. She requests that Margaret exhume her youngest son's body in Connecticut, have him reburied in the family plot in the Bronx. Margaret makes the arrangements. Margaret buys up blocks of tickets to Michael's lecture show and calls in favors from her friends so that the seats won't be empty while Michael stands onstage, all spindly weightless bone. A doctor calls to say that Margaret is causing Michael too much stress. Can she please refrain from visiting the theater?

28

At her home in Maine, Margaret hung a sign above the door to nowhere: MIND THE VIEW. She called the door the Witch's Wink. And now the hotel Witch's Wink was open, and now Margaret stood by it, holding Clara—opposing me and Michael as we stood in the frame of the door to the rest of the suite. A door directly across from a door. What was the word for a space between spaces? A purgatory? No, because the root word, *purgatorum,* meant a cleansing. A limbo? From the Latin *limbus,* a border or an edge. That wasn't right either— this wasn't an edge, it was an in-between, an other. A photonegative appearing between one life and the next, between one self and the self that would come after. A great green room. In music, a rest.

Margaret held Clara, and they stood there at the edge of the open door, and I still couldn't make myself go to them.

Through that door I could see the lake, thickly frozen, the snowflakes falling fat and luscious, collecting on the surface like cream at the top of good milk. They were meandering, lazy. Every so often the wind would hurry them along with a quick, walloping roar, and Margaret's dress and stockings would be dotted with new melt. Clara's onesie was damp with drool and spit-up, hardening into an icy shell. She would not survive the chill; already I could hear her coughing in the chesty, wet way that raises the hackles on a mother. Here I was, wheezing in sympathy, and I still couldn't make myself go to her.

When I was pregnant, they said: Don't drink wine, don't eat sushi or lunch meats or soft cheeses, don't lie on your back. Don't have coffee or clean out the litter box, don't go in the hot tub, don't sit still for too long, don't jump. Refrain from all of these things, and your reward will be a perfect little baby. When Clara was new, they said: Don't put her in the car seat in a puffy jacket, don't let her sleep with blankets, don't lie her in bed on her stomach, don't give her honey or water or juice. But I could follow these directions to a T, and still lose her. I could build my life around making sure she was protected, the crux of my life could be the maintenance of her health and her perfection, and still I could lose her. There were so many ways I could lose her, and here she was, the door wide open, coughing, cold, now scrabbling across Margaret's chest.

They never said: Do not invite a ghost inside you. Do not invite a ghost inside your home.

I didn't want to be waiting, forever, for disaster. I didn't want to be stuck living in *before*, in thrall of some impending *after*. I was ready for the *after*.

Margaret was looking out at the lake, and Michael was looking at Margaret. In her book, Michael had written: "My father's death had been my father's death, but my mother's was in some strange way a part of my own." How long would Clara belong to me? Without her there to suckle, my milk would swell my breasts to veiny, blown balloons, but would eventually dry up. Women who lost their babies didn't lose their milk immediately—they had to use cabbage leaves to help the milk stop, had to sit with the pain. Women who delivered stillborn babies still had to reckon with their postpartum bodies. Even childless, they were bloody and ragged and swollen and sore; in their bodies lived the ghosts of these babies. Where would Clara's ghost go?

"If only someone would marry you." Michael sighed. "If only some rich man would come and take you off my hands."

If only someone would come take you off my hands.

Margaret took a step closer to the edge.

Who would Michael be, without Margaret? It didn't seem fair that Margaret—who'd lived only thirty years when she met Michael, who would live only two more years without her—had to sacrifice herself so that Michael could find out. I saw now that if I wasn't going to write the story Michael wanted from me, she was going to let herself live it. She'd make Margaret smaller. She'd make Margaret nothing. She'd erase the story that biographers had told—the story that was written around Margaret—in favor of a story in which she was the star: the story of a benevolent poet queen, her body corrupted by the depravity of her most loyal servant.

Or was that my story? Was that me?

Who would I be without Clara?

"Your art lacks a certain sophistication, Bun," said Michael. "Like you, it's unserious and trite."

"I disagree," I said half-heartedly, but Margaret seemed not to hear me. This was a battle of both wills and wits, and if I chose to play seriously, I would be playing with the lesser hand. Michael was known for her persuasion, her rhetoric. She'd convinced wealthy men to back her plays, to publish her, to marry her.

"You're already dead," I said. "Both of you."

Margaret's one leg was out the door, dangling from the frame.

"Michael will change her mind," I said, one last perfunctory attempt. Michael shook her head to signify she wouldn't. "This isn't how things end for you, not really. This isn't actually how you die in real life."

Margaret stepped out the door, looking back at me, mouthing *I'm sorry.* And though I knew I should feel something, I felt nothing. Just the long flight of a body, the downward drop of a body, holding Clara.

I HAD CHOSEN. I knew which one I was.

Michael turned to me; she took me by the shoulders. "All you have to do now," she said, "is close your eyes."

Part IV

The Rabbit poet in me has always longed for another language before it is too late—a more fearless baldness of the heart to say the things we never say and the other never knows. Sometimes we ourselves know only too late what we wanted to say.

—Margaret Wise Brown, in a letter to
Michael Strange, November 1947

29

No parachuting, luminous fall. No skirts swirled up around me, no motes of light. Just the relentlessness of gravity; a steep, sickening plunge. And luck—the bushes skirting the cabin had doubled themselves since their original planting, invasive honeysuckle multiplying faster than it could be rooted up, opening its arms to us, heavy with snow. A popping lurch in my ankle upon landing was soon overwhelmed by the cold.

I LAY ON my back, broken branches a halo around the leaden sky. My tailbone hurt. A tiny bead of blood welled on my wrist. Soapy snowflakes hovered in the air. I rose to my knees, looking for Clara, my leggings cold and wet and clinging. A nearby tree had spouted icicles of pinesap; its trunk seemed to be weeping.

And then there she was in the bushes in front of me, her eyes open, her lashes starry from the wet, her cheeks a phosphorescent pink. She was looking up at the extraordinary slate of the afternoon sky. I was bent over her, and she was looking up at me.

NEVER HAD I been so in love and never had I been so afraid and never had I been so aware that Clara and I were alive, and that we were alone.

30

Ben found us in the car, wheels spinning out in the snow. I'd gotten stuck on the turn from the back roads to the highway, aiming for the hospital, driving wildly, my only thought saving my child. My ankle was swollen, bruising a mottled purple, possibly broken. Clara seemed unharmed—just very cold, so cold that her fingers were bloodless and white.

Luckily we were only sitting for about half an hour before Ben pulled up in a rented off-roader, its massive wheels salt-streaked and angry. I had my blinkers on, and I was, as always, nursing Clara. I'd been watching the highway for headlights, listening for a motor, waiting for some rural soul to pass so I could lean hard on my horn. If that didn't work, I was preparing myself to double Clara's blankets, grit my teeth and walk into town even though it was ten miles away. When I saw Ben, the stupidity of either plan unraveled. The stupidity of all of it unraveled, and I felt myself awash with self-disgust, mortified and afraid and suspicious and silent on the way to the Wisconsin ER.

Ben didn't seem mad at me, then. He said, "I'm mad at myself for not knowing." Even when they had to cut off the tip of Clara's frostbitten left pinkie, he said, "I'm not mad at you, Megan."

THEY LET CLARA stay with me at first, when I transferred to the mother-baby unit in Chicago, because I was nursing. The doctors thought it was better to keep us together, both for the breast milk and to minimize the immediate trauma. We had a nurse beside us constantly, observing, but I didn't mind the company. I didn't trust myself alone.

The doctors talked to me about my symptoms. They talked to me about my moods. They made a plan for me, which included a prescribed course of pills and spending time apart from Clara. I couldn't nurse her anymore because of the chemicals. They wanted me to focus on myself. They said they took her away so that I could sleep, so I could begin my recovery. The prognosis was good, and if I kept taking the pills, they said she soon would be returned to me, but a minute is an hour is a day when she is still so young, and though it was only forty-eight hours of sustained separation, I calculated that I'd be missing one percent of her life thus far. I lay at night with my eyes open—the city below me, around me—remembering when I lay at night with my eyes open in a different wing of this same hospital complex, watching Clara's first outside-my-body sleep. I could take the pills, but I couldn't get better until she was back with me. I said that to the doctor, and he nodded and told me that was good.

At first I couldn't understand why this had happened to me, or even whether this had happened to me. What had happened to me? Margaret and Michael, according to my doctors, had not. I'd been in a fugue state, broken psychotic, experienced a "flight of ideas." This wasn't necessarily common, postpartum, but all assured me it wasn't totally unusual.

It had been me, and not Michael or Margaret, who'd hurt Clara. I didn't think I'd wanted to hurt her; I was also sure I hadn't done all that I could have done to keep her safe. I was angry at my ineptitude, my warped instincts. I felt profoundly ashamed.

This wasn't what my life was supposed to look like. This wasn't what motherhood was supposed to look like. I wasn't supposed to need so much: not doctors, not medications, not Clara, not Ben. I wasn't supposed to cause so much trouble.

I wasn't supposed to be Michael, or Margaret.

Eventually the pills dulled my delusions, and along with them my feelings about my delusions. My feelings about my behavior, about other mothers who hadn't been broken, about my own mother. Once I was dull enough, they gave Clara back to me.

I still had thoughts. I still had needs. But these were thought and needed under the new, thin, hazy layer of my treatment—a growing scar tissue of antipsychotics and mood stabilizers that would thicken.

I went to the group therapy sessions in the common room at the end of the hall, and felt impossibly lonely. The explanation for my postpartum behavior was hormones, and genetic predispositions, and stress. None of these other women knew me, and none of them knew about Michael or Margaret. One had tried to drown her baby, another was severely depressed, and then there were three empty seats for whoever might next be made mentally unstable by motherhood. Apparently we were in one of only three hospitals in the country to provide this level of postpartum psychological care.

When the pills made my heart race, they gave me lithium and ECT—knocked me out and rewired me with electrical currents. They told me I might experience memory loss or temporary confusion, but I remembered everything.

MARGARET ONCE SAID that she felt her whole life was spent falling "deeper and deeper into the illusion that one is separate and so far away from others that only by playing a part could one meet one's fellows." Accounts of her by friends, all given after her death, seemed to corroborate this worldview. Many said they loved her, but felt they didn't really know her. Everyone thought maybe the others knew her better, but it turned out that nobody did.

Maybe Michael had been the one to know her. Or maybe it was Pebble, the boatbuilding Rockefeller heir she'd been engaged to when she died. But he'd never shown up for me anywhere—not in the cabin or the condo, not in my dreams.

BEN CAME TO visit, at first without his laptop, then with it. He would answer emails in the corner while I cuddled Clara, or watched TV, or slept. He'd come with us to the hospital's baby massage sessions or splash play. I was trying, with the help of the pills and the therapy, to be the person I'd been when Ben first married me. From the way he looked at me—approving, relieved—it seemed like maybe I'd succeed. Annie came to visit with magazines and stories about her dates with Garbage Greg. Seth and Linda brought a ficus, and some chocolates, and more sympathy than I had expected. My father didn't come, of course, and neither did my stepmother or Kelsey.

I was an inpatient for six weeks, and only at the very end of my hospital stay did my mother come to visit. I was packing up the cards I had pinned to the wall, and throwing away the dead flowers, and she walked in just as the credits were rolling on a *Golden Girls* rerun.

"I want to apologize," she said, and I laughed. I couldn't remember a time in which my mother had uttered those words in that order: more often it was "Young lady, come apologize to me at once." I left Annie's hydrangeas to make wet stem-prints on the paper tablecloth and sat down at the edge of the bed. Clara was cooing in the hospital bassinet, the same wood and clear plastic as the one they'd given her at birth. Her left hand was still wrapped in gauze, which she was busy trying to get off. I sat looking at her, waiting for what my mother would tell us.

"For?" I said finally. But that was it. That was all we were getting, me and Clara, as our maternal family legacy.

I didn't think about my mother's mother much—I'd never met her. She died when my mother was ten, and no one ever bothered to tell me and Annie how. I'd assumed something like cancer; now I wasn't so sure.

"What a shame," my mother said, stroking Clara's forehead and removing a wet strip of gauze from Clara's mouth, "that she won't ever be able to play the piano."

WE DIDN'T TALK about the things that were difficult to talk about. We, meaning my family—Annie, my mother, my father, myself—and we, meaning me and Ben. I would like to say that my reticence changed after Michael and Margaret. I would like to say I left the hospital emboldened, but I didn't. As it had been with my mother, so it was with me: some time away, a regime of medication, a finger stuck back in the dike.

But evolution is a slow climb, trekking eons of the same until finally, something different. And Clara was now missing a finger.

31

Ben took FMLA and bought us a month of togetherness. We brought Clara to the aquarium. We watched more HGTV. When they began my medications, I'd stopped nursing—the labs tested my breast milk and called it contaminated. After the ECT they lowered my dose, but when I offered myself to Clara, she declined me. This seemed an appropriate punishment. After everything I'd done to her, I wouldn't have trusted me either.

Using formula meant Ben could be a more active parent, that Ben could forge a real relationship with Clara. She was now sleeping up to seven hours at a time. Ben was back to sleeping beside me, and he'd lift Clara from the bassinet when she woke crying and take her to the living room, put on sports highlights, and feed her.

They'd had two nights together without me at the beginning of my treatment, and something had altered in that two-night separation, had left a scar more prominent than anything that had occurred with Margaret, more obvious than even Clara's finger. She still preferred me to Ben, but she seemed wary of me. And I had learned what it was like to be without her—the stiff hospital sheets, the sudden crying jags, the sense that I'd become an echo of myself.

I didn't think, now, that I would ever finish my dissertation. The fantasy I'd entertained in the throes of my "flight of ideas," of having both motherhood and a career, was a pipe dream. But maybe it was less that I didn't want to finish, or that I couldn't finish, than that I was afraid to finish. I was afraid I would find them again, Michael and Margaret. I was scared I would jump-start the old circuitry, undo all of what my doctors had been calling my good work. Corine, my outpatient therapist, said it would be fine, that most women took up their former occupations, most new mothers found their way back to themselves. She said that it's generally a good idea to finish what you start.

Corine had a white noise machine in her office, the same brand we used for Clara. She had little individually wrapped mints in bowls at strategic locations, and whenever I looked at them, I thought about little individual mint wrappers piled in some landfill. Corine wasn't interested in psychoanalysis, or if she was, she pretended that she wasn't. This pretending was something that had struck me about therapists even before Margaret and Michael, something I'd pointed out to Annie when she'd first gotten involved with her own. A therapist hears you say all sorts of crazy things and then has to pretend that they don't think you're crazy. A therapist has to come to work every day in a sweater set and sensible shoes and maybe pearls and a mask of what they think that you should see. I felt like putting on that mask was setting a bad example for those of us who'd considered telling our own truths, but weren't sure about unmasking. I felt like the resources Corine was giving me were all in service of adapting to society, and not necessarily in service of figuring myself out. But I played along, because I needed to live in society, because we all did, and also because I had Clara.

"Let's talk about your daughter," Corine would say, and I would try not to cry. "We can wait until you're ready," Corine would say, but I was never ready.

We made a plan for what I'd do if I heard noises, or saw things that I suspected were not actually there. I had to go see Corine twice a week at first, then once, then once every two. I saw my doctor every two weeks to talk about my medications, and my sister was supposed to come by to look for warning signs. Ben was supposed to look for warning signs.

"Let's talk about your husband," Corine would say. This I could do. I knew the answers here, or thought I knew them. Because of what we called my "lapse," Ben had a chance at getting custody of Clara if I ever decided to leave him. He said he wasn't mad at me, but he said it so often, I knew that he was. I wanted him to come out and tell me, and I said this to Corine, and she suggested couples counseling to air ourselves out, but when I brought it up to Ben, he wouldn't have it.

"We're doing well now," he said. I wasn't allowed to be mad at him, because I was the one who'd fucked up. But I was mad at him, and I said so to Corine, who was sworn to secrecy as long as I didn't seem violent. I was mad that he hadn't helped out more with Clara when she was brand-new, and mad that he was helping so much with her now that she was older. I was mad that he needed so little to be happy, mad that he would say things like "It's okay if you want to go back to work" or "Do you think the milk is spoiled?" I was mad that I didn't love him passionately, that I would never feel for him what Margaret felt for Michael.

I'd been raised on the idea that everyone would get one true, deep romance in their lifetime. My mother had fallen in love with my father. My father had fallen in love with Claudia, the preschool teacher who ultimately left him for a wealthier man. Ilsa got Rick and Cathy got Heathcliff and Rachel got Ross. I realized suddenly, sucking on a Life Savers mint in Corine's drafty office, that I wasn't going to get anyone.

EVENTUALLY THE MANDATED therapy turned into occasional sessions by choice. At Ben's request we moved to the suburbs, a fifteen-minute drive from Seth and Linda, a four-bedroom house with a yard. In the winter I could open the door and let Solly do her business out back—we would find frozen feces in the snowmelt when spring came.

Ben wanted Clara's room painted pink, which seemed too much to me, but in the long run didn't matter. We put on overalls and paper masks and classic rock and painted the walls. We forgot to put painter's tape down over the molding and dripped Misted Rose all over the rug, but Ben thought it was funny and put his hands into my pockets and we had sex for the first time in months on the nursery floor while Clara was downstairs with his mom. It wasn't bad, but it did feel like a tax I was paying in order to keep living in my body.

The microwave in this new house closed tightly. The air vents were silent.

Clara was seven months old when I finally wrote to my dissertation advisor: "I've had a family emergency and won't be able to complete the program." He wrote back: "This is not unexpected." *Expect*, from the Latin *ex*, meaning thoroughly; *spectare*, meaning to look.

For my birthday, Ben bought me a replacement for the ruined volume of my Oxford English Dictionary.

AND THEN IT was Clara's birthday. She'd dispensed with the pacifier and instead sucked on her littlest left finger, the one that had healed to a smooth stub. She had thin dark hair, and her eyes were fully brown now. Her cheeks had filled out. She could take two or three steps on her own, and could say "Mama."

We had the family over in a housewarming/birthday celebration, and Annie brought the garbageman, who she was now seeing seriously. I welcomed him in with a smile. I was still taking the lithium, and it dulled any judgment. It allowed me to live in the suburbs. It disguised most of the pain.

Of course Seth and Linda came to Clara's party and stayed the whole time. Linda stood at the sink and cut grapes into quarters. Seth let Clara smudge his glasses with her fingers.

Kelsey and Jeanie came with presents, and stayed longer than I would've expected. My dad, they said, had to work, but he sent his regards. My mother showed up late with a Barbie dollhouse, a giant magenta choking hazard that said "Awesome" and "Totally rad" when you closed the oven or opened the closet. We put it in storage in the garage.

After the party, Ben and I bathed Clara together, and lotioned her all over, and brushed her hair. I dressed her carefully in her pajamas and turned on her sound machine and let her choose two books. All of her books made me cry now, because they reminded me that she would one day have to learn about the world, and the world wasn't what I wanted it to be for her. There were floods and diseases, there were hurricanes and fires, but mostly there were cruel people, selfish people, people who didn't care what kind of legacy they'd leave.

We said goodnight to her lamp, to her stuffed doggie, to her sleep sack and her mobile with the colorful felt fish. We said goodnight to Grampa and Nana, to Aunt Annie and to Daddy and to Solly, to the garbage trucks and the birds in the sky. We said goodnight to all her toes and her belly button, to her ears and her eyes and her one special finger.

I kissed her on each cheek, then on the forehead, and I laid her in her bed and I turned off the light.

Epilogue

When Clara was fifteen months old, she looked right at me and said "Mommy more doggies," and we called it her first sentence. Ben was in Seattle, but I FaceTimed him three times in a row in the middle of the day.

"What's wrong?" he said, breathless, when he finally picked up. I could see his worried client in the background, framed by a whiteboard full of mathematical formulas.

"Listen to our daughter," I said. I held the phone up so Clara could see him, but she only wanted to look at herself in the corner of the screen. "Tell Daddy," I said. Of course she didn't.

I JOINED A local mom's group, and hosted monthly playdates. We would sit with our coffees amid puzzle pieces and baby doll dresses and stickers and talk about how to schedule naps or how much we should be paying for preschools. It was all very surface-level, though occasionally someone would talk about how hard it was to still be waking up with her son in the night, how hard it was to discipline her daughter, how sometimes after a particularly difficult day she'd skip her nightly pinot grigio and just cry. Each time I felt the moment in which I might tell them land like a bird in hand, and each time I let it take flight without comment. I thought that I was likely to be lonely for a very long time.

■ ■ ■

WE GOT A play set in the backyard, and I could stand washing dishes at the kitchen sink and keep an eye on Clara. The set had two parallel swings, and she spent hours on it, pumping her legs. Every few minutes she'd get down and give the other swing a push, then return to her own seat—her joy manifested like the inscrutable inner mechanics of an old clock, requiring that both swings be constantly moving.

WHEN SHE WAS five, I went alone to Clara's first parent-teacher conference. Ben was in Siena, Italy, for work. The teacher said that Clara was observant—she waited until she understood precisely how to do things before jumping in and trying them. This fit pretty well with my own understanding of my daughter, so I nodded. "When she messes something up, she says 'Nuts,'" said the teacher. "It's so old-fashioned. Most of the other kids swear. It's very sweet."

IT WAS IMPOSSIBLE to believe that days had once seemed endless, that nights had seemed endless, that I had been able to sit and just look. Clara was easier than Ben's brother's kids, objectively, and easier than Annie's kids. The rest of them bounced off the walls twenty-four seven, while Clara could sit still and color, or read books for hours on end. But she asked questions I would never be able to answer, questions like "Why are clouds so far away?" or "Who made the rocks?" Her pajama pants were quickly too short, her shoes too tight.

I GOT A part-time job when Clara was in second grade, which was also around the time when Ben and I officially decided that we wouldn't have more children. It had been a tacit agreement, made easy to keep tacit by the fact that we barely had sex. He was still gone a lot for work. It was possible that he was cheating on me, but the thought of him with someone else didn't burn the way it once had, didn't even offend me—he was still paying our mortgage, he was caring for our child. My symptoms hadn't recurred but the hormones could certainly rev them back up. I'd have to go off all my meds if I got pregnant. And then we were older.

My job was as a copy editor for an academic publisher, mostly social sciences but also some history. We got a manuscript in from a member of my former grad school cohort, but the publisher nixed it.

"Too obvious," he said between large bites of croissant, "and he should have toned down the language."

SOMETIMES CLARA WOULD tell me that she felt a tingling in her littlest left finger.

"It isn't a big deal," she would say, which made me feel like it was a big deal. Which made me wonder how many times she didn't tell me.

AT TWELVE, CLARA takes the bus home from school and lets herself inside the house when I have to work late. She keeps track of her key, and she knows how to make herself a snack and will get started on her homework, which to my surprise she genuinely enjoys. Of course I won't let her bring a friend home without some adult present, or do any actual cooking, or use the fireplace. Most of the time I'm home by five thirty to find her sitting on a stool at the kitchen island, working on her algebra.

Now it's November, but still pushing sixty degrees. I dawdle at work, aware the clocks will change soon, aware that I am nearing the last of my early-evening light. Ben is in Omaha, and I stop to pick up dinner from the Thai place he doesn't like. When I get home, the front door is unlocked, but I don't think much of it. And then I notice that the downstairs windows are all open, each lifted just an inch. Clara's geography textbook is spread out at the kitchen table, open to a map I don't recognize. She's put water on for tea, her mug is waiting. Steam sings from the electric kettle, calling her back.

Solly whines at the bottom of the stairs. She is getting too old to climb them. Her warning feels familiar.

Again derives from the Old English *ongean*, which can mean "in exchange for."

My daughter never apologizes when clomping through the house, not even when she slams the door so hard she'll frighten Solly into peeing on the hardwoods. I've always been quiet. My mother's generation has been quiet. Linda will say, "Can that racket really be Clara?"

The noise I hear now can be Clara; it is Clara. In stocking feet I climb the stairs and follow her, careful to avoid the creaky floorboards, stifling a cough.

Clara stands by the linen closet, her dark hair in a topknot, her school uniform wrinkled, her hands reaching toward the wall. A door is there—turquoise—where before there was not a door. Clara breathes in, and turns the handle. Behind it stands Margaret, on her ladder. The same tweed jacket with the chuffed elbows. The same red lipstick. The same serious, dreamy expression.

"What are you doing?" Clara asks her.

Margaret smiles, and the largeness of it makes her incandescent. "Why, I'm building a house," she says. "For Michael."

Author's Note

Although this is a work of fiction, I've done my best to inform the characterizations of Margaret Wise Brown, Michael Strange, and their associates with extensive research. The seeds of this book began with a desire to see these women have their due in popular culture—each was a trailblazer in her own right, and my hope is that giving them this fictional space will encourage readers to seek out more about their real-life counterparts. Mine is by no means a definitive analysis of their relationship or their work; to fictionalize recent historical figures is to do a strange dance of conjecture and interpretation, relating actual events through the lens of this particular novel, and my own impressions and experiences. I have the utmost respect for both women, their estates, their friends, family, and colleagues—it's been an honor to learn from them over the past several years.

This novel owes a massive debt to two particular Margaret Wise Brown biographies: Amy Gary's *In the Great Green Room*, and Leonard Marcus's *Awakened by the Moon*. Gary's buoyant narrative account of Margaret's life provided rich characterization, and her attention to Margaret's emotional range was a huge inspiration to me. Marcus's philosophical examination of Margaret's work and the literary world in which it flourished—as well as his highly detailed analysis of her career—provided the theoretical backbone for

Megan's dissertation and strengthened the intellectual heart of this novel. Both biographies are excellent reading for anyone interested in further exploring Margaret and her legacy.

Michael's writing—including the autobiography Megan references—is available to those who like a good scavenger hunt. Margaret's books are readily available from your local bookseller. Please do dig in—*The Little Fur Family, The Noisy Book,* and *The Little Island* are particular favorites at our house.

I'm in awe of the work of the many doctors, journalists, scientists, and mothers on the front lines of postpartum psychosis. Many aspects of Megan's experience are based on information gathered from women brave and generous enough to share their stories. Megan's treatment, and the fictional mother-baby unit in which she begins her recovery, is based on best practices I discovered during my research. Many of these resources are still unavailable to the majority of women in the United States, but in taking liberties with my description of available postpartum care, I hope to highlight the need for expanded treatment and the opportunity for change. Although my own postpartum experience was vastly different from Megan's, it was, in its own way, traumatic and isolating. I wrote this book to shed light on those first few weeks of parenthood, in the hopes of normalizing the intense, conflicting emotions women may feel in those early days. The more we actively discuss the multifaceted experiences of new mothers, the better we as a society can care for women and their babies during an incredibly vulnerable period of their lives. I'm excited and honored to use this novel to push that conversation forward.

Sources

Part I

"The Dark Wood of the Golden Birds." *Kirkus Reviews*, June 1, 1950.

Eliot, T. S. "Ulysses, Order, and Myth." Review of *Ulysses*, by James Joyce. *The Dial*, November 1923.

Gary, Amy. *In the Great Green Room: The Brilliant and Bold Life of Margaret Wise Brown*. New York: Flatiron, 2017.

Marcus, Leonard. *Margaret Wise Brown: Awakened by the Moon*. New York: William Morrow, 1999.

"Margaret Wise Brown." US BookScan. Accessed June 15, 2019.

Mitchell, Lucy Sprague. *Another Here and Now Story Book*. New York: E.P. Dutton & Co., 1937.

Murkhoff, Heidi and Sharon Mazel. *What to Expect When You're Expecting*. New York: Workman Publishing Company, 2008.

Part II

Barrymore, Diana. *Too Much Too Soon*. New York: Henry Holt & Co., 1957.

Correspondence from John G. McCullough to Gertrude Stein, 8 February 1939, Gertrude Stein Collection, Yale Collection of American Literature, Beinecke Rare Book and Manuscript Library, Yale University, New Haven, Connecticut.

Gary, Amy. *In the Great Green Room: The Brilliant and Bold Life of Margaret Wise Brown*. New York: Flatiron, 2017.

Kahn, E. J. "Tallyho!" *New Yorker*, March 8, 1941.

Larkin, Philip. *Collected Poems*. New York: Farrar Straus and Giroux, 1988.

Maiorana, Ronald. "Buckram Beagles Harass Hare, But Are Cheered By Its Escape." *New York Times*, January 13, 1964.

Shaw, Charles Green. "Through the Magnifying Glass." *New Yorker,* December 3, 1927.

Stein, Gertrude. "Poetry and Grammar." In *Lectures in America*. Boston: Beacon Press, 1935.

———. *The World Is Round*. New York: Harper Design, 2013.

Strange, Michael. *Who Tells Me True*. New York: C. Scribner's Sons, 1940.

Part III

Brown, Margaret Wise. *Goodnight Moon*. New York: HarperFestival, 2007.

———. *Goodnight Moon* manuscript notebook, The Kerlan Collection, Elmer L. Andersen Library, Minneapolis, Minnesota.

———. *The Little Fur Family*. New York: HarperFestival, 2005.

———. *The Noisy Book*. New York: HarperFestival, 2017.

———. *The Runaway Bunny*. New York: HarperFestival, 2017.

———. "Stories to Be Sung and Songs to Be Told." *The Book of Knowledge 1952 Annual*, ed. E.V. McLoughlin. New York and Toronto: The Grolier Society, 1952.

Gary, Amy. *In the Great Green Room: The Brilliant and Bold Life of Margaret Wise Brown*. New York: Flatiron, 2017.

Marcus, Leonard. *Margaret Wise Brown: Awakened by the Moon*. New York: William Morrow, 1999.

The Margaret Wise Brown Papers. 1910–1952, Special Collections. Wyndham Robertson Library, Hollins University, Roanoke, Virginia.

Strange, Michael. *Who Tells Me True*. New York: C. Scribner's Sons, 1940.

Part IV

Action on Postpartum Psychosis. "Personal Experiences." https://www.app-network.org/what-is-pp/personal-experiences.

Carver, Catherine. "Postpartum Psychosis: I'm afraid of how you'll judge me, as a mother and as a person." *Mosaic Science*, July 3, 2017.

Hill, Rebecca, Daphne Law, Chris Yellend, and Anne Sved Williams. "Treatment of Postpartum Psychosis in a Mother-Baby Unit: Do Both Mother and Baby Benefit?" *Australas Psychiatry* 27.2 (April 2019): 121–24.

"A Mother's Mind." *Earshot*, BBC Radio 4, November 3, 2018. Audio.

Twomey, Teresa M. *Understanding Postpartum Psychosis: A Temporary Madness*. Westport, CT: Praeger Publishers, 2009.

Acknowledgments

Thank you, always, to Stephanie Delman, who regularly makes my dreams come true. Thank you to Erin Wicks—your eye is impeccable, and your compassion is endless. Working with you two, yet again, has exceeded all possible expectations.

Thank you to the team at Sanford J. Greenburger Associates—Stefanie Diaz, Heide Lange, Sami Isman, Abigail Frank, and more—for your continued support. At Harper: Jonathan Burnham, Doug Jones, Christina Polizoto, Elina Cohen, and so many more. I appreciate how you've all gone to bat for me, and I'm so lucky to be in your hands. My immense thanks to Miranda Ottewell, copyeditor extraordinaire, for all your help with yet another structural puzzle.

Thank you to everyone who expressed enthusiasm when, three months postpartum, I decided that I had to write a ghost story about Margaret Wise Brown. Sophie Brochu and Brian Zimmerman, your early reads once again got me on track and asked the questions I needed to hear. Adam Morgan, please never stop hounding me about when the next book is coming—I promise always to do the same for you.

My "mom friends" who very quickly became good friends: Sam Dawson, Cara Turner, Mara Winston Grigg, McKenzie Roman, Kristen Seward, Katie Harte, Kailee Kremer, Rosemary Pritchard—you've saved me so many times, and in so many ways. I'm proud to be raising our next generation alongside you.

Thank you to Hannah Lee, for talking candidly, for reading carefully, and for being a wonderful role model. To Allison Somogyi, for teaching me about history PhD programs and reading my "dissertation."

Thank you to my parents, who are nothing like Megan's parents, and my in-laws, who are nothing like Megan's in-laws. I love you all, and you've helped me grow into the parent and person I am today.

Thank you to Elliott, who napped so nicely while I worked on this book, who brings me such joy, and is so (relatively) patient. And thank you to Margot, who has turned our lives upside down yet again in the most beautiful way.

Lastly, thanks to Rick, who juggles parenthood and career and good citizenship with overwhelming grace and generosity. It all works because of the work you put in. I love you deeply, and could not do this without you.

About the Author

JULIA FINE is the author of the critically acclaimed debut novel *What Should Be Wild*, which was shortlisted for the Bram Stoker Superior First Novel Award and the Chicago Review of Books Award. She lives in Chicago with her husband and children.